THE TASTE OF WORMWOOD

THE TASTE OF WORMWOOD

A JOHN EISENMENGER FORENSIC MYSTERY

Keith McCarthy

This first world edition published 2012
in Great Britain and in the USA by
SEVERN HOUSE PUBLISHERS LTD of
9–15 High Street, Sutton, Surrey, England, SM1 1DF.

British Library Cataloguing in Publication Data

McCarthy, Keith, 1960–
   The taste of Wormwood.
   1. Eisenmenger, John (Fictitious character) – Fiction.
   2. Detective and mystery stories.
   I. Title
   823.9'2-dc23

ISBN-13: 978-0-7278-8190-8 (cased)

All Severn House titles are printed on acid-free paper.

Severn House Publishers support The Forest Stewardship Council [FSC],
the leading international forest certification organisation. All our titles that
are printed on Greenpeace-approved FSC-certified paper carry the FSC logo.

MIX
Paper from
responsible sources
FSC
www.fsc.org FSC® C018575

Typeset by Palimpsest Book Production Ltd.,
Falkirk, Stirlingshire, Scotland.
Printed and bound in Great Britain by
MPG Books Ltd., Bodmin, Cornwall.

To the girls, all four of them.

ONE

It was a long crossing, but they always were. He hated sea crossings, but they came with the job and the job was good. Not good as in interesting, but good as in well paid, good as in keeping the circling predators at bay. And not the job as everyone thought it was, but the job as he had taken it and tweaked it; yes, that was a good way to describe it: he had *tweaked* the job, so that the returns were a little bit better.

He could never sleep on these crossings, no matter what he did; the ferries these days were full of entertainment – a bar, a games room, slot machines, even a cinema on the more modern ones – but the lure of such enticements had long ago wheezed its last. He had once been in the habit of spending money on a cabin, but that had been pounds sterling wasted; the cabins on these ferries bore an overwhelming similarity to prison cells, and he did not wish to be reminded of those. Not that he could get away from those memories on these night crossings, when he was confined below decks and where he was surrounded by painted steel, as he breathed other people's air, smelled their scents and heard their chatter, unable to escape from it.

He only made the journey once a month or so now, which was a source of both comfort and distress. It was a comfort because a year ago he had been on this ship – or one fucking identical to it – three times more often, and that had been killing him; distress because he was desperate for the money. The recession had hit hard, he was told; those who told him didn't know the half of it. He had remortgaged his house to raise the ninety thousand he'd needed to buy the truck – a beautiful three-axle Volvo with a superb in-cab hi-fi and a quite amazingly comfortable cab – but then fuel prices had really started to rise, and the amount of work had started to dive, and he had started to look around for other ways to make money. Hammy had suggested a way and he didn't know to this day if he had been joking. Hammy had only relatively recently come into his life, but they had struck a strong, firm friendship almost right away, even if he was a follower of Islam, who didn't drink and had what seemed to Arthur to be an unreasonably big family. 'If you want to make some easy money,' he said one day, 'I've got a cousin who could do with a lift.'

He hadn't understood at first – in truth, he was fairly pissed – and it had taken a fair few hints and nods and winks from Hammy – who was on orange juice – before he had understood. Actually, Hammy had practically had to tickle his ear lobe with his beard and lay things out in one-syllable words in order to make things clear.

It wasn't possible, of course. People-smuggling was far from easy and it was getting less so all the time. It wasn't just a question of hiding the passenger behind a sack of spuds whenever they came to a checkpoint; he had been driving long haul for a fair few years and was well aware of all the procedures the border authorities now employed in order to deter such entrepreneurial activities. Twice he had seen unscheduled hitchhikers unearthed – once by dogs and once by some sort of sensor device, a thing that looked like an emaciated metal detector. He also knew about the fines that they levied on the drivers, whether or not they were aware of their extra cargo; if one of those got slapped on him, things would really go shit-shaped.

Still, the idea, once it was in his head, just wouldn't budge; moreover, not only would not budge, but stayed put, and *grew*. And the colder the financial climate became, the more it grew, as if it were an arctic creeper, evolved to thrive in the bleakest of places. Eventually, this hardiest of perennials had its tendrils intertwined around every single synapse in his head, so that he couldn't think beyond it, so that it seemed to be the greatest idea he had ever had (because by now it had become very much his own idea).

With Hammy's help, he did some research, which wasn't easy, since he couldn't find a 'People-Smugglers' website, but eventually, after doing what people had done for years (that is, talk to people who talked to others, who talked . . .), he had a plan and he had someone who would carry it out for him. He had converted the two spare fuel tanks on the trunk into cabins; it was done for cash, and it was done in a large shed in Wiltshire under cover of a new moon's reign. True, the accommodation was a trifle cramped, each cabin measuring no more than a metre and a half in length and half a metre by half a metre in cross section. They were actually fairly comfortable inside, but that was only a by-product of the soundproofing. Most of the time, air came from a simple snorkel apparatus that opened on the underside of the chassis behind the cab; it didn't provide the freshest of air, but he wasn't reckoning on there being too many complaints. When he came to danger points at borders, he could seal the tanks down completely from the cab, so that neither the sniffer dogs nor the carbon dioxide detectors would register anything amiss, which meant the occupants relied on masks fed by compressed-air tanks. Water was merely from bottles that he gave them at the start of the journey in Turkey; they had to agree to be catheterized which took care of one route of excretion; as for the other, well, they were told just to grit their teeth and hang on for the two-day trip. It wasn't comfortable for them, but Turkey to England in forty-eight hours was none too easy for him, either. It required a lot of concentration, no sleep and a carefully 'adjusted' tachometer. By the time he got on the ferry, he was totally knackered.

It *ought* to have been a good income; it *had* been a good income; actually, it was *still* a good income. Trouble was, the other side of the business – the legit side – was continuing to dwindle. He was running loads at a loss now, just as a cover; after all, it would have looked slightly suspicious, even to the average European immigration officer, if he was running all over the Continent with an empty lorry. And it hadn't been cheap to set this all up. In fact, he'd had to remortgage the house again to raise the ten thousand required to make the necessary 'customizations'. Since property prices had dived into the shit-pit, this three-bed semi on the outskirts of Newent in Gloucestershire had been in serious negative equity; another source of argument with Joan the Moan, his 'till-death-do-us-part' wife.

This man's name is Arthur Meadows. He is fifty-seven years old, has a marriage of thirty-two years' duration and a single daughter who is a hairdresser in Newent, Gloucestershire. He has been a long-distance lorry driver for twenty-one years, although there was no cake and there were no cards when the actual anniversary had passed three months before. In their stead, there were yet more rows with his wife, Joan – she had been a striking blonde when they met, thin and voluptuous; now she was a bone-hard, grey-haired bitch with venom for saliva and hot, hungry coals for eyes – and yet more demands from the finance company. How had it come to this? It was a constant tattoo in his skull – a question repeated by a voice he didn't hear, but that was insistent and inevitable nonetheless – and one that, he was sure, was slowly driving him mad.

TWO

He was tired and, although he was always tired these days, on this day, on this trip, he seemed to be particularly exhausted. He'd promised Joan a holiday this year and she had been enthusiastic about this – distressingly so; she'd talked of Greece, or perhaps Turkey, while he had smiled and closed mental eyes, thinking about what that would cost, thinking that he should have told her there and then that Scotland or Wales was going to be nearer the financial mark. But he hadn't. He had been too afraid of another row, and so he had let her believe that they were going to have a week (maybe even two) in the Mediterranean sun. This trip – ostensibly bringing back rolls of cheap cotton cloth from Turkey – was to pay for that holiday; in his head, it was a penance for all the shit he had brought her; for the lost dreams.

It was, though, a risk, and one so for several reasons. Firstly, it was out of routine; he was well aware that such a break from the normal pattern might be suspicious, although it would only be so if he were to come to the attention of the UK Border Agency – much as his low-level but persistent defrauding of the Inland Revenue and the customs service was safe because they never noticed he was doing it. Secondly, this was a new client; he was sufficiently acquainted with criminal practice to know that strangers were always a risk; he was sufficiently prejudiced to know that foreign strangers were doubly so. Only the fact that Hammy had assured him that this guy was OK gave Arthur some degree of confidence. Thirdly, the cargo had not looked well when he had picked them up in that coastal town of Silivri, to the south-west of Istanbul, although there had been nothing that he could have put his finger on, other than the curious coincidence that they both limped stiffly and looked just plain *ill*. Apart from that, this pair were like all the rest: two girls of middling beauty, perhaps fifteen years old, fronting up as best they could, while beneath the bravado he could see silently screaming terror. He wondered what was wrong with them, but he didn't see it as his job to vet them. Anyway, by now he was used to the varied demeanours of those he transported; these two were nothing out of that particular ordinary, certainly not in their degree of bewilderment (a degree of bewilderment that would be a fucking sight greater when he finally let them out at the end of the journey).

They were willing to undergo any degradation or discomfort in order to get to the UK, it seemed; it was, he supposed when he came to think of it, a shame that when they realized their dream, the cost of transit that they would be expected to pay back would mean they were unlikely to enjoy their dream. He never asked what happened to his cargo, but he knew, just the same. He had rarely transported boys, and never anyone who looked over twenty, or any undeniably ugly ones. He might just as well be paid for carrying rubber sex dolls, for all the humanity his cargo was allowed.

The man who had been with them – Yussuf had been his name – had been slightly different, too. His normal contacts – he had built up a clientele of five – were always clinical and cold when treating the clients – an ill-chosen term if ever there was, implying as it did that they weren't being treated worse than animals for slaughter, that they were actually getting pretty good treatment – but this one's attitude seemed tinged with something more than the normal contempt for the cargo. He couldn't decide quite what it was, though. The closest he could come to describing it was 'pity', which was patently absurd. The men who arranged these 'transfers' were by definition strikingly lacking in that particular emotion, the lacuna filled in by greed.

This guy was, so he had been told, the friend of a friend of a friend; by the time you got to that many degrees of separation, you could effectively have been dealing with anyone in the world. This was not how he wanted to do business, because this kind of arrangement laid him open to attention from the authorities, but he had needed the money, and none of his usual contacts had been in a position to supply. It had all gone well, though. The transfer had been made at the back of a dilapidated and now empty supermarket on the edge of the resort, watched only by a group of feral cats. The cargo hadn't looked too keen when he had shown them their accommodation for the next couple of days, but that was pretty normal; explaining about the medical procedure that is catheterization hadn't been easy, especially as their English was pretty crap, but Yussuf had helped both by translating and suddenly producing a pistol; Arthur didn't like guns, but it wasn't the first time he had seen one wielded in such situations, and it had worked its usual magic.

And everything had gone well. Nothing had gone wrong; nothing had even come close to going wrong. There had been no problems at the various borders he had crossed; there had been no scares with flashing blue lights appearing in his side mirrors; there had been no car that had followed him for mile upon mile, leading him into a frenzied paranoia that it was tailing him. He had just driven for hour after hour, playing CDs endlessly on the multi-change player, keeping almost exactly to whatever the speed limit was, trying not to fall asleep, occasionally stopping for a quick meal or diesel (without spare fuel tanks to call on, he had to do so quite often) at some motorway shit-pit in any of the six – count them, six – countries he had to endure on his way back to Blighty.

Everything was hunky-funky-fucking-dory.

Except that he felt fucking awful.

Ostend, as ever, was no carnival. It was, in fact, the last place you would want to find yourself at the end of fifteen hundred miles of motorway; actually, it probably wasn't if your interests included heroin, STDs, detritus and sexual depravity, but he had never counted those particular vices as parts of his portfolio. He was lucky, though, because he had timed his arrival (as he had tried to do) so that he could more or less go straight through customs – as far as it was possible to 'go straight through customs' when you were hauling freight. These days, the default position was that you were smuggling something, and you and your vehicle were treated accordingly. It hadn't quite got to the point where he was expected to undergo a personal body search, but the rig sure got some pretty intimate going over. On quite a few occasions he had witnessed success from these actions, but thus far he had managed to outwit them; he had every hope of continuing so to do.

At least the number of children on this route was minimal. Not that he hated children; far from it – he loved them. He would have loved grandchildren – he and Joan had been devastated when, three years before, daughter Carol had announced defiantly that she was 'setting up home' with Theresa, a piece of news that had sparked months of mutual recrimination – but, by the time he got on to the ferry, all he wanted to do was rest. After buying a copy of the *Mail*, a couple of pints of Tetley bitter and a plate of fish and chips, he would claim a reclining seat, then inevitably fall into sleep. No matter how much he wanted to prolong the Meadows family lineage, at those moments he did not need the disruptive, screaming, giggling chaos that was children.

And he could never escape a feeling of claustrophobia on these crossings. Despite the carpeting, he knew that he was effectively in a cage composed of iron girders given a thick cosmetic coat of gloss paint; no matter how many bars and slot machines and pool tables and self-service restaurants they put in, he was imprisoned. He was always reminded somehow of his time in prison, not least because he was confined with no hope of escape until the ship docked; true, provided the weather wasn't too bad, he was theoretically allowed out on to deck, but there was no way he was ever going to do that, because his seasickness would not allow him to.

He wasn't a good sailor; actually, that was 'not good' as in 'crap'. Sometimes the four-hour crossing seemed to go on for ever, a sort of frigid, nautical Hades that went constantly up and down, side to side, forwards and backwards. Mind you, that irregular irregularity of movement wasn't the worst, because, after an hour of that, he found himself hating not that but the pauses, the infinitesimally small moments that separated the oscillations. His brain seemed to come hyper-alert at those moments and, no matter how tired he was, he would awake instantly to the realization not only that his whole immediate world was about to crash down in a nauseating, vertiginous slide, but also that this was likely to happen also to his whole, immediate future, that he was up to his neck in the proverbial slurry. Yet despite the relative calm of this trip, he felt slow, sluggish; if not actually sick, then sickening. It was probably those two in his lorry, he decided. They had something and he had caught it. Some tropical disease or other. He had heard about that kind of thing; some of them made you bleed from the eyes, others turned your insides to bloody slop, like minced offal. Jesus, that was a worrying thought . . .

Suddenly, gorge rose into his throat and he just knew that he wasn't going to be able to keep it down. He struggled to get out of the chair because of his arthritic knee as the first bitter tang of acid began to sting the back of his throat and tongue; a middle-aged couple looked up as he rushed past, their expressions showing what he thought might be derision, presumably because he was showing himself up to be a poor seaman. Well, fuck them if that was their dream of entertainment. Anyway, he doubted that they had just driven across the entire fucking continent without proper rest and with the constant draining fear of being pulled over and his extra, strictly unofficial cargo uncovered.

He heaved into the toilet bowl again and again, his vomit covering the skid marks left by a prior, oh-so-caring customer, chunks of partly digested fish plainly visible. There were streaks of blood, too, he realized after he had finally opened his eyes and the tears had gone; his stomach hurt as well, and not just because of the strain of upchucking. There was a deep ache within him, one that reached to his spine, one that was squeezing his guts with bony fingers and sharpened nails.

Fucking dirty foreign cunts.

At least the profit from this trip would pay for the holiday and relieve one particular pressure in his life. Only one, though. He was bright enough to know that there was no magic, one-size-fits-all solution to his problems, that he was buying only a respite. Beyond that, there was just a return to the cycling, cycling shit that his life had become.

In his head he felt his stomach whisper to him that it was about to hurt him again.

THREE

B ritish customs were the worst. On the Continent they had less of an uptight, suspicious attitude to importers; you were innocent until proven guilty. Not in the UK, though; in the country of his birth, there was a supposition that you were guilty, end of, and they were going to prove it, and then they were going to make you pay through the nose and through the arsehole. Even before he'd started earning a bit of the untaxed, he'd always got twitched by the attitude of the UK Border Agency. You learned pretty quickly that jokes were verboten; in fact, any kind of conversation outside that which was strictly business was verboten. These days, though, when he had a couple of extra and strictly unsanctioned passengers squashed under his cab, his stress levels generally went cosmic. It was all he could usually do to hold it together, to stop the shaking, to answer the questions without a tremor in his voice. Generally, his bowels did bad things at this time and, once it was over and he was at last driving away from the portside, he would have to find the nearest public toilet (he knew exactly where it was by now) and have a good, but overly liquid, shit.

Tonight, though, things had been oddly different. He didn't care any more, for some reason. There was actually something within him that wouldn't have minded too much if they had somehow managed to discover his secret; it would be a relief, a tremendous release. No more bitching from Joan about the lack of money, no more stress, no more having to deal with distinctly dodgy dark-skinned customers in far-flung lands who were just dying to do him over, or even slit his belly open.

In fact, tonight he felt like a robot, operating on a level that was beneath conscious thought. The level wasn't a good one, though. He felt feverish, whilst his insides were not so much doing the conga as writhing in slippery agony. He couldn't be bothered to be stressed by the uniformed goons whose job it was to make his life difficult; let them play their games. If they found his guests, then so be it.

Yet they didn't. He drove out of the port at Ramsgate not quite sure what had happened, aware only that he had got away with it one more time and that, despite his apparent lack of stress, he still needed to shit like he had never needed to shit before. He barely made it in time and, as he sat in the damp, smelly cubicle with his kecks around his cheap Adidas trainers and white towelling socks, he had the feeling that, while the bottom was slowly falling out of his world, here in a dubious public convenience on the outskirts of Ramsgate, the world was torrentially falling out of his bottom. It was an impression that was enhanced when he looked down between his hairy thighs and saw not just brown sludge but also bright red blood and a sort of dark crimson tarry substance that smelt metallic. The porcelain was splashed with watery carmine.

What the fuck?

He felt a shimmer of vagueness, the world becoming faint, bleaching in colour and dancing away from him. A deep breath and he was back again, or perhaps it was the world that was back, but he felt weak, listless. It was an effort to clean himself up, to resist the urge just to sit there slumped against the graffiti on the cubicle's side panel and let the darkness subsume him in sweet oblivion. He couldn't give in to that urge, though. He still had a three-and-a-half-hour drive ahead of him, a rendezvous to make.

FOUR

Arthur had known Paul Lynch for a long time, since school-days, in fact. Once they had set fire to a fairly large tract of the Forest of Dean when experimenting with matches, firecrackers and a rather large magnifying glass that Paul had stolen from the science cupboard at Cinderford Comprehensive School. On another occasion, when they had grown a bit older but perhaps not wiser, Paul had been the only one who had been willing to help when he had been done over by some diddicoys over a car sale; they were never going to get the money back, but the satisfaction in creeping on to the campsite at four in the morning, then pouring the paint stripper over the car so that the bastards wouldn't profit, had been immense. Paul and Arthur had shared too much pleasure and just enough pain to be bonded for life. He could trust Paul.

It was unalloyed coincidence that they had both ended up in the haulage business, although Paul had proved the more adept businessman; whereas Arthur had only one lorry to his name, Paul had a business that ran fifteen rigs varying in size from fully articulated, forty-tonne trucks down to vans. His headquarters was a large yard in which there was sporadic but twenty-four-hour activity; Arthur's lorry turning up in the early hours of the morning would not be seen as out of the ordinary or suspicious, especially as Paul frequently subcontracted Arthur when his own fleet was fully booked. Paul had never asked Arthur why he asked to have the sole use of the yard on these occasions, although Arthur suspected that he guessed the reason; it was a discretion for which he was grateful. For a two-hour spell, the yard would be unmanned with all arrivals and departures suspended, the security guards taking a prolonged break, the camera screens unwatched. Arthur had been entrusted with a spare set of keys and had also memorized the code of the electronic lock; the yard was on the edge of Andoversford, about a mile from the A40 and half a mile from any human habitation; it was perfect for the rendezvous.

In the event, he arrived eleven minutes late, because he'd had to stop three times – three fucking times, count them – on the way from Kent. As he pulled up outside the heavy iron gates, there was a dark blue Ford Transit van already there; a nervous minute followed in which he waited in the cab to see who it was and whether it was police and immigration officials, or whether it was his contact.

Abdullah, he had been told. He will be alone and he will have the other half of your money. The first time he'd done this kind of thing, he had been worried that they weren't exchanging passwords and that he had no way of recognizing his contact – perhaps a copy of the *Mirror*, or a pink carnation – but he'd soon come to realize that such cartoon exercises were a childish waste of time; after all, if the Old Bill (or whatever colour of uniform it was) had got to the point where they were imitating his contact, then it was all blown to shit and back anyway.

A man got out of the van. The security lights in the yard were on as they always were – and they were fucking bright, too – but they looked the wrong way; in, not out. All he could see was a high-contrast profile and, when the stranger turned his head, a silhouette of the deepest dark. He had a beard and he seemed to be Asian, but that was all he could tell; he was huddled against the cold of the night, wearing a leather bomber jacket that could have hidden an AK-47, for all Arthur knew. *Oh well*, he thought. He got out of the cab and climbed down.

'Abdullah?' he called.

The man came forward, eyes dancing around, looking first into the bright lights, then into the night that was on three sides of them, although Arthur guessed he wouldn't be able to make out anything. He wasn't into polite niceties and asked brusquely, 'You got them?' He was nervous, but Arthur was used to that by now. True, he had never met this one before, but they all followed a pattern. They were all proud, yet terrified; all a second away from erupting in righteous anger; all convinced that the British owed them and it was about time they were paid.

This was the tricky part, the part where it could go wrong; it never had before, but the fact that he didn't know this bloke kept coming at him from somewhere near the back of his head. He said, 'You got my money?'

Abdullah – if such it was – didn't look as if he trusted him and stared at him very hard and for a long time before he finally withdrew his left hand from the jacket pocket; there was a Jiffy bag in it. He held it up. Arthur said, 'Open it. Let me see the notes.'

The man calling himself Abdullah hesitated, but Arthur just waited and eventually he complied. Arthur held out his hand to take it, but it was at once snatched back. 'Not yet.'

Arthur shrugged.

He said, 'OK. Looks good. Let's go inside.'

He meant the compound. Abdullah became a bit arsey. 'Why? Why can't we do it here?'

'We go inside, we lock it up again, and then we're all nice and private.'

'What about the cameras?' Abdullah indicated one that was perched fifty feet up on a steel pole.

Arthur said confidently, 'I know how to make sure they're not looking our way.' He did, too.

Abdullah was tall – over six feet – and angular; when he was in profile against the lights, his Adam's apple stuck out from his throat as if he'd swallowed a diamond and it was only halfway down. He was staring at Arthur, his face betraying how afraid and how belligerent he was. The stare lasted so long that it became almost farcical in Arthur's head, as if the poor sod was hypnotized. *It's your first time, isn't it, old son? You're shit scared.*

Not that he wasn't also scared almost to death, but this young man – no more than twenty-five, Arthur reckoned – did not have the benefit of experience, of having been here (or somewhere like it) before. For just a moment, Arthur didn't mind how fucking awful he felt, didn't mind the feeling of roiling shit in his belly and the ever-increasing lethargy that hung like curtains of lead about his bones; he was the one in control here. At last, Abdullah, or whoever it was, nodded, although he did so reluctantly.

FIVE

It was another fifteen minutes before they were inside and the gates were locked behind them. Arthur had used the combination code to get into the security compound and turn the cameras around so that the near right-hand corner of the yard (and, just as importantly, a corridor to it from the main gates) behind the small loading bay would not be in range until he chose otherwise. Once the gates were open, the alarms deactivated and the cameras arranged just so, he drove slowly through, hoping fervently that Abdullah would do as he had been told and just follow him. He was relieved to see that he did, although he had had to explain what was required of him three times. He climbed down again from the cab, then locked up the compound again. 'There,' he said, returning to the lorry. 'All nice and cosy.'

Abdullah had not calmed down to any great extent as far as Arthur could see. 'Can we just get on with this?'

Arthur eyed him, thinking how much he disliked this twat; he had built up a bit of a sixth sense for the people he dealt with on these occasions, and it was telling him that here was a fucker who might be trouble. It was ironic that he was none too keen on people his grandfather had cheerfully and loudly referred to as 'darkies'; mind you, in those days, such language had been the norm, even expected. He didn't think that most of them even minded much because they saw it then for what it was – affectionate; it was no worse than calling short people 'Lofty' and slapheads 'Curly'. It was this fucking political correctness that, in his opinion, had ruined the country.

'I'd like a proper look at the money first.'

Despite his hurry, Abdullah – if that was his name, which Arthur very much doubted – was again suddenly coy. 'How do I know you've kept your side of the bargain?'

'Don't be so fucking stupid.'

'I want to see them first.'

It had often been like this in the early days, when he was a stranger to the strangers he dealt with, without the foundation of trust to ensure that things went smoothly. He'd have expected this kind of situation would occur; a Pakistani stand-off. 'I only want,' he said slowly, 'to make absolutely sure that you've got proper money, as agreed. All I've seen so far is one note and a bag of paper. I don't expect you to hand it over to me just yet.'

Abdullah thought about this. My God, he's green, thought Arthur. He revised his estimate of Abdullah's age downwards – he couldn't be more than twenty, he guessed. What kind of age was that to get mixed up in this kind of thing? Where would Abdullah go from here? Because, Arthur knew, it was only going to be down. It didn't bother Arthur, because he could see an end, and that end didn't frighten him any more; a kid like Abdullah, though, he couldn't see an end, because he would be scared shitless to raise his eyes to the horizon. Arthur had once been like that; he had been scared of the future, swaddling his terror in bravado, not realizing that by doing so he was walking purposefully and happily into the furnace.

And, now that he could feel the flames licking his face, he no longer cared. Something – call it peace of mind, or resignation, or exhaustion – had taken hold of him, and with it came a sort of emotional anaesthesia. Death was no longer an enemy to be fought; now it was a bed in which to lie, and it was feather-soft, too. The other's nervousness was at a remove from him, seen through a glass if not darkly, then certainly blurrily. He thought idly of reassuring this man who wore the name 'Abdullah' so awkwardly, but six decades of living – decades in which life had been applied to his skin like heat-resistant lacquer so that the empathies with which he had been born were now just blunted squibs of staunch disinterest – held him back. Why should this greedy little cunt have it easy?

After what seemed like hours of sullen unspoken debate, Abdullah said at last, 'I suppose.' He felt in the pocket of his black leather jacket – they always wore black leather jackets, straight out of the movies; but then everything about this poor shit-kicker came from there. He had learned from Hollywood and Bollywood, and learned it far better than anything he'd been told at school. He brought out the Jiffy bag, once more reached in and pulled out a wad of currency about halfway. This he held out to Arthur, making sure that it was out of Arthur's reach. In the drenched, drained brightness of the compound lights, the details were curiously indistinguishable. Arthur said, 'Pull out one from the middle and give it to me.'

Abdullah frowned at him. 'Why?'

'So I can get a proper look at it.'

'No.'

Arthur's guts turned, like a dying whale – perhaps even one that was starting to rot – thrashing on a dirty, polluted beach. 'Fuck you, arsewipe. I want to see one sodding note. I'm not going to do a runner if you give me twenty fucking quid, am I?'

Abdullah was sweating and there was a tremor in his right eyelid, one that spread down his outstretched arm like a palsy. He seemed to be a man in the grip of perfectly balanced, perfectly opposing forces. Arthur sighed. 'Don't be a wanker, Abdullah.

Just satisfy me in this one little thing, then we can conclude our business and we can each be on our way.'

Still nothing from the other.

'Look, Sunshine, the longer we stand here, the more likely it is that someone's going to see us and wonder what we're doing, and then all hell will shit down on us.'

To Arthur's relief, the young Asian saw the sense of this. He plucked a note from the middle of the wad and fluttered it at Arthur, who took it from him. It was a used twenty-pound note; so used it had a small piece out of the corner, but Arthur was fairly sure it was genuine. He crumpled it up and put it in his breast pocket. Abdullah said, 'Hey!'

Arthur gave him a look of impatient scorn. 'Don't be a fuckwit. Let's just get this over with, then you can give me the rest of the dosh and you can be on your merry way.'

He turned back to the door of his cab, climbed up and felt under the seat. He had, he thought, been clever and had the switches disguised so that they looked exactly like all the other nuts that held together the frame of his seat. It would take a lot of detailed examination to discover that they did nothing structural. Once twisted exactly three-quarters of a turn, they released the locks on the two tanks, allowing these to be opened from the outside.

He climbed back down, at once aware that there was a stink. It was a rank, disgusting smell of shit and sick and God knew what else, and it was coming from the tank at the back of his cab. Abdullah, too, could smell it and, judging by the look around his eyes and on his forehead, he was no fan, either. What the fuck had gone on? Even as he asked the question, he could make a pretty good guess.

He reached in between the tank and the back of the cabin, far in, having to stretch until his finger tips found the second switch. There was a whooshing noise and the top of the tank clicked up; the smell became intolerable, one of utmost degraded foulness, a foretaste of the hell for which he was bound.

Abdullah turned away, looking as if he was going to be sick; Arthur wasn't any too sure he wasn't going to join him, actually. He didn't want to, but he knew he had to look inside the tank, so he lifted the top half back on its hinges. He was very afraid that he would find a dead body inside, but she was still alive, although perhaps that wasn't much of a blessing. From a pool of liquid faeces, blood and what looked mighty like sick, the girl slowly, painfully raised herself up on her hands, looking blindly out on the bright compound lights, her eyes bloodshot, her face grey, blood and slime dribbling from her mouth.

SIX

DCI Beverley Wharton told herself, and not for the first time, that she ought to have been a fucking sight happier than she was. Her mother was always telling her to count her blessings – precious few in her mother's case, as far as Beverley could see – but it made no difference. Blessings were ephemeral things, soon melting into the morass of experience that she held in her head as memory, doing little but diluting the pain that, in its multitudinous forms, assailed from the safe bunker that was her subconscious. Blessings were little more than vodka shots, flung down her throat at the end of a shitty day, on the eve of a potentially even shittier one, without even the pleasurable burn at the back of her throat.

She looked out across the early morning riverscape that was Gloucester Docks, now turned from run-down dereliction to an anaemic, ersatz tableau of sophisticated city living, with its boutique shops, museums, warehouses converted into blocks of flats, and scattered, moored narrowboats. It wasn't even particularly clean any more, she noted in the dying evening sunlight; there was too much litter both in the water and on the land, too much of the brick surface covered with random graffiti. There was an air of passive decay about the place; millions had been spent on the renovation, yet little could now be found to stop the degradation that followed apathy like a canker. It was a depressed and depressing place, and this realization was not just due to her mood.

She should have moved a couple of years ago, she knew now. Or perhaps she should never have moved here. She had wanted to live in Gloucester because there was something about the air of Cheltenham that she found distasteful. Perhaps she detected superciliousness and arrogance in its faded architecture, qualities that were absorbed and exaggerated by certain of its inhabitants. Not many, though, and more and more were vanishing every year, replaced by common or garden, borderline lawful citizens, the ones that formed the loam from which she took her precious harvest.

And that's what it was all about. 'Harvest', 'yield' and 'crop' were so semantically close to 'quota', a word that was never uttered so that it could be heard, but which was forever there. She was now senior enough to hear the conversations that went on amongst the higher echelons of policing, the ones that rubbed brocaded shoulders with politicians and their civil servants, those to whom murder and rape were important not because they were bloody, cruel, disgusting and ruinous, but because they were the tests on which they were judged, on which they could build their careers.

She remembered a phrase that John Eisenmenger had once used – 'feasting on carrion', by which he meant that many people took their living from murder – from any crime, although murder was the richest fare; all of them (*all of us*, she reminded herself) were to a greater or lesser extent parasites – at best, symbiotes – on others' miseries. She had enough insight to appreciate that she had been amongst the most avaricious of feeders at this trough of abject despair. Not any more, though. The race, she felt, was now run, or nearly so. She was in her early forties, but those few decades had seen too much deceit, dishonesty, barbarism and misery to allow her sleepful nights; would that they had merely been at the hands of others . . .

John Eisenmenger was the problem. He had been the problem for a long time now; an irritation, an itch, but, above all, a tease. He didn't even seem to know that he was a tease, God rot his miserable soul. Why him, though? Why had she fallen for that man? He wasn't particularly good-looking, nor physically imposing; if anything, he was too self-effacing, too detached, too *other-worldly.* She laughed at this thought; 'other-worldly'? John Eisenmenger was, if anything, too much of this world. He was just . . . well . . . *uninterested.* She considered this, then decided that this was an accurate description. He was uninterested and it was that which gave him the air of other-worldliness. All around him – herself included – there were people who took an interest in too many things; they distracted themselves, failed to see a purpose, because all around them was a plethora of potential purposes. Eisenmenger seemed naturally to pick and then possess his purpose and, having done so, was supremely capable of hanging on to it until the end. During this time, diversion was unknown to him; he was blinkered but, unfortunately, blinkered in not only an intellectual but also an emotional sense. Fuck, he was blinkered in an emotional sense perpetually. Even Helena, the Ice Maiden, had grown tired of that, which was ironic, now she came to think of it.

He was supercilious, too. Not, she thought, that he meant to be; it was just a symptom of his lack of involvement. He was incapable of understanding how infuriating he could be, and frequently was. She knew from experience that he was often surprised at the reaction of others to his more abstruse or unusual pontifications; in the right mood, such a reaction could be taken as delightful, even endearing; in the wrong mood – the mood in which human beings so frequently find themselves – it could be aggravating to the point of seething anger. For years she had only shown an interest in him because he had been Helena's; it had been nothing more than a game to tempt him away from the bitch, but one that she failed in. And the more she had failed, the more determined she had become to succeed; looking back on things, she hadn't at the time even been aware that this change was happening to her. With Helena gone, it should have been easy; he should have looked up, peered around and seen what the blinkers of a steady relationship had hidden from him. He hadn't done that, though. The stupid bastard had just carried on as before, whilst she told herself that it didn't matter, that she could have any man she liked; trouble was, whilst that might once have been true, she suspected – fuck, she *knew* – that this piece of optimism was no longer true. Once, she had given out her favours equally between those who satisfied her sexual desires and those who satisfied her career ambitions; the latter had almost always been with men whom, under normal circumstances, she would have crossed the street – the globe, even – to avoid, even in social circumstances, let alone the rather more foetid and intimate confines of a bed, an office or even (God help her) the back seat of a car. Now, even these seemed less inclined to take up any implied suggestion or even vague hint that she was open for business on the right terms, while those who were still willing to enter into sexual congress with her purely for pleasure seemed somehow less attractive to her, seemed almost now to be rather old, overweight and ugly. Was she any of those? She didn't think so, but who was she to judge? If her lovers could be seen as a mirror for her own appearance, then she was clearly a very deluded woman. In the reflection of the window glass, she could make herself out to be still fairly slim, still fairly smooth-skinned, but she was well aware of how deceptive was the translucent image in front of her. There were times when she glimpsed in the corner of her eyes the mirror's evidence that she was not immune to the way of all things, that even good make-up and a starvation diet did not grant her an eternity of youth.

What she saw wasn't that bad, though; she was convinced that her self-delusion didn't completely blind her. In which case, what gave Eisenmenger the right to refuse her? Was he really so blind or arrogant or stupid as to have missed or deliberately ignored her signals? She sighed. She was rather afraid that he might well be; if not stupid, then conceivably arrogant and certainly blind enough to be wittingly or unwittingly oblivious of what she was trying to say to him.

And the chance may be slipping from her. Eisenmenger had suffered another breakdown, she had been told; certainly he was no longer undertaking forensic work, a hole that the police in general, and she in particular, were finding it hard to fill. Precisely why, though, she did not know, although she well remembered his problems following the suicide of Marie, his partner of so long ago. The loss of Helena had not seemed to affect him so much, but then she had always appreciated that Eisenmenger was a deep pool indeed. The last case had been tough, too. She considered herself to be made of a metal that had been well and painfully tempered in humanity's inhumanity, yet even she still found herself occasionally back in the middle of the soul-seeker's insane quest for evidence of God's special blessing upon man. At the time, Eisenmenger had not seemed to have been overly distressed, but there had been personal cost in the case for him, and she guessed that it had been this that had finally tipped him again into depression. She wondered if, this time, it would be a final illness and what, if anything, could tempt him back to work. She rather suspected that it would have to be something special.

She turned away from the window. It was late, but she had no major cases on; there was only paperwork to be done when she got into Cheltenham police station. She didn't feel tired, only exhausted in a way that sleep would not heal. Perhaps she would read something. She hadn't read a novel for years.

Yes, that's what she would do.

SEVEN

Arthur's trip to his house in Newent took forty minutes, but it passed in an instant. When he finally reached the yard where he parked at nights, he was unable to recall any details of the journey, save one; he had had to stop just north of Gloucester to be violently sick. He had only just made it out of the cab in time, even though he had stopped the lorry in the middle of the road. Fortunately, no other traffic had come along at the time, because he had blocked the highway. He didn't know whether he had been sick because he was under the weather, as he had been for much of the journey, or whether it was because of the sight of his cargo. That was enough to make anyone feel ill, even if they didn't have gut rot beforehand.

Jesus, he thought. *What the fuck did they have?*

Both of them had been the same; same as in barely alive, covered in puke, shit and blood, and looking close to death. They were jabbering something that was lost on Arthur; Abdullah seemed to understand them and apparently plied them with questions, although he kept well back whilst doing so. Arthur was bright enough to know what was going to happen and, sure enough, it did. Abdullah had turned to him and begun being a bit naughty. He'd got on his high horse first of all, shouting a lot and invading Arthur's personal space – which, when it came

to the coloured brethren, was pretty large – demanding to know
what was wrong with them, as if Arthur was a fucking quack.
When Arthur had told him that he didn't fucking know what was
wrong with them and, what was more, he didn't give a flying
fuck, Abdullah had taken it badly. He had become even more
aggressive; Arthur might even have said that he had been distinctly
threatening. Worse, he had said that he wasn't going to pay up.

Arthur wasn't particularly violent by nature, but he knew how
things worked and he was quite a big man. That he wasn't feeling
any too good didn't help his temper, either. He wasn't about to
let this arrogant little arsewipe do the dirty on the deal, so he
put his point of view across with a few smacks that had left poor
little Abdullah with a funny-looking nose and tears in his eyes.
When the cunt had reached into his back pocket, Arthur had
sucker-punched him and then, when he staggered backwards and
fell over, had knelt on his chest; the knife had fallen on the
tarmac of the yard and Arthur had picked it up. Then, with the
two items of cargo having staggered out of the hidden compartments, but still on all fours and smelling like sewage gone bad
in the background, Arthur had explained how things stood.

'OK, Sambo. All I do is transport them. They get into the lorry
in Turkey, and then they get out here; that's all I do, and that's
what I've done. If your Paki friends have decided to ship duff
goods, I suggest you take it up with them, understand? Now, I
would like my money, please.' He had felt in the inner pocket
of the leather jacket where he had seen Abdullah put the Jiffy
bag, pulled it out and put it in his jacket pocket. Then he said,
'Thank you very much. Now, you take your friends and fuck off,
and I'll go my way, and with any luck I'll never see your shit-
ugly face again. Comprehendez vous?'

Abdullah could hardly breathe because of Arthur's weight,
but he had refused to speak for a long time; when at last he
had, he hadn't looked happy, but he had nodded slowly, his
eyes alive with resentment. Arthur had taken the knife – it
was just a fucking kitchen knife, for fuck's sake – and stuck
the point under Abdullah's chin. 'Tell your chums to get in
the back of your van.'

A stream of gobbledegook came out of Abdullah's mouth.
Arthur looked up; his passengers were by now standing and

looking at them; they were shivering and crying, clearly in pain. They didn't move. Arthur said quietly, 'Say it again.' He jerked the point of the knife a little bit deeper into Abdullah's neck. After a wince, Abdullah complied, hoarsely spewing out another splurge of rapid, slightly breathless and totally incomprehensible gibberish; for all Arthur knew, Abdullah could have been reciting the names of the Pakistani cricket team. But slowly, and clearly painfully, they did as Arthur wanted.

'Right,' he said then to the man under his knees. 'This is how we're going to do things.' He felt in his pocket for his mobile phone, then held it up for Abdullah to peruse. 'I'm going to dial nine-nine-nine for the police.'

This announcement had an interesting effect on his captive, who gasped and said something that sounded obscene. Arthur smiled, although he wasn't feeling particularly joyful. 'There's a nick in Andoversford, so I reckon they'll be out here in no more than ten minutes; my mate who owns this yard has had a lot of trouble with break-ins here over the years, so they'll be keen to see what's going on.'

Abdullah sneered, 'What about you?'

'I'll be long gone. If you're a clever little black bastard, so will you.'

Abdullah struggled a little, but it was half-hearted and ineffectual. Arthur punched in the numbers, waited, then said, 'Police,' in a loud clear voice.

Abdullah spat up at him, falling short so that the gobbet of spittle hit Arthur's jacket, whereupon Arthur leaned forward so that more of his weight was on Abdullah's ribs, causing him to groan and swear, this time in English. Arthur said into the phone, 'There's something odd going on in Lynch's haulage yard, the one just off the A40 near Andoversford.' He paused, listening. 'The gates are open and I thought I glimpsed a dark-coloured Transit van with three figures around it. Looked like they were up to no good.' A second pause. 'My name? No thanks, mate. I don't want to get involved.' With that, he cut the connection and, leaning down to Abdullah, he said, 'Ten minutes . . . if you're lucky.' He held the knife up in front of his face so that he would remember who was in charge, then stood up. He backed away as the other stood up painfully; once he was back at his lorry, he climbed quickly up. Abdullah was looking at him, pressing the heels of his hands into the sides of his ribcage. Arthur called out of the cab window, 'You'd better fuck off,' before starting the engine, releasing the air brakes with a loud *whoosh* and pulling slowly out of the yard.

He drove away but, instead of taking the first exit of the roundabout at the end of the long, curving lane – the one that led to the A40 – he took the third, travelled a hundred yards along it, then turned sharp left, pulling in at once into a parking area that was relatively well hidden. There he turned off the engine and killed the lights, waiting for twenty minutes; at the end of this time, he started the lorry again and drove on down the road until he came to the first turning on the left, which he took. Within two minutes, he was back at the compound.

He was relieved to find it was empty. Feeling rather pleased with himself that his little ruse had worked, he closed the gates and reset the security system after making sure that there was nothing too incriminating in the way of evidence around the yard. There were a few stains on the tarmac – blood, some shit and not a little sick – but there was nothing he could do about that; if they were noticed, he was content that Paul would make sure that the finding was suppressed, or explained away, and that Paul wouldn't be too nosy himself. It was while he was climbing back into his cab that another wave of nausea and belly pain hit him, the worst so far, so that he only just avoided adding to the stains.

He found himself terribly afraid that he had what his two passengers had had.

Fucking dirty cunts, he thought to himself.

EIGHT

R ashid was so angry that he had trouble driving in a straight line. He felt his stomach to be churning, and he had to grip the steering wheel so hard that his nails drew blood from the palms of his hands. He had mentally practised the drive home many times; when he had done so, this part of the process had been a downhill, over-the-hard-part bit, what with the handover completed, the transaction with a total and potentially treacherous stranger – one who was not of the faith, one who was condemned – finished satisfactorily. Yet it was anything but. He felt cheated, defiled and angry. The scum had humiliated him, made him eat dirt like a pig; he had stolen his money and abused his race and his beliefs. And the goods were soiled; there was something wrong with them. He could hear them now, in the back of the van, retching and moaning; he had tried telling them to shut up, but to no effect.

He should never have listened to Mohammed; the stupid bastard was too fond of faithless infidels. The only time he wanted to have contact with white trash was when he took their money, and then he was happy to take as much of it as he could. Not that the two in the back were likely to earn him much; not at the moment, anyway. What the hell was wrong with them? He hoped it wasn't catching; he hoped it was just dysentery from drinking dirty water, but that would be bad enough. He'd spent a lot of money and if they both died – or even just one of them – he would be seriously out of pocket; he'd have to work the survivor hard to stand any chance of recouping his investment even within six months.

He suddenly braked as he realized belatedly that he was just coming into Highnam where he thought there was a speed camera; the last thing he needed was to get photographed in case someone started asking questions. It took a big effort of will to keep below thirty, though, because he was acutely aware of houses not too far away to his left and he felt that by driving so slowly he was increasing the chances of someone just happening to glance out at the wrong moment . . .

At last, he was through the low-speed zone and could safely increase to just under fifty. Then he joined the A40, a dual carriageway that led eventually into the centre of Gloucester. He was calming down at last as the danger of being seen began to decrease. If he saw a police car, the only thing he could do would be to pray that they didn't get it into their thick skulls to take an interest in a navy-blue Ford Transit that was driving just within the speed limit at three in the morning. He knew that he was never going to outrace them.

He saw no police, though. He spotted a few people – probably drunk, he reckoned sourly – walking with hunched, defensive shoulders along Bruton Way, and there were a few huddled shapes in shop doorways on either side of London Road, but nothing that he thought to worry about. He turned right into Great Western Road, now feeling easier in keeping his speed not too fast nor too slow. The bulk of Gloucestershire Royal Hospital, with its dull grey prefabricated tower block, loomed up on his left; even the casualty department seemed quiet, with a host of idle ambulances clustered around the forecourt, like sleeping drones. At the end of the road, he turned right but had to stop almost immediately because the gates of the level crossing were closed.

He immediately began to panic again. What was going on? It couldn't be a train, not at this time of the morning. He looked around the van, in the wing mirrors and out of the side windows, certain that he would see police uniforms closing in on him, finding nothing. *Calm down*, he told himself. *Keep your breathing steady. This isn't a trap.*

He found himself gripping the steering wheel too tightly again, but he fought down the feeling of panic. Then, from somewhere, he heard a rumble; the gates *were* closed for a train. Oh, the relief.

After what seemed like an hour of the noise gradually increasing in the cool night's fragile air, until the ground itself seemed to tremble, the train arrived, trundling past with a counterpoint of slightly higher but louder, intermittent 'clacks'. It was some sort of freight train, the trucks huge and covered in dirt, curiously shaped like enormous iron flasks; perhaps it held nuclear waste, he thought. He had heard that such trains passed regularly through Gloucester, on their way up from Bristol to Cumbria. It went on for ever, continuing until he felt the tension returning to his hands; he kept checking the mirrors, just in case. There was only silence from the back of the van. Even after the train had gone, the gates remained closed for no apparent reason; he knew well that they always did this, but it was hard to bear, nonetheless.

At last, the gates opened and he could move forward, relieved that he had seen no one and no vehicles whilst he had been stationary, hoping that this meant, in turn, no one had seen him.

He drove all the way along Derby Street, under the bridge carrying Metz Way, then turned right again into Barton Street. It was a long way round, but he had reckoned that it was safer that way. He stopped the van outside a house that was not untypical of the neighbourhood. It held an air of neglect close to itself, like a faded, crabbed and dehydrated spinster; the small front garden was open to the road and paved to make a narrow and barely adequate parking space. The front door was rotting badly and someone had made free with a spray can; the net curtains at the windows were all too obviously of an older age, although they were defiantly clean, even in the glaring yellow neon light of dark morning in the centre of Gloucester; one of the upstairs windows was boarded because two years before someone had thrown a brick through it.

Rashid drove the van on to the parking space and stopped the engine. He waited for five long minutes, forcing himself to be still and calm, hoping that his arrival had excited no attention or, if it had, that it would be fleeting and bored; cars and vans – even lorries – coming and going in the middle of the night were not an uncommon phenomenon in Barton Street, where there was a code of deliberate disinterest amongst the residents. Only then did he climb softly out of the van, look carefully around and go to the front door.

Within a minute, Rashid and his cargo were inside the dark house.

Within another minute, Rashid was dead.

NINE

Harry Weston had had a good night. Harry Weston's idea of 'good' was not everyone's, in that it involved anything from poaching to petty theft; tonight it had involved doing a bit of redistribution of fuel oil, taking it from three unfortunate and unsuspecting homeowners and giving it (for a cost) to some of his clients, those in the community who were less than interested in where their heating oil came from and

who were not in the least surprised that it was delivered at four
o'clock in the morning. He would make a profit of three hundred
or so from tonight's enterprises.

He was on his way back to his cottage, and he was driving
carefully along a dark, wooded country lane (wouldn't do to
attract too much attention) when he saw headlights suddenly
appear some fifty metres ahead, coming around a bend. He
barely had time to register this before a dark van – a Transit,
he thought without really thinking it – appeared. It didn't slow,
didn't even seem to think about slowing; he wasn't going fast
and this fucking loony was going much too fast, but then he
didn't have his headlights on (he had always been of the opinion
that the better option in all situations was to remain as invisible as possible, and most especially when he was well over
the legal limit for the proverbial), so he was forced to admit
subsequently that he might share some guilt for what happened
next.

They didn't collide, but only because at the last moment they
both veered off the road. Harry was lucky, because on his side
there was a bit of a grass verge and no trees, whereas the other
guy was unlucky, because on *his* side of the road, there was a
bit of a grass verge and one tree. Which he hit.

Harry's pick-up truck had brakes that were, like his knees,
past their best-before date; in fact, they were past their sell-by
and use-by dates too. He managed to stop, though, although it
was perilously close to a drainage ditch. In a way, he was fortu-
nate because, although he wasn't wearing a seatbelt, it gave him
a chance to brace and to prevent serious injury to himself. It took
him only a few seconds to pull himself together and to recall
hearing the other van's impact with a rather sturdy sycamore
tree. He looked around over his right shoulder; the van driver
had done well, only clipping the wing, but doing so with enough
force to buckle it and cause it almost to come off. Harry got out,
feeling none too steady for all manner of reasons, not even sure
why he was doing so; something at the back of his clouded mind
suggested that his best course of action was not to be there at
that particular time. Perhaps it was an impulse born of humanity,
although he himself would have doubted it.

He walked slowly towards the van, looking around him as

much as where he was going; it was an area he knew well and it was well away from dwellings, but he was by nature a cautious criminal. He was about ten metres away and, not unnaturally, heading for the cab when the banging on the back doors of the van began. Startled, with confusion adding to his innate intellectual simplicity, he momentarily halted. The banging came again, and this time there was a muffled but undoubtedly anguished cry; he couldn't decipher what was said, couldn't even decipher if anything had been said at all, but he could tell a couple of things, one of which was that the cry denoted distress; the other was that it was the distress of a woman.

He frowned. He knew enough to know that there were degrees of infamy and that here was a degree that he did not like; pinching a bit of fuel oil or the odd river trout was just part of the hidden economy that kept things ticking along when things in the outside world went tits up; they did no harm, not really, and they kept people from the workhouse. There were some things, though, that stank of wrongness, that he couldn't abide at any cost. When he came close to the back of the van, he saw that the handles of the back doors were tied together so that they couldn't be opened from the inside, and he realized that someone had been shut in there. His first instinct was that was wrong, his second that it was possibly dangerous, the third that he should run; he might well have done so, too, but the cry came again, and this time it was accompanied by another.

Two of them? Two of what, though?

He hesitated, then looked to the front of the van; in the wing mirror he could see movement, but could make out no details. What was going on here? He asked himself the question and had no specific answers, yet the generalities were all too clear, and he didn't like the smell of them. He made a decision – the kind of decision he'd always made – and he turned, ready to run. Whatever was going on here was none of his business . . .

There was a thump on the back doors, just strong enough to move them and, at the same time, a hacking, bubbly cough; just the sound of it made his chest hurt. He found himself hesitating, some weak instinct of compassion kindled by the pathetic nature of what he saw and what he heard.

'Please . . .'

It was barely spoken, hardly even breathed, but he heard a young girl's voice and he heard agony.

There sounded a voice in his head and that voice said, *Shit . . .*

Unbidden and like a muscular reflex, he thought of Wanda. He felt in his jacket pocket, sorting with his fingers through the bric-a-brac that he always carried with him for his pocket knife.

Then it all began to happen at once; with a sudden, loud click, the driver's door of the van was forced slightly open; it was buckled by the collision, though, and would not budge more than a few centimetres. Immediately, there was another, but weaker, thump on the back doors. This only made the driver all the keener to get out, for his door was forced open a little further. Harry jumped back, the cough came again – this time even more agonizing in his ears – and for a third time the driver tried to get out. A face, barely discernible in the darkness, flashed briefly in the tall wing mirror as the door moved, and then was gone.

Harry was no hero, nor was he sorry because of this. He turned and ran.

But not before he had cut the cord that bound the back doors of the van.

TEN

She was jerked rudely from sleep, momentarily vertiginous, nauseated. Then she heard the van pull up on the drive outside the house and felt safe again; not happy, not comforted, just safe because she was no longer back in her childhood, with her father standing by her bed . . . She went immediately to the front room, standing to one side of the heavily curtained windows, peeking carefully out. They had disabled the security lights and the house was surrounded by thick woodland, so that there was little light to see by; but then there was little light to be seen by, as well. She could just about make out the outline of the van; it looked wrong, although she could make out few details. She waited, refusing to do anything precipitate, all too aware that caution was necessary at all times, especially now that they were so close. All the same, she heard herself whispering under her breath, *Come on . . .*

At last, the driver's door opened and a shape that she realized with some relief was Marty got out; and yet, even as she recognized him, she saw that something was wrong. He was moving awkwardly for some reason, and seemed to be holding his right arm stiffly. Still, she didn't move, just watched. He got out of the cab gingerly, leaving the door open, and came at once towards the house; only when he was five metres away did she leave her station and go to the front door. She opened it as he approached; no word was exchanged as he entered the small house and the door was closed behind him; no word was uttered as they went single file to the back room that had once been converted into a large kitchen. She made sure that the curtains were tightly closed before she put the light on, and that light was only a low-wattage bulb hung low over the pine table.

'What happened?' she asked. That something had happened was obvious, and that it had been something not good was equally plain. Marty looked shaken and pale, and he was holding his arm to his chest, his lips tight.

'I fucking crashed, didn't I?' He was murderously angry, she could tell. When Marty got like that, it took all her patience and skill to keep him from dangerous violence.

'Where?'

'I don't fucking know, do I?' he exploded. 'About a mile or two away, I suppose.'

'And the cargo?'

His reply was low, almost inaudible. 'They're gone,' he said bitterly.

It was her turn to react. 'Gone? What do you mean?'

He looked up at her, his eyes dangerously cold. 'What it says. They're gone.'

'How did that happen?'

Nothing.

She had once known him well, but not now, she appreciated. Now he was changed, so that, where once she had been sure of what kind of a man he was, what he needed, what he could give, what he liked, what he disliked, how to talk to him, and how to make him do what she wanted, now the rules had fundamentally changed. Now there were places inside him that were foreign to her; worse, they were forever unknowable. Now he was spoiled.

Someone would pay for that.

'Martin?' she said softly. 'You're hurt.' Still nothing; his face bore a grimace that she suspected was partly pain, partly frustration. 'Tell me what happened, my darling.'

She stood and came around to his side of the table to sit next to him. She took his head in her arms and gently pulled him towards her, so that she could kiss his bearded cheek. Slowly, he relaxed. 'It was going well. I was waiting inside the house when he came back; he never knew what happened to him.'

'The wife? Did you have any trouble with her?' If he thought she sounded oddly eager, he didn't show it.

'None,' he said, and there was some pride. 'She went down just like she was supposed to.'

'You wore the gloves the whole time?'

He nodded.

'And the cargo? Were they any trouble?'

He shook his head, but followed this up with a grimace. 'They're disgusting.'

She smiled. 'Of course they are. You knew they would be.'

'No, I mean really horrible. I hated it.'

She kissed him again and then whispered into his ear, 'Of course you did, Marty. Of course you did. But don't worry. It's nearly over.'

'He brought them in with him into the house.'

'Did you touch them?' she asked, her voice betraying concern.

'No. You told me not to, and I didn't. They were covered in . . . *stuff.*'

Marty had trouble with words; she loved him for it. 'I know, Marty. I know.' He nodded morosely at the memory, his eyes seeing the events of the recent past. She waited a heartbeat, maybe two, before asking, 'You got them back in the van without trouble?'

'They understood the knife.'

'And nobody saw you?'

'I don't think so.'

This had been – still potentially was – the weak point of the night's plan. Getting into the house after dark was likely to be fairly straightforward. Once inside, she knew that Marty would do his work easily and without noise; he was a large man with a lot of relevant training and experience. The only likely problem she had foreseen was – as had apparently happened – the cargo had gone into the house with Rashid Malik at once, rather than being kept in the back of the van; this would mean he would have to kill Rashid Malik, keep the cargo quiet, then get them back into the van. Fortunately, it sounded as if they had been too far gone to put up much opposition or make too much noise to alert nosy neighbours.

'So what happened?'

'I was nearly home when I almost crashed into someone coming the other way.' She didn't say anything, but he saw her face and it said much to him. He added plaintively, 'He had no headlights on.'

This surprised her, but she knew that Marty would not lie to her. This fact gave her pause for thought. 'Did you hit him?'

He shook his head vehemently. 'I managed to avoid him, but I hit a tree by the side of the road. I hurt my shoulder.'

She wanted desperately to know about 'the cargo', but she knew better than to rush him. 'Let me see, my angel.'

She had to help him unbutton his shirt; there was no blood but there was bruising over the end of his collar bone; he winced when she pressed on it but not in a way that told her it was broken. 'It's fine,' she told him reassuringly.

'You're sure?'

'I'm sure.' She kissed him on the cheek and he put his shirt back on. She made them both some instant coffee and put some whisky in his. Only then did she ask, 'How did the cargo get loose?'

'I was stunned when I hit the tree. The other driver freed them before I could get out to stop them.'

For perhaps the first time, she began to be really concerned. 'He set them free?'

Marty nodded and she could see that there was no point questioning him further; he was reporting all that he had seen, and Marty had not been made for deep speculation; that was her job in the partnership. 'The car was heading towards you? It didn't come from behind and try to force you off the road?'

'No.'

'And the driver freed them?'

He had.

'Was he on his own?'

He was.

'What did he do after he'd let them go?'

'He ran away.'

'Did you recognize him?'

He thought about this. 'I don't know his name . . .'

'But?'

'But I think I've seen him about, in the town. He was driving a white Toyota pick-up . . .'

'Good, good,' she said encouragingly. She gestured that he should drink up. 'Can you remember any more?'

But he couldn't, and it would soon be getting light. She said, 'Put the van in the garage, then get some sleep, Marty. You deserve it.'

'What are we going to do?'

'We'll go back to where the crash occurred tomorrow. See if we can track them down.'

'Supposing someone finds them?'

She forced more confidence into her voice than she felt. 'They won't have long to live, Marty. I expect we'll find them in the woods. We just have to make sure that no one else does.'

He nodded, taking comfort from her, as he always did. 'I did all right, though, didn't I?'

Jacqueline gave her son a tired smile, hoping that it wasn't too obviously worried. 'You did, Marty. You did.'

This is Jacqueline Millikan. She feels that she was nurtured by the instruments of the state, thought that she had grown into an understanding of the bargain; she now realizes that she had been wrong. She was raised in the certainty that her religion was a family; she married a man who had entered into a contract with the state that they both thought was fair and equal; she gave birth to a son who thought the same. She has now come to appreciate that everything she believed may well have been wrong; she thinks that she has been duped. She is past what was once called *epiphany*, what is now termed *paradigm shift.*

She feels that she has been scorned.

ELEVEN

Beverley clamped her teeth together, saying nothing, deliberately suppressing her immediate urge to unleash her temper and let loose some words of war. It was getting worse, this reaction. Yet a small part of her laughed, though this was not hysterical laughter, nor was it in even the slightest way amused; it was the laughter of monstrous irony, the only reaction when the fates that rule the cosmos play their games and, once again, prove how small and feeble humanity is in the face of the forces arrayed against it. She leaned back in her seat, pressing back against the headrest, trying to relieve the broiling within her as she listened to her new sergeant, as her anger accentuated the angle of her jaw and her cheekbones.

She could not believe that she had been saddled with this; not now, not after she had only just managed at last to escape years of being subordinate to incompetent, vindictive, lecherous senior staff. Her present commanding officer – Superintendent Richard Haines – had been a wondrous change to some of his predecessors as her boss; they had immediately struck up a good working relationship, one untainted by the smear of ulterior motive on either side; he was sociable when he wanted to be, businesslike when the situation called for it, and trustworthy. She had had an occasion a few months before – when he was quite newly arrived from Bristol – to ask him for support in a little jurisdictional battle she was having with an overbearing shit over the border in Monmouthshire, and he had come through for her spectacularly well. Looking upwards, then, everything could not have been better, so the fact that she was now forced to work with someone like Nathan Lever seemed all the more cruel.

To make matters even worse – in a way that was exquisitely apt, she had to admit – she recognized her sergeant's type.

As they drove along the A40 (the Golden Valley) that connected Cheltenham to Gloucester, every word he said, every tone he employed, every prejudice and piece of unpleasantness he betrayed, she heard echoed in her own memories. She was listening to an avatar of her earlier self, when she, too, had been uncaring, ambitious, ruthless and, above all, certain. She thought back a dozen years to another journey in a car, when she had been in the back and her then boss in front of her; when she had schemed and plotted, not how to seek out the killer of Nikki Exner at St Benjamin's Hospital, but how to use it for her own career advancement; how she had looked at her superior and seen in him only an old man in a dry month, someone to climb over and, if necessary, push away to fall to a dusty doom, uncared about.

True, Castle had been considerably older and much closer to retirement, but she knew the mindset of people like Lever too well. He would use every trick he could and take every opportunity that presented itself to advance not the case, not the course of justice, but his own career. He would look on the bodies and damage in his rear-view mirror not as regrettable, not as collateral damage, but as tokens of victory, like secretly taken phone snaps of sleeping sexual conquests.

'Fucking Barton Street,' he said loudly to no one and yet to everyone; to her, because he wanted to impress her, she guessed, and to the driver – Constable Melanie Harrison – because he wanted to screw her. 'Why they don't just nuke the place, I don't know.'

He had an uncultured tone, one that she guessed he had spent a lot of time perfecting, so that it would sound just right; nice and laddish for the boys, nice and rough for the girls. Beverley had seen his record and was well aware that he had been born and raised in Woking, had attended grammar school there, then obtained a poor degree in history at Sussex University. He had come into the police not because he had an overpowering urge to fight the good fight against the powers of anarchy and criminality, but because he wanted the privileges, he liked the idea of being allowed to be a bastard and get away with it, and he would be able to retire in his fifties. He wasn't alone in any of those, of course – if they excluded everyone who veered towards such tendencies, the entire country's police force could be billeted in a shed – and she herself knew that her motives for becoming a police officer had not been particularly high, but she was quickly discovering that Lever was something else. She had yet to find any redeeming qualities; even the fact that he was efficient was quietly alarming to her, because she appreciated that this meant he was going to be efficient at being a scheming, underhanded, cruel bastard, and that was something she could do without.

Once again, the ghosts of her past blew icy breath on her as a thought – unbidden and most decidedly unwanted – drifted into her head: *you were cruel and efficient at getting your own way, too.*

She saw him glance slyly across at Constable Harrison to see what reaction he got from his remark; Beverley couldn't see her face except in oblique profile, but the language of her head and shoulders suggested that she was agreeing with him. Idly, Beverley wondered if the young woman really did, or if she was playing the game to keep in with a superior officer, just as she had once done. Either way, she guessed that Melanie Harrison would do well, both because she was reasonably attractive and because she was just intelligent enough to use her physical attractiveness to advantage. She was a graduate entrant, one being fast-tracked to higher things; already she had done time on secondment to various specialist units. It would not be long, Beverley guessed, before she would be promoted, providing she didn't upset anyone. She would have a lot to put up with, though; people like Lever being just one irritation. She would be lucky to escape not infrequent sexual harassment, possibly even the occasional sexual demands of a senior officer. It was a scenario that Beverley knew well, her own career pathway littered with such episodes. There had been times when she felt that she was the victim of institutional sexual abuse; of course, she had early on realized that she could either use this fact of police life and gain a great deal, or buck against it and probably lose a great deal. It was a moral compromise that had looked mistaken on more than one occasion, but it had worked; she had played their game and endured to the end. That it had trapped her in a prison cell of self-loathing, that she carried with her an indelible reputation as being an amateur whore, and that she was secretly afraid that she needn't have resorted to such a strategy, was part of the tariff that she was now paying off.

She did not think that Melanie Harrison would have to endure such agonizing.

Lever said, 'It's a waste of fucking resources, anyway. Pakis killing their own isn't a crime.'

No, Beverley thought, *I was never this bad . . .*

Was I?

She said in a quiet but demonstrative voice, 'We don't know the nationality or ethnic origin of the killer – or killers.'

'They could be white, you mean?' he asked, but she saw his glance across to Harrison to make sure that she was paying attention to his wit. 'Maybe we shouldn't try too hard.'

Beverley had been holding her teeth so tightly together that it was hurting the sides of her face. She leaned forward so that her head was between Lever and Harrison. Staring straight ahead at the Cathedral in the distance, she said, 'If you don't shut the fuck up, Lever, I'll have you suspended and charged with incitement to racism. Then I'll give your name and address to a West Indian acquaintance of mine who has a particular allergy to snivelling white shits like you.'

There was a silence in the car as she withdrew her head; it wasn't just any silence, but one that battered the ears, made the heart beat faster. She saw from the slight bulge on the side of his head that it was Lever's turn to clench his teeth; Harrison had gone pale and was suddenly concentrating to an astonishing degree on her driving; Beverley could see in the mirror that her eyes were wide.

Into the shocked silence, she asked, 'What are the names of the victims?'

His voice was calm, dangerously so, as he read from his notebook. 'Rashid and Parveen Malik.'

The car had stopped at the lights outside the railway station. 'Who found the bodies?'

Lever took a moment to respond and his words were dull. 'Fatima Butt.'

'Who is?'

'As far as we can tell, the mother of the female victim.'

'And just what the fuck does that mean?' She thought for a

moment that he meant that they had been mutilated. He turned in his seat to face her, a deliberately aggressive act; on his face she saw cold anger and, just for a moment, she was afraid. Just for a moment, though; she had come up against bigger, uglier and nastier men than Sergeant Nathan Lever – most of them had been policemen – and she had survived. He said with the slightest hint of a sneer, the merest intimation that he wasn't going to let her get away with belittling him in front of a mere constable, that he would never forget and never forgive her for it, 'The bodies were discovered by someone we believe to be the deceased woman's mother. She's gone completely mental – the officers at the scene can hardly get anything out of her, and most of that's in fucking *Paki* talk. She's in no fit state to make a formal ID.'

His emphasis on the racist word was deliberate, she knew. She briefly contemplated taking up his challenge there and then, but quickly decided against; at least things were now out in the open. There had been underlying tensions between the two for a couple of weeks now, and he had only been assigned to her two months before. It had started when he had made a pass at her, and not just any pass. It had been at the end of an evening in a pub in Montpelier, Cheltenham, effectively the police station's official drinking den. It was at the end of a three-week trial of three men accused of the rape and murder of a seventeen-year-old prostitute; the jury had pronounced them guilty and the judge at Gloucester Crown Court had promised them long sentences. It was good and many of them were drunk; although Lever had joined the station only after the case had been prepared and submitted to the Crown Prosecution Service, he had been drunker than most, as if he needed the reflected glory to justify his arrogance. Beverley had long ago made it a rule not to get drunk in public – and most definitely not in public with other police officers – and had enjoyed the evening, the exuberance and elation of her team, reminiscing about such occasions in her past, occasions which had seemed to happen much more frequently then. Police work now seemed a peculiarly joyless thing, a process of avoiding bear-traps and landmines rather than doing something that felt worthwhile. She had taken a call from a contact of hers – someone who in the old days would have squirmed under the name of 'grass' or 'snout', but whom she preferred to think of now as 'sensors', people who (for a price, of course) listened and watched and sniffed, and tipped her the proverbial if there were things she might like to know about. It had been noisy in the pub and she had gone outside better to hear what she was being told. 'What is it, Benny?'

'Does the name Arthur Meadows mean anything to you?' The voice was thin and nasally. Benny was a sometime tattooist, sometime user of heroin and (decidedly small-time) sometime dealer of same. She dreaded to think what artistic results he produced when he was going through a minor withdrawal episode, which was a not infrequent occurrence.

'Should it?'

'I don't know.' Benny was like this: elusive and therefore irritating. She endured him because his work brought him into contact with a constant stream of the type of people she was interested in. Her hold over him was simple; she knew that he was hepatitis positive, which is generally frowned upon amongst the tattooing fraternity and liable to lead to his dismissal, if not the breakage of his leg bones.

'Tell me more, Benny.'

As she listened, Lever came out for a smoke. She looked across at him but didn't acknowledge his presence; she turned away, not wanting Lever to know too much of what was going on. Benny said, 'I hear he's short of money.'

'So I should pull him in for what, Benny? Running an overdraft perhaps? Or wasting money on the Lotto?'

'He's got his own HGV.'

'Why doesn't he sell that and live off the profit?'

Benny said slyly, 'I think the bank might have something to say about that, if he did.'

'What's your point?'

'I overheard someone telling someone else that he's found a way of boosting his income.'

'Go on.'

Benny paused and she knew what that meant; he was trying to salve his conscience by framing his replies in opaque, oblique terms, so that he could tell himself that he wasn't actually informing. She became aware that Lever had moved closer to her and she turned to look him in the eye as a warning. He was pouring smoke into the night in a blossoming cone; it was starting to drizzle just slightly. She turned away from him and moved a step forward as Benny said, 'He makes a lot of trips abroad.'

She said, 'Drugs.'

A pause. 'I don't think so.'

'What, then?'

'There's nothing definite . . .'

'For fuck's sake, Benny,' she hissed. 'I don't appreciate the fact that you're wasting my social time . . .'

Quickly, he said, 'I've heard he might be moving livestock.'

This made her pause. 'I see . . .'

'And he's not a farmer,' added Benny, just in case she hadn't got the point.

'OK, I get it.'

She cut the connection before he could ask her for any money; it was potentially interesting – in which case she might give him something for the information – but potentially just meaningless tittle-tattle. Benny had been known to provide her with some very useful tips, but if his funds were a little on the low side, he could prove unreliable as his desperation increased and his antennae became oversensitive.

Lever, again surprisingly and uncomfortably close, said into her ear, 'Anything useful?'

She turned abruptly. He was standing less than a metre from her, a knowing smile on his slightly too-full lips, his eyes dancing lazily with intelligence. 'Were you listening?' she demanded. Sources of information such as Benny were jealously guarded; Lever knew that.

'Not really, but it was obvious it wasn't your poor sick mother.'

She looked at him; it was something that would have caused many to feel uncomfortable but not, apparently, Lever. She wondered if he knew that her mother was in a nursing home in Hove with severe Alzheimer's and going downhill rapidly. It was then that she realized that he was very drunk indeed. She said, 'A word of advice, Sergeant. Play by the rules.'

His cigarette was nearing its end, a casualty on the battleground of human craving, and he now put it between his lips and sucked hard at it before flicking it into the gutter. 'I always do.'

'Good.'

She began to walk past him but he moved to block her; it wasn't an overtly intimidating gesture, but it made a point and it stopped her, giving him temporarily a political, physical, even sexual advantage. He said quietly, 'But what's the game, Beverley?'

She had to step slightly back to cease the contact. 'What the fuck are you talking about, Lever?'

He came forward to negate her evasion. 'Come on, we all know about you.'

She flared and, as was her habit, in her incandescence her voice became low and venomous, her face taut with hard-edged angles, her eyes brilliantly cold. 'Say that again,' she suggested.

But he didn't yield. Instead, he just remained in front of her, his stance one of intimidation and careless antagonism and, to make his indifference clear, he put on a sneer. 'Or do you only sleep with senior officers? The ones who can give you a bunk-up in more senses than one?'

She felt herself flushing and could not allow that. Nor would she give him the satisfaction of slapping him. She was reduced to saying, 'Get back inside, Lever.'

For a long moment, she was afraid that he wouldn't, that he would play this out for longer, that she would be forced to interact with him and, in doing so, sink lower into the faecal pit of her own past. Only after several cars had swung around the roundabout outside the pub, and several people had walked past in couples and small groups, did he turn away from her and do as she had ordered.

TWELVE

John Eisenmenger yawned, a reflex action born not of tiredness but of tedium. It was not yet nine in the morning and already he was bored. There had been numerous occasions over the past twenty years when he had prayed for a break in the steady stream of work that had assailed him from all directions – routine surgical biopsy specimens and cytology samples to report, specimens to dissect, Coroners' autopsies, hospital autopsies and Home

Office autopsies to perform, management tasks to undertake, lectures to give, lectures to attend, articles to write; now, of course, he had what he had wished for, and he was dissatisfied. Dissatisfaction, it seemed, was his inescapable fate, a bête noire that was always there, ever just out of sight, yet heavy in his awareness. It was just one of many, though; sometimes it felt to him as if there were huge herds of black beasts grazing just beneath his consciousness, cropping the grass of his memory, drinking dry the watering holes of his self-esteem; as if his head were filled in its corners with shades, spectres and spirits which, although silent, screamed in tormented pain for every second of every hour that he knew, whether asleep or no. It was screaming directed at him, too; these insubstantial players – those he had known and loved, those who had known and loved him, and those whom he had never known whilst alive yet had come to know in their death – would not leave him, neither because they could, nor because they would. They were his and he was theirs, and perhaps not even death would separate them.

He had started to write the book at the suggestion of Serge, his therapist. No, he corrected himself, his *latest* therapist, for Eisenmenger had had several over the months; he had become something of a connoisseur of therapists and their various forms of therapy. He had tasted hypnotherapy, neurolinguistic programming and cognitive analytical therapy; he had lain on couches or sat in chairs whilst people tried to hypnotize him and then ask him questions, and he thought about lots of things, but mostly about whether or not he was hypnotized, and how would anyone know? He had done silly exercises whilst feeling like a fool; he had been shown innumerable diagrams in the shape of circles or pyramids or glasses; he had been given homework tasks to perform, often in the form of mental exercises in cognition; and always he had felt slightly idiotic, or slightly unfulfilled, or both. It had taken him some months and some thousands of pounds to realize that there was a fundamental obstacle to this kind of treatment doing him any good at all; he only now appreciated that not only was it necessary for the therapee to have a close emotional relationship with the therapist, but it was an absolute prerequisite that the therapee should not be paying said therapist any money. During all those hours of earnest talking and dissection of his fractured psyche, he now saw that he had been unable to escape the suspicion that the other person in the room was only in it for the money, and that the resolution of his problems was secondary and, indeed, expendable. After all, a hardworking therapist might find himself or herself in penury were the client to be suddenly cured.

Ally that to the appreciation that training in therapy was available by distance learning, that it required for its practice no medical or psychological training, that it was only lightly regulated and that – no matter how screwed-up he was – he just couldn't see how walking towards a wall with his eyes shut, while joss sticks burned and whale music incongruously battled the Cheltenham town centre traffic, was going to help him come to terms with his life, loves and memories, and he came to the inescapable conclusion that he was wasting his money.

He had found Dr Serge Burbatov through contacts at his GP practice; it had not been a formal referral – making contact with a consultant psychiatrist was harder than talking to the dearly departed in the modern NHS – but achieved because he was a doctor and because Serge had a professional interest in psychiatric conditions amongst medical staff. Another bonus was that Serge Burbatov offered a kind of therapy – psychoanalytical in nature – that Eisenmenger had yet to try in his slow, tortuous course through the maze of psychological nostrums; there had been times on this journey when he felt as if he were trudging through some sort of labyrinthine bazaar, being tempted into dark shops to try treatments that were little more than coloured water. Now, perhaps for the reason that his subconscious allowed him to trust that this man knew what he was talking about because he had a considerably deeper and longer period of study behind him, and perhaps because Eisenmenger was no longer handing over a cheque for two hundred and fifty pounds every month, he felt as if he were making progress.

But not progress with the book. He had been at it for five weeks now, and had put down only six thousand words, and he still didn't feel that he had so much invested in the book that he could not abandon it, that he was yet seriously embedded in the book. It was supposed to be about his life as a pathologist – not just the forensic work, but the whole of it; how it had interacted – perhaps 'reacted' would have been a more apposite term – with his personal life, and how that in turn had affected him. All that he had found on the sheets of paper, though, were words about the *technicalities* of his work, the algorithms through which he now ran as automatically as a tube train on the Circle Line; he might as well have been writing a primer about how to practise pathology. That was the thing about medicine, though; it was a way of life that took one away from life, and no specialty more than his. Oncologists and palliative care physicians – who perhaps came closer to death more than any other non-pathological doctor – had the occasional respite of their treatments actually prolonging life, even effecting a cure. They had, too, the comfort of gratitude from their patients or their relatives; few pathologists have ever received a present from a grateful patient, even though most of his work had been for the living and had helped cancer patients and others with serious illness to receive the optimal treatment. The pathologist was ever the back-room boy, there to be blamed if things went wrong, not there to be remembered if (as they usually did) they went right.

And all he had now was a sense of bitterness; bitterness that his work for the living was doomed to bloom and waste for ever its sweetness on the desert air of Gloucestershire, while his work for the dead had left him crippled inside. He felt as if he were in a mental cul-de-sac without a reverse gear; one that had steep walls, and that was too narrow to turn round in . . .

He turned his attention once more to the screen in front of him, feeling again that he had lost control of all the most significant aspects of his life, not at all sure that he *wanted* to write the bloody book any more, that he could cope without reliving some of the less savoury moments that had come his way. Tomorrow he was on the rota for coronial autopsies – work he still continued in order to reduce the strain on his finances whilst he tried to come to terms with his situation. He was, as the biologists would say, 'terminally differentiated'; he was fit for only one job, but it was a job that brought him only distress; a job that had become an impossibly thin line between the boredom of routine work as a general hospital cellular pathologist – writing an endless stream of similar reports, examining the torrent of surgical biopsy specimens that flowed forever under his microscope – and the over-intense but more interesting, forensic work, the work that he knew would one day destroy him.

THIRTEEN

The crime scene wasn't far from the level crossing and they had to wait for a train to cross, ignorant that this was a faint echo of what had happened the night before. It had taken them thirty minutes to get here from the Golden Valley, even though Barton Street had been closed to traffic. There was a crowd around the house, filling the pavement on both sides of it and accumulated on the opposite side of the road, although they couldn't have seen much, for there were three police cars, a hearse, an ambulance with its rear doors open and, Beverley saw with some dismay, a battered Volvo estate that she recognized all too well. 'Jesus,' she breathed. Lever heard her, for his head moved involuntarily, although he said nothing. They parked behind the hearse and got out, aware that they were being scrutinized, that much of the murmuring around them was about them, and that they were not the most popular of people in this particular neighbourhood; Lever's way of coping with it was to stare venomously around him, as if daring someone to say something that he could take issue with.

Two men in black suits and ties waited in the hearse, unable and perhaps unwilling to shake the impression that they were nothing more than feeders on the corpse. As she walked past the ambulance, Beverley could see two paramedics tending to a short Asian woman who was clearly in great distress; she had on an oxygen mask and was hyperventilating; one of the paramedics was holding a plastic beaker of something – possibly water – close to her lips while the other struggled to get a blood pressure cuff on her arm. There wasn't room for the female police officer in the back of the vehicle; she waited patiently just outside, a notebook at the ready, presumably just in case this poor and hysterical woman should utter some priceless, never-to-be-repeated gobbet of evidence. Beverley received a nod from her as she passed.

They stopped in front of the house and looked at it. One of the upper windows was boarded, the front door was battered and had been spray-painted; try as she might, she could see nothing intelligible in this vandalism – not even obscenity or insult – and it just seemed to be some sort of primal expression. The minute front garden had been made into a single parking space, although it was now empty. There was one dustbin with an unmatched, ill-fitting lid at the end of this. Lever's expression told of mounting disgust, but she guessed he was enjoying the situation because of it; everything he saw ticked the little boxes in his head that told him his world view was the only reasonable one. She guessed that the stench coming from the opened front door was only adding to his prejudices in spades.

The front door opened directly into a living room, the stairs to the upper floor directly ahead. Inside, all the lights were on and she wondered if that was how it had been before the travelling law-and-order circus and funfair had descended on Barton Street; she couldn't blame someone for deciding that more light wouldn't go amiss – the net curtains were so thick and heavy that they allowed the admission of hardly any illumination, and those photons that did make it through were clearly exhausted by the effort. As long as they hadn't left their fingerprints on the light switch, and as long as they hadn't wiped any relevant ones off, and as long as they remembered exactly which lights had been on . . .

The room was crowded with ornaments, many large and brightly coloured; every surface was covered in framed photographs of groups of people – presumably family and friends – and various exotic beauty spots; the furniture was clean and looked comfortable to sit in, although showing its age; a large television – too big for the room – stood in the far corner, squatting down over a DVD player. Two forensics officers – Beverley knew them only slightly – were crouched down by the front windows, their disposable suits rustling as they did whatever they did. The stench was stronger in here.

She asked them, 'Where's safe?'

They both stopped and the older one – Stan? Steve? – said,

'We checked and hoovered the carpet from where you are to that doorway.' He indicated the entrance to the back living room that was in the corner opposite the television.

Lever asked, 'What are you doing down there?'

They both stood so that he could see what had been the object of their interest. It was a pool of faeces. Their attitudes suggested that they were slightly embarrassed, as if they had been caught doing something shameful. Lever's face didn't need accompanying sound, but he made one anyway. 'Jesus fucking Christ! The dirty cunts.'

Beverley might have reacted if Lever hadn't; all she did, though, was bend a little closer to the mess. 'Is that blood there as well?' she asked.

'We think so. We'll have to test it formally in the lab, but it's positive on dipstick testing.'

Curious, she thought. Was it relevant, though? Lever clearly wanted it to be yet another prop to his racism, but she doubted that it was. From the outside, this house might appear unloved and ill-used, but from what she could see of this room, that was a deceptive appearance. This had the air of a bolt-hole, a haven that was merely disguised as derelict; the people who had lived here had had standards, even if they kept them hidden from outside view. She couldn't see them putting up with something as disgusting as that on the carpet for very long.

She went along the path that the forensics team had already checked and, in a final attempt to make sure that not the smallest piece of potentially useful evidence was missed, vacuumed, stopping just inside the doorway. A middle-aged woman with bright red hair that peeped out from under the hood of her disposable clean suit was standing with a digital SLR camera pointed down over a body on the floor, although Beverley could only see the legs because the top half was obscured by a second figure, similarly attired, that was crouching with its back to her. It was a back that she recognized with a heart that not so much sank as plummeted.

She sighed more than said, 'Dr Sydenham.'

The figured looked back over his shoulder, saw who had spoken and immediately stood up to face her; his gloved hands were liberally doused with blood and, from a face that was curiously baby-like due to the elasticated hood that encased it, he exclaimed, 'Beverley! How the very devil are you?'

She didn't wince and she didn't flinch, but it was only through years of training. 'I'm fine.'

'Good! Good!'

'I thought you'd retired.' She meant, *I hoped you'd retired.*

He laughed. She knew it well; it was unpleasant and came down a nose that seemed forever turned up and looked down. 'I was but, what with Johnny going MIA, I was asked by the boys at the MOJ to come back and lend an expert hand.' By 'Johnny' he meant Eisenmenger.

Her opinion of the Ministry of Justice had never been high, but this snippet sent it into the sludge of the sewer. Had there been no one else they could turn to? She knew from Eisenmenger that pathologists of his ilk – those who were interested in autopsy pathology – were a rare breed, becoming endangered, but surely there had been someone else? Although she tried to keep these thoughts from her voice as she spoke, she was aware that her voice held more than a trace of irony as she said, 'I'm grateful.'

She needn't have worried, though; his beaming smile told her that Sydenham, as was characteristic of him, failed to notice her tone; he seemed to have the unalterable opinion that everyone admired his intellect and loved him for his charm. 'So you should be,' he proclaimed. Turning to the corpse, he opined, 'Not a good one, this.' He said it as if he were critiquing an art work.

Lever, from behind her and just to her left, asked, 'What can you tell us, Doctor?'

Anger burned bright within Beverley; Lever was being insubordinate and he knew it. Sydenham didn't give a fig; he loved performing and proclaiming like a loud and self-important actor-manager of the late nineteenth century. 'This man has been stabbed in the abdomen and also had his throat slit.' As he said this, he stepped backwards so that they could see for themselves. There was a lot of blood, but the slit in the stomach wall was clear to see; something yellow poked out of it, as if this were a form of biological stuffing; the wound across the throat was equally easy to see, although the amount of blood associated with it was even more shocking. The carpet – a lush, deep-pile thing of lustrous blue, was soaked through in the shape of a plume that had as its base the body's head, so that it bore a vague but distinct resemblance to an artist's rendition of an incarnadine flame. Beverley was used to such sights, but even she found the effect slightly shocking; Lever, though, didn't seem in the least disturbed. It was with heartless enthusiasm that he asked, 'How do you know it was in that order?'

Sydenham wore thick-rimmed glasses, although the lenses did not appear to Beverley to be particularly strong and she speculated that he wore them for effect. He now peered over these at Lever; she knew that he loved questions because they were opportunities to show off his knowledge and skill, and to put someone in their place, and 'their place' was always going to be considerably inferior to Sydenham's. 'Because . . .' He paused. '. . . Constable?'

Lever replied sourly, 'Sergeant.'

'Sergeant . . .' – and Sydenham's voice told all of them that he didn't really care one jot what Lever might care to call himself because, to Sydenham, Lever was an insignificant dullard – 'it is hardly necessary to stab someone in the abdomen after they've almost decapitated them.'

He had a point. The cut through the throat was deep and extravagant, reaching almost from ear lobe to ear lobe, and it seemed shockingly deep.

Lever persisted. 'It was obviously a frenzied attack. I don't see why the killer couldn't have just stabbed the victim in a sort of rage, even after doing that to the throat.'

Sydenham sighed, a signature sound; it conveyed exasperation and pity perfectly. 'My dear *Sergeant,*' he responded, with a nice touch of emphasis on the rank to make it plain that he was having trouble seeing how Lever had managed to attain even that paltry station in life, 'two strokes with a knife are not *frenzied.* Ten, twenty, fifty, a hundred or even more would constitute frenzy, a state of mind where rational thought is no longer part of the action, where the only criterion for ceasing is exhaustion. This is clearly a case where the attacker stabbed once into the abdominal cavity in a surprise attack, then, when the victim was completely disabled but not dead, the job was finished with the slice through the anterior throat.'

He smiled superciliously at Lever, who was blushing, Beverley noticed. She saw that perhaps Sydenham had his uses after all.

The pathologist went on. 'The first wound was made from the front by a single-sided, non-serrated blade about three inches wide at its base, at least ten, maybe twelve inches long. Then, when the victim was on the floor on all fours, the attacker came around the back, stood astride him, grabbed his hair to pull his head up, then cut the throat in a single stroke. As far as I can tell, it was the same knife.'

Beverley asked, 'Left or right hand?'

'Difficult to judge at the moment, what with the blood, but the wound appears to be deeper on the right-hand side, indicating a left-hander . . . a "southpaw".' He paused before looking up at Lever and Beverley. 'Very *sinister*, wouldn't you say, Chief Inspector?' He laughed heartily at his own witticism, one that seemed to leave all others in the room strangely unmoved. Not that this perturbed Sydenham. After a short while, he said, 'No sign to suggest a struggle, either; it was a very efficient killing.'

'Professional?' asked Lever. He sounded very keen that it should be.

Sydenham snorted. 'How the bloody hell should I know, Sergeant? I haven't found a receipt for services rendered, if that's what you mean.'

Beverley could almost hear Lever grinding his teeth. She asked, 'Where's the other body?'

'Ha!' Sydenham was delighted that she had asked. He stepped none too delicately over the body and strode to the back of the room. On the left was another doorway that she could see led into a galley-style kitchen; on the right was a closed door and, between the two, there was a small dining table against the wall on which was a closed laptop computer. Sydenham went to the closed door and turned to them as he grasped the handle, pulled it down to fling the door wide, a gesture of unnecessary theatricality. Behind it was revealed a built-in cupboard, and in that cupboard was a second body; it was curled into a foetal position on the floor and also covered in blood. All they could see at their distance from across the room was a curved back and long, black and wiry hair. Sydenham might have been a stage magician revealing the climax of his latest trick, albeit one that had apparently failed disastrously. He said, 'Before you ask, she's not in here getting the ironing board out. I would suggest that the likeliest explanation of this little scenario is that she was killed first, hidden in this broom closet, and then the killer waited to ambush the male.'

Beverley considered this a reasonable supposition, albeit one with a lot of guesswork involved. 'How was she killed?'

Sydenham didn't stint in showing his contempt for this question. 'I haven't looked at her yet, have I? You surely don't think I examined her and then bundled her back up into the cupboard, do you?'

She took the point, and perhaps she imagined Lever's enjoyment of her situation, but she doubted it; she stored the feeling of irritation for future use as a fuel when she next incinerated Lever, as she knew she surely would. She said to her sergeant, 'Check the rear of the house. See if it's secure.'

His nod was delayed by a look that, had she been cynical, she would have called 'insubordinate'. When he had left, she asked Sydenham tiredly, 'Can you give me any idea of when this might have happened?'

Years of such situations, memories of scores of pathologists treating corpses like dead sheep that were just fodder for measurement, had left her asking this purely from formulaic enervation. Sydenham looked down at the corpse, then at the clock on the wall, a cheap thing of plastic. 'Is that right?' he asked doubtfully.

'More or less.'

'Then I would estimate this poor chap died between two and four in the morning.'

Beverley had expected the usual dissembling that she always got from pathologists, the pseudo-scientific crap that they trotted out whenever they were asked for specifics; she had seen it a thousand times in court. This completely unexpected decision to be helpful – pathologists were renowned for being interested only in covering their arses, and Sydenham was famous for being one of the worst – was as shocking as an ice cube down her neck. She knew better than to comment, though; she had learned through long, arduous experience that Sydenham could be very good, or he could be almost negligent in his opinions; sometimes producing startling deductions that were almost too good to be true, as they not infrequently proved to be. Were she to question him, though, or often hint that she did not believe him in totality, and he would be merciless in his excoriative riposte, almost vituperative in his indignation that she should presume the authority to criticize him. She would have to accept what he said, but not base a case on it, at least not until some form of corroboration was open to her.

He was probably right about the order of the killings, though. The killer or killers had been waiting for the male victim, having already despatched his wife and tidied her away in the cupboard. These were violent killings and the motive was as yet obscure. Again, Sydenham was right in his assessment that they were not frenzied, which argued against race as a motive, but didn't exclude it completely. She doubted, too, that it had been done for robbery – the only possibility along those lines was that the killer had been after a specific thing of value that was hidden. If that were the case, though, why were there were no signs of searching? She had yet to look upstairs, it was true, but in the downstairs living room there was no sign that anyone had been searching for anything, and it was hardly likely that anyone undertaking such a search would be particularly interested in taking care to put things back as they were. Could it be that the item the killer was after was elsewhere? A combination number, perhaps? But wouldn't there be signs of an interrogation? This seemed to be a pair of executions, done swiftly and economically; the man, at least, looked merely as if he had been surprised, stabbed in the stomach and then had his throat slit, all done in ten seconds or less. Possibly it was the way that the wife had been bundled away that kept whispering to her that she had not been the target; she had merely been in the way – 'collateral damage' was the modern way of phrasing it, a seepage from the military's habit of coy euphuism about death. What, then – if not theft – had been the reason for the murders?

If she were discounting robbery – and she was only speculating as yet, quite ready to re-embrace any possibility should further evidence come to light – then she was left with sex or a murder related to some sort of criminal activity as her two likeliest motives. Normally, the fact that both a husband and a wife had been killed would argue against a sexual reason, but in this case she wondered if that were necessarily true; was there a possibility that this had been an honour killing of some sort? She thought that she would do well to research such a possibility. The concept that this was related to crime struck her as the likeliest, at least on present evidence. There was a touch of professionalism about all this that told her that the murders had not been the work of an outraged, offended uncle who imagined that a family's honour had been besmirched. That she was standing in a house in Barton Street, Gloucester, added weight to that theory, too; throw a stone around here and you'd be more likely than not to hit a thief or a prostitute, a young boy dealing in drugs or a group of two or three just back from stealing a car and then setting fire to it on Staverton Airport.

And yet . . .

Lever came back. She demanded, 'Well?'

'There's a small back garden without a rear gate; the fence is pretty rotten but nearly two metres high; the garden's a mess . . .'

'I don't give a shit about the state of the garden,' she said tiredly, and really just to put him down.

'. . . but the back door is secure and there's no sign of forced entry around any of the windows,' he continued evenly, as though she hadn't spoken.

So the killer hadn't broken in at the back; she had already noted that the front door hadn't been tampered with and that the front windows were secure. Presumably, something as simple as a knock on the door, then. If it hadn't been someone they knew, though, then what? Either the entry had been effected by subterfuge, or there had been some sort of violence involved, and that meant perhaps someone had seen something. She told Lever, 'Seize the laptop and get it to the computer lab. Then organize house to house, both sides of the street. I want to know if anyone saw anything between about six o'clock last night and six this morning. I want to know if the Maliks were into anything illegal and, if so, what it was.'

Lever said sneeringly, 'Like anyone around here is going to tell *us*.'

'Whatever, Sergeant. If we don't ask the questions, then we may miss something very important.'

He turned to go but she hadn't finished. 'After organizing *that*,' she continued, 'I want you to interview the mother. I want to know when she last saw them alive, when she found them, what she knows about any business activities, and whether there was any unhappiness in either her family or his family; get the names of all close relations so that, when you get back to the station, you can do standard checks to see if this is some sort of family feud.'

'What will you be doing?'

It wasn't the sort of question a sergeant should have asked a chief inspector, and certainly not in the tone he had adopted. In fact, she was going to search the upstairs rooms and recheck the rear access to the house, because she didn't trust him to have done a proper job. She said coldly, '*I'll* be waiting for *you* to do what I've told you to do, Sergeant.'

FOURTEEN

Marty drove Jacqueline to the site of the accident; he was good at that kind of thing, she knew – excellent spatial awareness – and his army training had improved what had already been a powerful, innate skill. There was some damage to the tree, although not much; probably not noticeable enough to arouse undue interest. What worried her more were the traces of blood and faeces that were present around the tree; they couldn't be seen from the road, but if someone noticed the tracks that led from the road to the damaged tree and followed them, they would hardly fail to notice the traces. She told Marty to get a spade from the back of their Land Rover and dig over them. It was a little-used road and she doubted that many people ever passed that way, but it would be wise, she thought, to hide what they could.

There was undoubted evidence that the traces led off into the woods.

'What do we do?'

She had spent the night trying to work out who the stranger could be, the one who had released the cargo. There weren't many white pick-up trucks in the neighbourhood. 'The man who let them go – could it have been Harry Weston?' she asked.

Marty responded at once. 'That's him. I've seen him in the Seven Stars a few times. He's a farmer, isn't he?' Marty was now like that, she had come to appreciate. He had never been able to make that final step up to cleverness; after what had happened, it was now a chasm he was doomed never to be able to bridge and she loved him all the more for it, even while telling herself fiercely that it wasn't pity but unbridled maternal love.

She snorted. 'He owns a smallholding, but I wouldn't call him anything as grand as a "farmer". He's too keen on poaching, thieving and drinking.'

'Shall we go and talk to him?'

'It's something that has to be done, for sure,' she said, almost to herself. 'But we've also got to find our little treasure trove, haven't we?'

He looked earnestly at her; the dilemma would, she knew, be difficult for him to cope with. Only she could make the decision of what to do; once made, he would do his best to carry it out but, until that moment, he was as feeble as a baby. 'From what I've heard of Harry Weston, he'll be in no hurry to talk to any police. I think that maybe we should search around here for a while, see if we can't recover our property.'

He acquiesced at once, without argument, without even thought of argument. It was a reaction that she'd become familiar with over the recent past, yet one that never failed to cast her into a depression so deep even all her tears could not fill it. She put out her hand to touch his arm, surprising him. 'What is it?'

Yet she didn't know what to say, which was perhaps why she asked, 'Do you ever think about Daddy?'

She hadn't asked him this before; perhaps, she suddenly realized, she'd never asked it before at all. It wasn't surprising that this question did not immediately bring forth an answer; she saw with some pain that the immediate reactions in his eyes were first bewilderment and then, quite clearly, pain. His nod was slow, agonizingly so, as if the movements of his neck were arthritic and inflamed. 'All the time.'

She smiled, even though her cheeks did not want to and her

eyes were interested only in sorrow. She squeezed his arm gently. 'Good.'

But all things have consequences. He asked of her, 'Is he with God?'

Now there was a question. It had all been simple when she had been young, when she had had a husband and Marty had had a father, and the world had allowed her to have imbecile beliefs.

'He's at peace,' she replied evasively, pathetically.

'With God?'

She took a deep breath, regretting her stupidity in asking the first question. 'With *his* God,' she said.

He frowned. 'But why are we doing—'

She cut him off. 'What we're doing has *nothing* to do with God, Marty.'

Her voice would brook no polemic. If he had thought to argue, he didn't. Instead, he considered what she said with a depth of concentration only a child could ordinarily summon; he was, though, a child, she reminded herself cruelly. She was blessed in that way; she had a son who would never grow up. If only that were all there was to it . . .

He said eventually and with heartbreaking seriousness, 'Good.'

Before they set off into the woods, she made him move the Land Rover well over a kilometre down the road, so as not to invite suspicion. When he was back, she said, 'And remember, Marty, don't go anywhere near them unless you absolutely have to.'

He nodded solemnly. He knew how dangerous they were.

FIFTEEN

'Arthur?' Joan Meadows couldn't keep the trepidation from her voice as she called up the stairs. There was no response, even when she repeated her call. She turned away, unsure what to do, and stood for a moment, completely still as she pondered her next move, a statue paradoxically built

out of uncertainty. He had woken her when he had come in; he
always did, but this time there had been something – many things,
actually – that had been different about him. His breathing for
a start; it had been loud and rasping, as if he were both exhausted
and incubating a steaming cold. And then there had been the
smell; that had troubled her the most, because she could not
avoid the conclusion that it had reminded her of cold meats that
had gone off, just past their sell-by date. It had been nothing
rank – not an odour of rotting or outright decay – and she might
have imagined it, except that when she had risen quietly and
carefully from his side that morning, it had still been there. There
had been a pallor to his face, too, one that was dampened by
sweat; and had that been blood at the corner of his mouth? She
hadn't dared wake him – after his long trips, he was always bad-
tempered and demanding of peace and sleep – but she had been
very tempted this time.

Now it was late afternoon and he was still asleep – a long
time, even for him. She didn't know whether it was for the best
to leave him to wake in his own time or to slake her anxiety and
check that all was OK. She didn't want another row, although
what she wanted – what he wanted, too, she suspected – didn't
seem to enter into it these days. She still loved him, but the years
had somehow eroded her ability to say it, had transmuted affection and a light heart into drear cynicism and irritation that was
too easily triggered. Did he still love her? That simple question
would not leave her, and added its own barb to her fears.

What did he do on those trips to the other side of Europe?
That was another needle of worry that was slowly pushing its
way through into her heart. In the old days – when he had been
happy or, at least, happier – his main work had been to and from
Germany, the Netherlands or France; he had been happy to discuss
the loads and talk about his tribulations. Now, though, he made
more and more of these mysterious journeys to Turkey, or even
Russia or the Ukraine. They were long trips that exhausted him
– of course they did – but there was more to his resentment and
anxiety and nastiness than mere physical tiredness, she knew.
There was a hint of paranoia, she suspected.

She suspected, too, that she knew the cause.

His decision to 'upgrade' the lorry had taken her by surprise, especially because it was at a time when money was getting rarer in their household. He had never told her exactly how much it had cost, but she thought it had been a lot. Shortly after, he had begun to make the occasional longer trip and he had also begun to change into what he was now, and she saw a clear connection. He was smuggling drugs. There was a bit more money, true, but she feared the price he was paying for it. She wondered what Paul knew about it.

The relationship between her husband and his best friend from way back had always been as much a source of fear as reassurance for her; she knew the details of it, but not the spirit of it. Certainly, she did not understand the depths of it; sometimes she felt giddy and sick as she gazed into it and was unable to see the bottom of it, the limits of it . . .

Perhaps, too, she could not see the limits to which they would go.

She and Angelica had become friends only because their husbands were bonded so deeply and so irrevocably. Fortune had played its part and they had become *good* friends, although, as with all such relationships, she knew that there were limits. Perhaps she should talk to her, try to find out if Arthur's recent behaviour was connected with Paul in any way; she would have to be tactful, though, because Angelica was touchy and protective of her husband. She would ask her, too, specifically, if this last trip had been different, because it seemed to her now that it most certainly had been. Arthur appeared to be physically ill, not just fatigued or worried. She was more scared now than she had ever been. Had he been stupid enough to try a bit of what he had been carrying? Had he overdosed?

'Arthur?' she said again, this time very loudly and in a tone that was almost pleading with him to answer, as if to end some intolerable cruelty he was inflicting upon her. Yet – and not, she knew, because his heart was hardened and he was deliberately prolonging her agony – he again failed to answer, again remained mute and, in doing so, might just as well have been screaming in physical pain.

She began to climb the stairs, no longer afraid of angering him, merely terrified that he might be too sick to be capable of such a reaction.

SIXTEEN

Lever emerged from the ambulance and Beverley was too cynical not to be gladdened by the look on his face, not to experience *Schadenfreude* that she thought was well earned, although she didn't show it on her face. She had just come out of the house, Sydenham having finished his examination of Rashid Malik's wife, Parveen. She had been killed in an identical way to her husband, which said only one thing to all of them – some sort of professional killing. It was progress of a sort, but it gave no clue as to the motive.

'Well?' she demanded of her sergeant.

'Nothing.' He was disgusted, as if this lack of help were yet another example that proved his race prejudices correct.

Her smile was so tight it nearly disappeared. 'I want to know exactly what she had to say, Sergeant, not what you *think* of what she had to say.'

They were already well on enough in their relationship for Lever to take the rebuke without obvious reaction – save for studied insolence – as he consulted his notebook. 'She last saw her daughter-in-law at eight last night, leaving after she had eaten dinner with her.'

'What about the husband, Rashid? Was he there?'

'No.'

'Where was he?'

'According to Mrs Butt, he ran some sort of general transport business. You know, "a man with a van", that kind of thing. He was out on a job.'

She knew exactly what kind of thing; no questions asked, strictly cash terms; see no evil, hear no evil, speak no evil. 'And she doesn't know what that job was?' she guessed.

He shook his head and said sourly, 'So she claims.'

'What time did she discover the bodies?'

'She called round at just after eleven. She'd been to the hairdresser's.'

'How did she get in?'

'She has her own key.' They were both aware that there was a degree of verbal sparring about this exchange.

Beverley changed the subject, although she knew it was far too soon. 'Anything from the house-to-house enquiries?'

'Not yet.'

She considered her options. 'OK, I'll coordinate things here. You go back to the station to organize database searches on the victims.'

'What time will Sydenham do the post-mortems?'

'*Doctor* Sydenham will do them tomorrow morning at the Royal.'

Joan Meadows had watched enough *Casualty* and *Holby City* to recognize where she was. This was the special room where they took you to have only one kind of conversation, the kind of conversation that nobody ever wanted to have, the one that was about a life; that was, at the same time, about a death. She was lost in an emotional typhoon, an inert and frightened soul, operating on only a basic level, yet curiously alert to all around her, even as she felt that she was at the bottom of a deep funnel of furious feeling. She saw that the room was painted in a light, pastel shade, that the window admitted dying evening light, that the carpet was pale grey and marked by too many relatives' shoes, and that the man who was talking to her was too young to be telling her the tales that came from his lips. He wore what she knew from the television were called 'scrubs', and he had around his neck a grey-tubed stethoscope, exactly as her knowledge of the world told her he should, yet it was all *wrong*. She shouldn't have been sitting on that orange, wipe-clean upholstery, listening to what he had to say, unable to take in the details, only the significance; she should have been at home with Arthur, watching this play and half held in its thrall, half reading a magazine; she should have been interested yet safely detached, able to put herself in the place of the people on the screen, yet knowing that there was a safety rope by which she could be rescued.

There was no safety rope in this place.

'I'm afraid your husband's got what we call "multi-organ failure", Mrs Meadows. His kidneys and liver have shut down, and his heart's having trouble pumping the blood around his body, so that his lungs are filling with water.'

She nodded, a poor imitation of comprehension. 'Why?' she asked, unaware that it was a very good question for which the young intensivist – a fourth-year specialist registrar called Angus Cartwright – had no answer.

'You say he's just come back from a trip abroad?'

'He's always abroad,' she pointed out. 'He's a lorry driver.'

'Do you know which country or countries he went to?'

She shook her head. 'I never know; somewhere in Europe, I think.'

'Who was he working for? We really need to know where he might have been.'

But she didn't know and, at that point, was well beyond understanding the importance of the questions; she had never wanted to know much about what Arthur did and why, and, in truth, since she had begun to wonder if what he was doing was illegal, she had had even less inclination to pry. She shook her head. 'I don't know.' Even to her own distracted ears, it sounded pathetic.

She could not know that it didn't really matter, that Dr Cartwright and all of the medical and nursing staff in the intensive care unit were completely at a loss as to what, precisely, was the cause of Arthur Meadows' malaise, could only surmise that he had some sort of rare and devastating infection; hence the interest in his recent trips abroad. He said as kindly as he could, 'You need to understand, Mrs Meadows, that your husband is seriously ill.'

'Will he die?' she asked. She was quite abrupt about this, and it momentarily surprised him. He could not read her tone, wondered for a moment if this were an option that she was particularly keen on and, following this, a brief vista of an unhappy marriage blossomed and then faded as he saw the pleading fear in her eyes. 'We're doing what we can,' he assured her, even as he knew that it was an empty phrase. Of course they were doing what they could; they were doctors, for God's sake; she would know that, although it had to be said on every occasion such as this. 'We're supporting his kidneys, and we're giving him drugs to help his heart cope. We're administering the most powerful antibiotics we have . . .'

He couldn't stop his voice trailing off, though; he wondered if she heard the emptiness at the heart of his assurances, and if she realized that he had failed to answer her question.

SEVENTEEN

'**N**othing.' Lever was disgusted, as if he were naive enough to believe the television programmes and films that portrayed post-mortems as inevitably illuminating, and pathologists as mystical wizards who were able somehow to dig under reality and unearth insights that led eventually to the downfall of the criminals. Beverley knew different. Too many times she had stood and watched the dirty, nauseating and grisly process that was the post-mortem dissection of a corpse to expect life to imitate art in any useful way. Most of the time, the autopsy merely confirmed what she already knew, and all it achieved was to eliminate the unlikely, the unexpected and the unnecessary. These had been a case in point: the Maliks had been killed exactly as she already knew. Unless the toxicological samples and various swabs that Sydenham had taken returned completely surprising results, they were no further forward, although perhaps at least they were slightly more assured of their footing.

They were standing in the body store at the mortuary, having just come out of the dissection room. She asked, 'What did you expect?'

He was surprised by her question and didn't answer. She took pleasure in exposing his naivety. She said mockingly, 'We have to be here for procedural reasons, nothing more. It's not likely that we'll learn who the killer is.'

'Is he competent?'

Beverley wasn't sure that Sydenham was, actually, but she was not about to discuss the man's failings – real or imagined – with Lever.

'If I were you, Sergeant, I'd worry about my own competence before I start questioning the pathologist.'

He gave her a cold stare but said nothing.

Beverley wondered if he had expected it to be easy, if he had perhaps imagined that the death of the Maliks would be simplistic; she had known better as soon as she had seen the manner of their deaths. Unlike most killings – those that were born of avarice, sexual anger, stupidity (nearly always there was stupidity) – she had suspected that here was a member of the small subset of murders that were not almost immediately solvable. Had most homicides been this difficult, the clean-up rate – the statistic by which she was measured, by which she was potentially to be hung – would have been pathetic. Most killers killed and then ran away, leaving traces (hell, a lot of them leaving fucking great gobbets) of evidence which they hadn't even thought about. She had the feeling that this time she was up against someone who knew what they were doing, who knew why they were doing it and how they were doing it, and who knew what they might be leaving behind when they did it.

They walked out of the mortuary to their car parked just outside. 'Anything yet from the database searches on the Maliks?' she asked as she settled into the front passenger seat and he started the engine.

'What you'd expect. They were on every benefit going; according to the Revenue, the wife was a cleaner but earning only minimum wage, whilst the husband didn't earn at all.'

'Criminal records?'

'Nothing.'

'Immigration?'

'Everything checks out.' He sounded slightly incredulous. 'Rashid Malik was born here; his wife came over when she was three.'

He wasn't saying anything that she hadn't already half guessed. Whatever was going on here, it wasn't straightforward; people didn't die at the hands of trained killers – and this one was clearly, to Beverley, highly trained – every day in Barton Street, Gloucester. Something was going on.

'What's the lab come up with from the laptop?' Forensic analysis of computers was now an inevitable, and not infrequently useful, part of most investigations.

'Nothing yet.'

She couldn't believe this. 'How fucking long does it take to hack into an email account and print off a list of contacts, for God's sake? I could find ten kids in any school in Gloucester who could have done that in ten minutes.'

'They say the hard disk's been wiped, so it'll take a while.'

Which brought her up short, so that for a moment she was wordless. 'Really?'

He nodded, pleased to have caught her out. 'They may have something for us tomorrow.'

What was the significance of that? Who had done the wiping, and why? She sensed a new dimension to the case, but it was one that stretched into as yet impenetrable mist. She asked, 'Anything from the phone company?' The Maliks' mobile phones had been seized and, as was routine, were also being examined forensically; the mobile phone company had been contacted and records of all their calls for the past three months requested.

'Harrison's got them. She's going through them now.'

'What about the house-to-house enquiries?'

'Not one of the neighbours saw anything odd last night. Those who didn't claim they'd never heard of them said that the Maliks were the nicest people you could ever wish to meet. Nothing shady or nasty about them.'

'Saints?'

'Or whatever the Paki equivalent is.'

He didn't believe any of that, but then neither did she. Communities in places like Barton Street were fractured, but if there was one force of nature that united everyone, it was the one that acted repulsively when the police came into view, the one that was stronger even than electromagnetism, the one that caused everyone to act in a cohesive, cooperative and uncommunicative mass. 'Have you checked at the local nick?' Barton Street police station was only two hundred metres or so up the road.

'The Maliks were pretty law-abiding, considering the area. They didn't make trouble and no one knows of any disputes with the neighbours. There was an incident last year in which that upstairs window got broken; someone chucked half a brick through it. The Maliks reported it, but no one was ever found. It was put down as a random act of vandalism. There's been nothing like it since.'

A wiped hard disk suggested that maybe they weren't as law-abiding as all that, she mused; assuming, of course, that it was they and not the killer who had done it. There was silence between them until they got back to her office. Her desktop was covered in pictures of the crime scene taken by the scenes of crime unit; she had spent a lot of time staring at them, as she always did, but nothing was whispering to her from them. Lever was sitting at his desk, sipping coffee, looking at her; hostilities were in abeyance, at least temporarily. 'What about this "business" that Rashid Malik ran? Have you unearthed anything about that?'

Once again Lever had to shake his head. 'It wasn't in any way legit. There's nothing registered for VAT, and Revenue don't know anything about it. Maybe he kept his records on that computer.'

Lever was probably right, she conceded. 'And nobody knows where he was yesterday evening?'

'They say not.'

She didn't show her frustration at this woeful catalogue of negatives; she was missing something, she knew. It wasn't a pleasant feeling; indeed, it was an awful thing to experience, but one she knew too well. She looked at Lever. 'What's your theory?' she asked him.

He was surprised, she could see, and this pleased her. Keep the bastards off guard, make them uncertain of where they stand with you, what you might have hidden in your pocket, half convince them that it's a knife, reassure them that it's just a helping hand; keep a smile on your face the whole while, and make sure it spreads to your eyes as they seek the vulnerable spot. He said, at first uncertainly and then with more conviction, 'I reckon it's an honour killing. One or other of the families reckons they blackened their name.'

She thought this unlikely, but she was wise enough not to dismiss his suggestion at once, and certainly not to dismiss it with contempt. It was beneficial to have people to talk to about cases like this, even if some of those people were trouble, even if they were as thick as cow shit. Even some of the zombies she had worked with over the years had occasionally come up with an idea that she hadn't thought of. 'The Maliks have been happily married for, what, four years? A bit late for someone to get antsy about the dowry, isn't it?'

Lever shrugged. 'You don't know what goes through their heads, do you?'

Beverley was fascinated by that remark, made much as a Victorian scientist might have made when discussing the tribal rituals of peoples in New Guinea, sure in the knowledge that here was a different (and inferior) species that only happened to look like human beings. Rather than tackle Lever's attitudes head on, she decided to make use of them. She looked at her watch, then said, 'It's time to knock off for tonight. I suggest that tomorrow morning you should look into that possibility. Do a little research on the two families. See if they have connections back in Pakistan.' He looked suspicious of this apparent change in her attitude to him and, to make sure that he should remain unsuspecting of any ulterior motive, she added, 'You needn't worry, Lever. If you find anything of importance, I'll let you have the credit.' He thought about this and she could see that he was still wondering if she could be trusted, so she sweetened the placebo with a spoonful more of sugar. 'Get Constable Harrison to help you.'

As she knew he would, he forgot his suspicions and agreed that this would be useful. *You're so predictable, Lever. That's going to be your undoing; I'll see to that.*

Marty and his mother returned to their cottage without success and, accordingly, frustrated and angry. The trail of blood and faeces had quickly faded and their hunt had turned into a random search of the woods which were untended and very old, so that the overgrowth of undergrowth of bramble and fern was in places almost impossibly thick. There were numerous fallen trees in varying states of rot, and the general topography of the area was hilly. Their progress had been slow and it was impossible to be certain that they had not missed two bodies lying in the middle of thick vegetation.

'What do we do now?' Marty, as was his way, was panicking.

As was *her* way, ever the mother, ever the thinker for the pair of them, she couldn't afford such a luxury. She went to a large carry-all bag that, although they had been there for a week now, she had yet to unpack. In it was a set of Ordnance Survey maps of the area. She opened the one that covered where the accident had occurred, examining the surrounding terrain. She had expected the cargo to be too weak to get far but, if they had proved more resilient than she had thought, then it was possible that they had reached a small farmhouse that abutted the woodland area, just to the north. The trouble was, they couldn't just go knocking on the door . . .

She told Marty to sit down at the table while she made them both some coffee and thought out some sort of plan. Assuming that they had not missed the cargo, and that they were not lying in the woodland somewhere, and assuming that they had not made their way back to the road or been found, then they were likely to be in that house. If they had been found on the road, or if they had made themselves known to the householders, then it was likely that they were out of reach. That didn't matter too much, though. As long as Marty had not left evidence behind in Gloucester to incriminate them, no one, except perhaps Harry Weston, could possibly link them to any of this business; the only other piece of evidence was the stolen van, and that was tucked away in the garage by the side of the house.

Effectively, finding the cargo could wait, then. They had to get rid of the van and see to the problem of Harry Weston. Marty didn't think Weston had seen who had been driving the van, but they couldn't just make that assumption; another killing was a complication she would rather not have had to deal with, but she knew that it was one of the things that Marty was good at, God bless Her fucking Majesty. The van was, if anything, more of a problem; moving it, even in the middle of the night, was potentially a very risky thing to do, especially as she couldn't drive and she would have to accompany Marty in order to ensure that he disposed of it properly. Then there was the problem of getting back here . . .

Damn their luck!

She forced herself to stop because, although it felt like anger, she realized it was panic. The van was not a problem; let it rot in the garage. It would not be long before its discovery would be of no concern to her. He was agitated, but she calmed him with her words and her soft tone, as she had done for so many years; it made him feel better, made her feel better, too; she was doing what she felt she had been born to do, doing all that she felt had been left to her. Eventually, after they had drunk some whisky together, he calmed down enough that she could send him to bed, leaving her in peace to read the local paper on the cold wooden surface of the kitchen table, under the gloominess of the single bulb that hung from the ceiling. The murders in Barton Street dominated, and she read eagerly of all the paper had to say about it; there was precious little fact, a whole heap of speculation, and she was relieved to see that it was all completely wrong. The police were obviously clueless; she could not help smiling to herself as she read what they had to say; Chief Inspector Wharton clearly knew all the right phrases – 'enquiries are proceeding', 'we believe the killer or killers to be highly dangerous', 'there is no evidence that this crime was racially motivated' – and, equally as clearly, was uttering meaningless garbage designed only to cover up a lack of any true knowledge. She found a sense of some pride in knowing that Marty was a good soldier.

The inside pages contained the usual parochial inanities. She was interested to read the latest news on the upcoming Highgrove House bonanza; the guest list looked impressive, she thought. She looked at the details of the upcoming Sunday service at Gloucester Cathedral; she had been attending the Cathedral regularly ever since she had returned to the county. There was to be a special service in celebration of 'the Glosters', one of the most decorated regiments in the British Army, now renamed (unhappily, she thought) the 'Royal Gloucestershire, Berkshire and Wiltshire Light Infantry'; she thought she might go, if things worked out and she overcame their present problems.

EIGHTEEN

'It's quite unique in my experience.'
   Eisenmenger forbore to comment on the poor use of language, or on the rather preposterous sense of pomposity

it conveyed; the young intensivist was probably under thirty and, as far as Eisenmenger was concerned, his experience was almost certainly woefully inadequate and extracted mostly from text books and lectures. Eisenmenger was now old enough to appreciate that, as good as books were, they represented a mere shadow on the wall of life. The only problem was that the case was also unique in Eisenmenger's experience, which didn't seem entirely fair.

The new medico-legal facility was located to the south of the city centre, rather incongruously next to a hotel; it didn't *obviously* contain a mortuary and dissection room, but the guests staying in the rooms on that side of the hotel could not have missed the endless succession of mostly black 'private ambulances' that called during daylight hours. There was also a courtroom in which Her Majesty's Coroner for Gloucestershire could hold inquests, a facility that had been lacking in the county for many years. Unfortunately, the project had been begun against the background of intense financial hardship that had strangled the world and, accordingly, the budget had been cut and squeezed and downsized and, at the end, hacked into a small stunted thing, so that the materials had been second-rate and already, after only a short while, beginning to show undue signs of wear. He had noticed a steady, perhaps correlated, decline in the morale of the staff.

At one end of the dissection room was an area that was slightly separate and had a viewing area, so that clinicians could attend and peer down as the pathologist dissected the organs from a case. This had always been a rare occurrence, even when the post-mortem examinations had been conducted in the hospital and the clinicians had had less far to come, and since the move it had become unheard of; after all, they were very busy people and, if they unfortunately lost one patient, there were always several more calling urgently for attention. That Dr Cartwright had made the two-kilometre journey to the new facility suggested that here was a very perplexed young man. Perhaps, Eisenmenger reflected, he should be charitable towards him.

'Take me through the story again,' he suggested.

'There isn't much. Mr Meadows came in with a blue light after his wife phoned that she couldn't rouse him. The paramedics had done what they could to resuscitate him, which wasn't much, unfortunately. By the time he got to us, he was in multi-organ failure; everything was going down.' *Going down*, whilst not exactly normal medical parlance, was an apt description of what had happened to Arthur Meadows' organs. 'There was nothing we could do, except offer symptomatic support, but that was clearly never likely to pull him through. He kept dropping his sats, even though we were practically pushing pure oxygen into him, and his kidneys packed up, even though we managed to keep his blood pressure off the floor by running gallons of dopamine into his neck.'

This was the speech of an intensive care physician, who did his miracles not so much by looking at the patient as looking at the read-outs of increasingly sophisticated machines; Eisenmenger couldn't help feeling that it was the medical equivalent of driving a car with the windows blacked out and only television screens for information. He didn't comment, mainly because he was bothered by something, although the identity of the irritation was as yet a mystery to him. Dr Cartwright opined, 'It must have been overwhelming sepsis of some kind, but so far everything's come back negative.'

This seemed a reasonable assumption to make, Eisenmenger had to admit, and yet . . .

'Something viral, do you think?' asked the young doctor. 'I suppose it could have been an atypical bacterium – especially in view of the fact that he's so recently been abroad – and his bone marrow had practically packed up by the time we got to him, so it would be no surprise that the antibiotics didn't help much.'

'You don't know where he went, though?' Eisenmenger had read the notes before starting the autopsy.

A shake of the head. 'He was a long-distance lorry driver, but his wife is rather vague about where he'd been. It could have been anywhere in Europe, or even further abroad.' There was something about the way he said this last that suggested 'further abroad' was a place where hideous disease lurked. He lapsed into silence for a moment, but then could stand it no longer, asking, 'What do you think? Perhaps a fungal infection?'

Eisenmenger had finished the dissection, and the organs, separated from the 'pluck' and neatly opened or sliced (according to the nature of the article in question), now lay on a board on the stainless steel bench. He took a deep breath, trying to put it all together in his head, to separate the changes that extreme medical intervention had wrought from those that the disease (whatever it was) had caused. In cases such as this, such partition was not always easy. He said slowly, 'The lungs are heavy and wet; probably that's mostly ventilation and dopamine effect . . .' He knew that intensivists could be slightly touchy about pathologists pointing out the damage they had done in order to attempt to keep patients alive. 'The heart's basically just a bag, the kidneys are like sponges, and the liver's falling to bits,' he added.

Dr Cartwright said nothing; in truth, there was little he could say. Eisenmenger took pity on him. 'What did you make of the rash?'

But, it appeared, they had been unable to make anything of it. 'We asked the dermatologists for an opinion, but they were foxed.' It was, undoubtedly, a strange rash. It was intensively erythematous and blistering; oddly, it appeared to be centred on the buttocks. 'What do you think?'

But Eisenmenger had no definite opinion; he thought he could offer speculation, but he was not the type of man to voice it without more evidence and he contented himself by murmuring merely, 'I'm not sure.'

'Could it all have been due to some sort of gastroenteritis? Something he ate whilst abroad? He certainly had really offensive diarrhoea, although it hasn't grown anything in the lab.'

Eisenmenger frowned; that had been bothering him. 'I don't know,' he admitted. Then, really because he thought he ought, 'Possibly.'

'Viral, you think?' suggested the young man again, perhaps without realizing that he was becoming a tad repetitious.

'Perhaps.'

There was a fly buzzing around the room. Surprisingly, flies were fairly rare in mortuary dissection rooms, a tribute to the cleanliness that mortuary technicians sought so relentlessly; a couple of days before they had performed a post-mortem examination on a badly decomposed body and, inevitably, a few maggots always got away to hide in the corners. It was dozy and, when it settled on a pool of blood by the spleen, Eisenmenger squashed it with the base of a steel bowl.

There was no doubt that the lining of Arthur Meadows' intestines had been severely inflamed, in places completely ulcerate, in others totally necrotic, and such a thing could be caused by infection . . . Other things could do it, though; ischaemia, for example, which tended to produce confluent areas of sloughing of the gut lining, as was present here, at least in one or two places. That was the problem: all of the possible causes he could think of for this strange disease – lack of blood supply, microorganisms, autoimmune disease, chemical toxins – did not produce quite this odd pattern of tissue damage. For a start, the rectum was particularly severely affected, followed by the caecum; the transverse colon was relatively spared, and some of the small intestine was bad, other parts less so.

It was all very odd . . .

And yet, he felt as if the answer were simple. That, though, he knew to be a truism; there is no difficult question once you know the answer. He said, 'I'll have to take samples for histology.'

Dr Cartwright left, if not satisfied that he had an answer, then at least not dissatisfied that he had missed something obvious.

Eisenmenger took his samples, and one of the four mortuary technicians who worked at the facility came in to start sewing the body back up. He had been introduced to him as Sam. He was thin and scrawny, covered in tattoos and had not only two earrings per side but also a nose stud; Eisenmenger judged him to be perhaps thirty-five. As was his way, Eisenmenger had tried to make conversation with him. 'How do you like the new mortuary?' he asked.

''S'all right.'

'It must be busy with just four of you.'

'You can say that again. Especially when there are forensics being done. There's not enough room, and it takes one, maybe even two of us, off the rota for the next day if they're done late, like yesterday's.'

Eisenmenger told himself that he wasn't interested, even as he enquired, 'You did a forensic yesterday?'

'Two. The Barton Street killings.'

Eisenmenger had seen news of them on the television. 'Who did them?' By which he meant, 'Who was the pathologist?'

'Dr Sydenham.'

Eisenmenger hadn't realized that Charles Sydenham was again

practising in the county, unaware that it was his own absence that was responsible. 'Do you know what he found?'

'I wasn't there, but it was apparently pretty straightforward. They were both stabbed and their throats were cut.'

Instincts that, try as he might, Eisenmenger could not suppress stirred sluggishly. 'Really?'

Sam had finished sewing up the scalp and was just threading the needle to begin closing the body cavity. 'Apparently. Neat job, too.'

Subconsciously, Eisenmenger ran through possibilities, inferences, even on these small data. Sternly, he pulled himself up and told himself silently but imperatively to stop it. It was nothing to do with him.

NINETEEN

The realization of how stupid she had been made Beverley feel sick. It had come to her on the way into the station that morning, as suddenly as a stroke, and having much the same physiological reactions. She swore out loud to herself, and anyone observing her through the front windscreen would have been totally perplexed to have seen her apparently so angry and distressed for no discernible cause. How could she have been so stupid? It was a question that would not go away, because it was unanswerable.

It was only ten minutes before she was in her office. Lever was already there, sipping a cup of Costa coffee and eating a Danish pastry; somewhere inside her, Beverley wondered if he were styling himself on US cops as portrayed on television. *It'll be chilli dogs for lunch, next.* She said without pre-emption, 'Where is Rashid Malik's van?' It caught him by surprise and he just looked up, mouth full of flaky pastry and sucrose, eyes questioning. She went on, 'He was a "man with a van", wasn't he? Where's the fucking van?'

To his credit, Lever didn't hesitate. 'I'll get on it right away.'

*   *   *

Harry Weston's smallholding was little more than a large allot-
ment, running to only an acre or so. Once, he had tended it
carefully, making economical use of every square foot, and
keeping a pig and chickens; at that time he had been almost
self-sufficient, as well as earning an income as a part-time farm
worker, together with occasional work as a beater for local shoots
and as a forester. Now that his daughter, Wanda, was dead of
meningitis, his wife had left him and osteoarthritis had set in,
the land was neglected and the livestock long gone. His income
now came from benefits, some occasional legitimate work, and
crime. He considered himself a victim of circumstance, as anyone
in the Rose and Crown could have attested, for it was one of his
favourite subjects, although the same was not said by the other
patrons of that establishment, who regarded him as a 'fucking
bore' on the topic.

His house was small – two rooms and a tiny kitchen downstairs, two bedrooms, a bathroom and a separate toilet upstairs
– and it hadn't been properly cleaned for five years, since two
days before his wife had left, in fact (although his sister did her
best); there was a sort of cosmic symmetry in the fact that he
hadn't been properly cleaned for about as long, either. He shopped
at the local petrol station, opting for a diet that was based on
pre-prepared meat pies, potato-based snacks and beer; variety
came from having a different flavour of pie or crisp, and cycling
through the diverse types of canned beer that were available. He
had noticed of late that he had constant gut ache, but had only
done so in a sort of distracted way, much as he might have noticed
that the tyres on his pick-up were becoming threadbare; something
to be dealt with at an unspecified future time.

He had other things to think about now. Like what had
happened the night before. He was poorly educated and bright
only in a sort of unintellectual way that was ill-disciplined and
wildly random, but he had sixty-two years of experience of his
life, and that told him that he had stumbled across something
that was seriously *wrong*. He kept hearing that word of pathetic
entreaty that had come from the back of the van, and there had
been something unholy about the way the driver of the van had
forced the door open without any sort of vocalization . . . Harry
wasn't given to night terrors, and his imagination had never

roamed very free, but he hadn't liked the look of that little scenario. The question was, what should he do about it? The concept of going to the police, although it occurred to him, did not entertain him for long; his relationships with the constabulary had never been good and had deteriorated quite a lot in the last few years. They might ask what his business had been, and if he knew anything about people waking in the morning to discover that their central heating and range cookers were no longer working.

Those cries for help, though . . .

Of course it hadn't been Wanda, but in his head there remained the stubborn assertion that somehow, in some time and place, it *could* have been, or it *might* have been. The distress had not been good; until a year ago he had had a dog – a border collie called Tess – and, although he had never pampered it, he would not have stood to hear such distress from her. And if not in a dog, then surely doubly so in a human, and one who sounded so young?

Yet, what could he do? Whoever had been in the back of that van would be long gone by now, either under their own steam or in the hands of that driver. He had done what he could to help them, and he could do no more.

Or was that true?

The flashed vision of the reflection of the driver's face was something else that would not leave him, had been nagging at him. It was not, he was sure, entirely unknown to him; not a face he knew well, but one that he had seen before. Where, though? And, if he could recall it, could he use this information?

He smiled grimly. Maybe he could. He didn't know what he'd stumbled across during the night, but it sure as shit wasn't legit, and where people were doing things they shouldn't be, there was always a little pocket money to be made.

He rose from the table and went to the cupboard under the kitchen sink. Where most people would keep cleaning fluids such as washing-up liquid and bleach, Harry kept demijohns of cider. He hefted one out and took it, together with a pint glass, back to the rickety table. Cider, he knew of old, helped him concentrate.

TWENTY

Eisenmenger could not find it within himself to love Newent. He could see that it had once had charm and character, and that remnants of these lurked, wraithlike, under the ravages wrought by time and ill-considered building done under the name of 'development', but it was not enough. The 'development' of Newent (for which Orwellian phraseology he knew the correct term was either 'disfigurement' or 'exploitation', or perhaps 'destitution', or even a combination of the three) had led to a few original (or, at least, characterful) houses and buildings being interspersed with a bewildering variety of dwellings and business premises that were, to put it simply, ugly. They sat there in this unsightliness, glaring at him every time he went through the place, daring him to complain about what had happened to the town, insolently silent yet seemingly unabashed. Being an old town, the high street was not designed for cars, let alone for parking, and consequently driving along it was an interesting, punctuated experience, with frequent stops, occasional near misses and a lot of stress. It was not directly on his way back home from the county medico-legal facility, and he would therefore normally have happily avoided it, but today he braved its rigours because his interest had been tweaked. Whereas some men are said to be led by their penises, Eisenmenger was led – in a way, just as mindlessly – by his intellectual curiosity.

Arthur Meadows had lived in a small semi-detached house – an ex-council house, Eisenmenger judged – just off one end of the high street, quite close to a doctor's surgery and a small, rural police station. The outside brickwork was painted in a slightly lurid shade of pale yellow that might have looked good on a Mediterranean isle, but which in Newent looked somehow wrong, as if it were an illegal immigrant failing to fit in with the environs. There was a large community school just down the road and, when Eisenmenger called, he could hear the chaotic yet somehow cheering sounds of the pupils on their lunch break. The front garden was mostly lawn with a single flower bed along the front; it was bounded by a low chain-link fence and was neatly tended.

He pressed the cheap plastic doorbell and was rewarded with a cheap, electronic chime sounding loudly but, for a long while, nothing more. His assumption that the house was empty, though, was proved wrong when, just as he was about to leave, he heard the sound of someone coming down the stairs; the door was opened quickly afterwards by a woman who was patently in deepest mourning. Her eyes were painfully raw to behold, her mouth drawn into a thin, anaemic line that was curled tightly down at the ends; she seemed drugged when she looked at him.

'Mrs Meadows?' he asked unnecessarily.

Her hair was long and, he suspected, had once been lustrous, but was now slightly wiry and slightly grey; her skin was dried by tobacco, the skin beneath her chin had become just a little pendulous. 'Yes?'

Eisenmenger was used to the dead, and he was becoming experienced in the ways of bereavement; he knew how she felt, knew it too well. 'My name's John Eisenmenger. I'm helping to look into the death of your husband.' He said this as gently as he could, aware that he could never be gentle enough.

Interest sparked in her face, although it was vague and veiled by crushing melancholy. 'Oh . . .'

'Could I speak to you? Is it convenient?'

It wasn't and could never have been, but a combination of deference to his implied authority and a need to bring some understanding to her situation overcame her desire to be left alone by this man who was a stranger to her, who wouldn't even have looked twice at her under any other circumstance. In her sitting room, they sat opposite each other, to his left the fireplace in which there was a flame-effect heating appliance, a thing that had limped into the new millennium with an unwarranted degree of bravado and dedication despite showing its age. She had not thought to offer refreshment and he had not thought to ask for any, as if it would have made mockery of the occasion. 'I performed the examination on your husband,' he began, waving euphemisms around like flags of surrender.

For a while, she said nothing, merely looked at him as if she were terrified by this admission, perhaps because she thought him a monster or something; it was a silly idea, of course, but one that was born of his own ambivalence about what he did. With her eyes wide and lips dry, she asked, 'What did you find? Why did Arthur die?'

He felt awful having to disappoint her. 'I don't know yet, Mrs Meadows. It's why I'm here. To find out a little more about the last few days.'

She leaned back in her chair quite abruptly, almost as if pushed, her head down and shaking slowly. '*I* don't know,' she said in anguish. 'They kept on at the hospital about what he'd been up to, but *I* don't know.'

'He was a lorry driver?'

She nodded, beginning to cry again, pulling tissues from her sleeve, as if she were a conjuror producing flags from her clothing, flags of her distress. 'I don't know where he went, though; not this last time.'

'No idea at all? Was it in Europe or further abroad?'

'I'm sorry . . .' Then, presumably because she felt she had to explain her ignorance, she added, 'He's been going over the Channel so long, it's just routine . . .'

But it wouldn't be routine any longer, and this realization – brought home by her mistake in using the present tense – was too much for her and the tears took over. Eisenmenger looked on awkwardly, aware that he was doing no good to either of them. Then the front door opened and a voice called, 'Mum?' just after it closed again.

Mrs Meadows stood at once and left the room. There was a muffled conversation and then she returned, accompanied by a young woman who was clearly her daughter. Eisenmenger stood, but before he could say anything, he was on the receiving end of angry questions. 'Who are you? What's all this about? Can't you see how upset Mum is?'

Eisenmenger explained, just as he had done to her mother. 'I'm trying to find out as much ancillary information as I can, you see.'

'Why?'

'It's possible that he caught something while he was abroad.

If we knew precisely where he went, it would help us identify the cause.'

'I don't understand why they couldn't work it out. They did enough tests.'

He agreed to try, but only to assuage her anger. 'Which is very odd, I know. Sometimes, though, these things can be very hard to track down. Some viruses – the rare ones – can be almost impossible to identify without specialist equipment.'

She was calming down. Mrs Meadows, perhaps suddenly aware that she had neglected the formalities, asked, 'Would you like a cup of tea, Dr Eisenmenger?'

'Yes, thank you. That would be nice.' He didn't particularly desire one, but it seemed tactically a good move.

'What about you, Carol?'

The daughter nodded. 'Do you want me to make it?'

But Mrs Meadows needed to do it.

Alone with Eisenmenger and now considerably less intimidating, the daughter said, 'We don't know the details of what Dad did. We never did.'

Was there a trace of sarcasm in her voice? 'What was he carrying? It might give us a clue as to where he went.'

'We don't know.'

He believed her when she said this, but he believed also that this was merely a piece of a truth, a facet of it, and he wanted to know what would happen if he tried to peer at things from a slightly different angle. 'Really? But surely he's got paperwork. The lorry was his, wasn't it?'

'Dad wasn't very talkative about his work.'

'Yes, but surely . . .'

'We don't know, Mr Eisenmenger.' She was losing her temper again, a defensive anger designed to warn him off. Her mother came back with the tea; it was weak and she had clearly made it with full-fat milk, so that it failed to ignite the fires of love in Eisenmenger's heart, and his cockles remained unwarmed. He sipped it, considering the situation. She *did* know – that was plain; or at least she *thought* she knew, or she knew about a bit of it, or . . .

'Is there someone who might have more information?'

Mother and daughter exchanged looks, and he couldn't tell

whether they were significant or otherwise. Carol said, 'He didn't have a partner, if that's what you mean.'

'How did he get his business, then?'

Unaccountably, there was yet more reluctance, but eventually he was told, 'He got most of his business from Paul Lynch, especially of late.'

'Where's he based?'

'Andoversford.'

'Could I have a contact phone number?'

He was given one. He hadn't finished the tea but didn't care to stay to do so, both because of its awful taste and because the atmosphere had suddenly become difficult. He put the mug down – *Keep on Truckin'*, written on the side – and asked, 'Is that where his lorry is? At Paul Lynch's?'

Mrs Meadows shook her head. 'If he arrived back here late at night, he'd park it just outside of Newent, then take it to Paul's the following day.'

'So it's close by?' Again, there was that reluctance, but Mrs Meadows eventually nodded. 'Where is it? May I see it?' he asked.

'Why?' was the demand from Carol.

Because you're behaving oddly. Because you're worried about something. Because you aren't behaving as I would expect a bereaved family to behave.

He said calmly but firmly, 'Because it might give me a clue to what Arthur Meadows died from. That's my job.'

It worked. Although still clearly unhappy about something, the daughter, Carol, agreed to walk with him to the lorry. They left her mother gently weeping in the kitchen, washing the tea mugs. The wind was whipping a few spots of rain into their eyes as they walked at first in a slightly hostile silence, until Eisenmenger remarked, 'Was business getting hard for your father?'

'It is for everyone, isn't it?' It was as much a rebuke as a reply.

Tired of this unearned antagonism, he enquired, 'What are you and your mother afraid of?' She stopped suddenly, staring at him, as if he had made an improper suggestion, something that he considered improbable since he thought her rather dowdy. Seeing that she was about to respond angrily, he went on, 'All I'm trying to do is find out how your father came by his death. I'm not out to judge him.'

She didn't reply, but she did start walking again, her face set. He kept pace with her, saying nothing more, feeling that he didn't have to, hoping that he was right. She said suddenly, 'We're not lying, you know. We honestly don't know where he went, or what load he was carrying.'

She was quite tall but still wore high heels, as if she wanted to dominate the world. Dressed in unwisely tight blue jeans and an orange pullover, her perfume was strong, even out of doors. 'But you wonder . . .?' he asked.

She said nothing more and he didn't push her. Although it wasn't far to the place where the lorry was parked, he would have had trouble finding it alone, since the route she took was tortuous. It turned out to be a patch of hardstanding just off the Newent-to-Ledbury road that was hidden from the road by trees. She said, 'There used to be a barn here, but the farmer pulled it down. He used to let Dad leave the rig here when he couldn't get it back to Paul's.'

Eisenmenger knew nothing about a great many things, and lorries and trucks formed a subset that was wholly contained within this ocean of ignorance. He could only look on it as a thing of incongruity, as impossible to understand as a flying saucer would have been, and perhaps as beautiful, too; that he could not enfold it with his comprehension did not mean that he did not appreciate it as a thing of achievement, even if the culture and learning that had produced it were as foreign to him as those of Jupiter would have been. It appeared impressive – bright and shiny and big (which was about as technical as he could get) – and, looking at it, he wondered why he had insisted on coming. What was the point? Maybe, he had thought he would inspect the tyres for evidence of clay only found in Moldavia, or pick out the mummified remains of an insect indigenous and unique to only one of the Croatian islands? Or was he hoping for some sort of supernatural intervention to help him, to shine a light on the darkness that surrounded the dying of Arthur Meadows? If so, it was failing to pierce the layer of high cloud that diffused the drab sunlight in that early afternoon.

Carol stood by his side, looking at the lorry, although he sensed that for her there was more emotional overlay than he could feel in the sight. For her, he guessed, this was a hulking symbol of fatherhood, of family, of a past just died, of grief all too present. She said suddenly, 'He changed about eighteen months ago. He stopped talking about where he'd been, what he'd seen, some of the out-of-the-ordinary things that had happened.'

Eisenmenger waited; he had nothing else to do. She continued, 'It was about the time that he spent a load of money on the lorry; he remortgaged the house and everything. Mum was worried sick about spending so much. He said it was to upgrade the cab, and to put in extra fuel tanks, so he could do longer runs; he said that was where the money was, but I could never see it. What the hell did he need extra tanks for? It's not as if they don't have filling stations on the Continent, is it?'

'So what do you think he was up to?'

She took a long time to answer and, when she did, she had to do so with a sigh, as if her answer had had to be dragged to the top of the hill and now it was pushing off down the slope. 'Mum and I think he was smuggling drugs.'

TWENTY-ONE

'What about the shit on the carpet?'

Beverley was talking to Sydenham on the phone; was it possible, she wondered, that it was an even more unpleasant experience than talking to him in person? There was an intimacy about a phone conversation that he somehow seemed able to exploit; she could hear his sighs and innuendos too closely, and her mind conjured his leer too easily and too vividly. His reply to her query was typically crushing, stereotypically uncaring. 'How the devil should I know? I'm a forensic pathologist, Chief Inspector, not a laboratory technician.' He didn't say '*mere* laboratory technician', but then his tone said it for him and did so far more eloquently than the syllable would have done, its enunciation clear and ringing, a denunciation that could not be missed.

'Are you saying that it didn't come from either Mr or Mrs
Malik?' His report hadn't said it had, but then it hadn't said it
hadn't, either; she had learned not to take anything in a pathologist's autopsy report for granted.

Sydenham did not often pause before ejecting a reply, did not
often have to search too far down in his arsenal to find the right
verbal warhead, so the pause was ominous. 'Does my report say
that it did?'

'No . . .'

'Is there any part of my report that is unclear, or *ambiguous*?'

'Of course not . . .'

'So, let me get this straight – for the record, you might say.
You have read my report and you acknowledge that it does not
contain any direct reference to a wound or condition that might
have caused the faecal staining seen on the carpet in the other
room. It makes no reference to faecal staining of their clothes,
would you not agree?'

'Dr Sydenham, I just thought it important to make sure.'

'My dear young lady, I have written a great many autopsy
reports for a great many police officers. I would have said that
you were among the – how shall I put it? – *sharper* of the various
police implements I have had to deal with; please don't spoil
that delusion.'

He cut the connection abruptly, leaving her frustrated, humiliated and angry to the point of self-immolation. *John Eisenmenger;
wherefore art thou . . .?*

It left her with the problem of that staining, however.

The Maliks were childless, and the forensics team – the 'laboratory technicians' – had managed to determine that it was human,
but there was too much contamination to tell anything more. It
hadn't grown any bacteria, though, which was apparently odd.
The lab suggested that some sort of antiseptic on the carpet had
killed them off. Overall, there had been nothing useful at all
generated by the painstaking investigations of the forensic team.

If the faecal staining hadn't come from the Maliks, had it come
from the killer? Surely not; she was unable to conceive any
concatenation of circumstances that would make that a possible
scenario and, unlikely as it had seemed, she had already checked
with the grieving mother, Fatima Butt, and made certain that the

staining had not been there when she had left her daughter on the night she was killed. Which left another person. More importantly, it left a potential witness.

For some reason, Beverley had some lunch, and – as she ate the waterlogged, lifeless and loveless thing that 'Dean' of 'Dean's Delicious Deli Delights' assured her, via an encomium on the side of the packaging, was lovingly hand-made using only the best ingredients he could source – Lever returned to the office. He was excited; it was, she decided, a gauge of the depth of her depression that she found reason for hope in this. Perhaps, though, he had successfully managed to breach Constable Harrison's underwear barrier. He announced, 'Rashid Malik's uncle is wanted on suspicion of heroin smuggling. He absconded to Pakistan three years ago, then just vanished into the countryside, according to the Pakistani police.'

He made it clear what he thought about that last.

She considered this new information. She could not deny that it was interesting and might well explain the style of the killings, which had clearly been done by someone with experience of murder, if not training. 'But we've got nothing to link either of the two dead people to drug smuggling, have we?'

'Not yet.'

She ignored the implication that it was just a matter of time. She knew that she could not ignore what Lever had discovered, even if she desperately wanted it to be irrelevant to the double murder. She considered what to do, fully aware that a large part of her motivation was not bent towards discovering who the murderer was, but towards ensuring that, whatever happened, she came out of the business ahead on points and – the ideal scenario – Lever came out badly wounded. She did so with no compunction, because she was a professional and what she did was be a police officer; if being a police officer resulted in finding the perpetrators of crime, all well and good, but it wasn't all that she had to do to get ahead in her career. To succeed in her chosen job, she had to come out of any investigation a little bit more in credit than when she had gone into it.

'Have you got a photo of him?'

'Not yet.' The answer gave her a small pleasure because it was a tactical victory over him, if a somewhat insignificant one.

'Well, get one, Sergeant. Then I want you to organize a second house-to-house specifically to ask if this man has been seen recently in the neighbourhood.' Before he could raise an objection, she added, 'And find out from the mother and the neighbours if it's possible that there was a small child in the house the day they died.'

'Why?'

'The shit on the carpet,' she explained in a patronizing tone. Before he could react, she asked, 'What news on the van?'

'It's gone without a trace. Rashid Malik would normally park it in the front garden. He went out in it at about six on the night of his killing, and it hasn't been seen since.'

She felt something that was struggling to be elation at this news. It wasn't, though, as if the case were cracked, but it was another lead in an investigation that was proving worryingly hard to break; she knew from experience that soon she would be coming under pressure from above to produce results, and if all she had was Lever's titbit about the uncle, she would have lost position in the game. As an afterthought, she ordered, 'Compile a list of everyone Malik worked for in the last six months, then interview them.'

'He didn't keep records.'

'Ask the mother, and include it in the house-to-house questioning. What about mates?'

'He didn't appear to have any, if you can believe what we're being told.'

It wasn't unusual for small ethnic communities to turn inwards on occasions such as this, no matter how frustrating it was to the police, no matter how often and insistently they were told that it was in their best interests to cooperate (except that they didn't see it that way).

'Was he devout?' Lever seemed to be nonplussed and she rephrased the question. 'Did he attend the mosque?' But Lever didn't know and it was another small victory. 'Well, find out. Talk to the preachers and staff there.'

'They won't tell us anything.'

'They certainly fucking won't unless we talk to them, Sergeant, will they?'

TWENTY-TWO

Harry Weston decided to begin his investigations in the pub, both because it was the only place he could think of where he might have a chance of learning the identity of the van driver and because he fancied a drink. He thought to call in at Countrywide on the way, in order to stock up on cider for the evening; he also had his eye on a couple of vulnerable-looking fuel tanks near Painswick, and he would be able to check the layout prior to paying them a visit, perhaps even tonight.

The doorbell rang, but he knew who it was – it was Girlie, his sister, the one who had taken to looking after him when Wanda had died and Annie had left him. She called most days, although sometimes it was earlier because on Tuesdays she went into Painswick to have her hair done, and every so often she would go into Gloucester to 'do a bit of shopping', although what she bought he never knew; perhaps that was because he never asked, knowing that she would not have told him anyway.

He opened the door and knew at once who was standing there before him, and it wasn't his sister. This person he had seen only a few times in the Seven Stars and then seen once more in a glimpse in the reflection from a wing mirror in the dark on a country lane.

Apart from pain, that was the last thing he really knew, because then a knife pierced his belly, and, skewered, he crumpled as the blade was withdrawn; he was not, even then, to know peace, for he was swiftly turned and his throat was slit.

It was done just as Charles Sydenham had so easily described.

TWENTY-THREE

'I'm really sorry to bother you, Beverley.'

'You're not bothering me, John. I could do with a drink.'

There was, as there always had been, a tension between them; she had hoped that by now it would have gone, that he would have found within himself something more than good-natured reserve with which to see her, that he would offer her more than an occasional – and usually professional – relationship. If his phone call that afternoon had led her treacherously towards hope, his demeanour as they sat opposite each other in the Slug and Lettuce in Cheltenham town centre told her that she was a fool; as she grew older, so she grew more ingenuous.

But I was so much older then; I'm younger than that now . . .

'How are you?' he asked. 'What's it like to be a chief inspector?'

She laughed, a sign of merriment that she did not feel. 'More pay, but a lot more shit.'

He raised his glass of lager. 'I'll drink to that,' he said, and she saw that his merriment was as counterfeit as her own. She wondered why they had to lie to each other; she wondered, too, if everyone had to lie to each other, if too much truth, like too much oxygen, was toxic. 'And what about you, John?'

'Fine.'

She had interrogated – 'interviewed' was the term that was now preferred, in case of giving the impression that water-boarding and electrodes had been involved – too many people to miss the brevity of a lie; almost instinctively, she said and did nothing, waiting for psychosocial pressure to do its work and squeeze more out of him.

'I've cut down on work, for the time being.'

'I'd heard.'

'I just do some coronial work, to keep the wolf from the door.'

'You've been missed.'

'Have I?' He was surprised, and genuinely so, she thought.

The look on his face told her that she had hit some sort of nerve, although where the pain had struck was impossible for her to see.

'I've had to put up with Charles Sydenham.'

He laughed; this time she judged it was more genuine. 'Good old Charles.' This was the kind of sentiment held by someone who was past the aggravation; she knew that Eisenmenger had considered Sydenham, aside from his professional opinion of his abilities, excruciating to be with and personally unpleasant. 'I heard he was called in for the Barton Street killings.'

'Unfortunately.'

'Are you working on those?'

She sipped her wine, then nodded. 'I am.'

'Has he been helpful?'

'Pretty much so, yes. He's given us a reasonable time frame, and a fairly plausible sequence of events.'

'Good.'

'I just hope he hasn't missed anything . . .'

'Have you some reason to think he might have done?'

She hesitated. Strictly speaking, she should have kept her mouth shut . . . 'There's one odd thing, although Sydenham assures me it's not directly rated to the two deceased.' She told him about the bloodstained, faecal staining on the carpet by the front door.

'Odd,' he commented.

She found that she had been hoping he would come up with some magical explanation. 'But is it relevant?'

'Until it's proved otherwise,' he responded absently; the way he said it was slightly sepulchral, as if something were speaking through him. Still, she acknowledged, it was good advice. Suddenly, perhaps because the shade that had been inhabiting him departed and he was suddenly no longer under the influence of something enervating, he said, 'So you're pretty busy, then?'

'You could say that.' He didn't sigh, but the way he drank his beer suggested that this response had not delighted him. 'What do you want?'

'I was hoping you could run a few checks on someone for me.'

'I take it this isn't official, if you aren't doing forensic work.'

He smiled wanly. 'If you don't turn anything up, then, yes, it's not official.'

Which was always, she had to agree, the way of things. 'What kind of checks?'

He told her about the case that morning, how the death was as yet unexplained, about how it was perhaps important to find out where this man had been and what he'd been doing.

'You think it's an infectious disease?'

'It's possible.'

And yet, even as he said this, he found himself listening to the question anew, as if light of a different hue were being played upon it, bringing out different shadows, highlighting different contours.

That odd rash . . .

Such a strange distribution . . .

'You don't sound sure.'

But it needed to be excluded, and he told her as such. 'I thought someone could at least contact this chap, Paul Lynch, to find out what the itinerary of the trip was.'

'A Coroner's Officer could do that.' She saw the look on his face. 'But you think it might have been something less than totally legal?' she guessed.

'The family think so; the family are terrified it's so.'

She told herself that she was only inclined to help because John Eisenmenger had a track record in uncovering things that needed to be exposed; she told herself even more loudly that it was nothing at all to do with the barely appreciated suspicion that she was unaccountably attracted to him. 'I asked if you thought so.'

He tried to evaluate exactly *what* he was thinking, but couldn't come to a firm conclusion. 'I don't know.'

Which didn't help her. She ran through her options, which were to refuse or to stretch resources that were already beyond the point of tearing. She was quite convinced that she was not influenced by any emotions whatsoever as she said, 'I'll see what I can do.'

I'll get Harrison to do it; it'll keep her occupied, perhaps save her from Lever's wandering willy . . .

'Thanks.' He seemed strangely relieved, as if this triviality were important to him; she found that it just contributed to the air of unreality that seemed to surround him sometimes. Perhaps it wasn't trivial at all, she had to concede.

'On one condition.'

This made him stop and frown slightly. 'What?'

She smiled, she hoped reassuringly. 'I'm hungry,' she said as she looked around. It was a place of polished wood, and bustling, young waiters in black dress busied themselves and occasionally even served the customers; there was a hatch through which could be seen three chefs, one in a fetching check bandana and gold earring. The place was filling up, the atmosphere becoming loud and welcoming. John Eisenmenger, being John Eisenmenger, didn't immediately take the hint. 'Are you?' A moment later, when she hadn't replied, he said, 'Oh . . .' There was a pause before, 'Shall we get something to eat, then?'

It was a pleasant meal; not quite haute cuisine, but serviceable and well cooked. At the end of it, when she knew that it *was* the end, she asked, 'What's the name of this chap?'

'Meadows. Arthur Meadows.'

For a moment she wondered if she had heard that name before, but it was merely a moment, after which she decided that it meant nothing to her.

TWENTY-FOUR

She hated the house, but that no longer mattered. She hated almost all aspects of her existence and had learned to ignore the emotion; she had long ago reasoned that if you love everything, then everything is the same to you; it is the identical situation when you hate everything. In any case, she couldn't rail too loudly against the universe on this topic, because she had chosen where to spend the last few months of her life. In most ways, it suited her perfectly; in a few but important ways, she found it abhorrent. It was cold and damp, poorly decorated to the point of decrepitude, and dark – not perhaps surprisingly, since it was surrounded by leylandii hedges that had been allowed to roam unhindered for fifteen years and now were almost completely beyond taming. The furniture was twenty-five years and more in age; it had probably never been particularly attractive to look at, or comfortable to sit in or lie on, but age had wearied it all to an extreme. The kitchen was a bare minimum, the washing machine a twin-tub, the bathroom as inviting as a public convenience. The carpets had once been thin and cheap, and now had added value in being threadbare and dirty as well.

Had she been interested, she would have spent her last few thousands of pounds on a lease for a far more appealing property than this one.

Yet it did have its attractions for her.

The village of Cranham was isolated for a start. Situated in the south of the county, it was, in actual fact, not many kilometres from Stroud, where she had been born. A turn off the A46, then two more – one right, one left – and the road dipped alarmingly, becoming poorly tended and overgrown; within fifteen minutes, the world seemed isolated both in time and place. Secondly, the house did not induce anything in the way of sentiment in her soul. It was bare and cold and nothing more than the minimum; it took her back to the basics of existence, allowing her to believe with total conviction that reality was not the best, nor even the only, thing worth trying for. She woke every morning, feeling the damp and the ascetic hardness of the mattress, and through them experienced a sense of joy, one that she had not known since Marty's father had made his last footfall in the world. Thirdly, it brought back to her the years of her childhood, when her own father had worked all the hours that she was awake and her mother had killed her with passionless kindness, when she had first become to appreciate that perhaps she would never be allowed to draw enough comfort to sustain her from the sea of humanity in which she was now drowning.

She found herself helped by the discovery that she now looked on Stroud as a very strange place indeed; its setting was beautiful, combining the perfect English combination of rugged hillside and greenery of astonishing depth in which were dotted wonderfully harmonious stone houses; yet its development had been curiously uncontrolled, so that wherever she looked there was something to jar the eye – a hideous supermarket, a housing development that should never have been born, a 'traffic management scheme' that sank her heart.

In a fundamental, almost intestinal, way, though, she was glad to be back; it made her feel as if her final journey had been made, that the circle had been completed, and that things were as they should be. She drew enormous – not to say, overwhelming – comfort from this. It strengthened her resolve; she felt that she could do anything, and was happy to believe that she would.

'You're sure you weren't spotted?'

Marty shook his head, but she was only partly reassured; Marty would not lie to her, but he might not know that he was lying. She had known that it would be a risk to send him to tidy up the loose end whilst it was still daylight, but she hoped that it was one worth taking; the longer that Harry Weston was around, the more likely it was that he would prove a danger to them and to what they hoped to achieve. Even if he was unlikely to go directly to the police, he was still likely to blab to someone, somewhere, at some time. Anyway, Marty had been good at his job; it was unlikely that he had been seen anywhere near the scene, and there was no point in fretting about it. They now had to get the plan back on track, which meant that they had to locate their missing merchandise, and so, while she cooked baked beans on toast for her son, she made plans.

She had been listening constantly to BBC Radio Gloucester all afternoon; there was no report that anyone else had found them, either alive or dead, although the murder of the Maliks was big news; she listened to a precis of a press conference given by Chief Inspector Wharton, the officer in charge, not finding anything to worry about. The station was also making much of an upcoming royal gardening show at Highgrove House near Tetbury; it was being organized by the Royal Horticultural Society and was going to be attended by the Prince of Wales and the Duchess of Cornwall. Thousands were expected, apparently. Jacqueline smiled grimly to herself as she listened to the syco-phancy dribbling from the radio speaker, forgetting for a moment her own immediate problem. She had the power to upset their plans, but that was only if she overcame this particular hurdle.

Assuming they weren't in the wood – which was not impossible, though it was a scenario that could be held for later consideration if all other avenues led nowhere – then she reckoned that they had taken shelter in or around the house that bordered on the woodland. The first thing would be to determine whether that house was occupied. It was dark tonight – a new moon – which Marty would find an ideal environment in which to work.

Girlie hadn't been feeling well that day. Actually, she didn't feel well most days, but this day had been a bad day; the nausea had been worse than normal, the malaise more dragging. She had duties, though, and, although she didn't fully appreciate it, these were the only things for which she still continued; to her, 'duty' was synonymous with 'love'. She had asked the doctor in the hospital how long she would live – how long before the cancer in her gullet killed her – but he had been sly and evasive (although in a cheerful and optimistic way), and he had fobbed her off with vagueness, as if she were stupid. She knew that she wasn't schooled, but she knew also that she wasn't stupid. They had put a tube down her throat a month ago – not as bad as she had expected, and done within the day – which had helped a lot with swallowing her spit, and it meant that she didn't have to cut her food up so small any more. Today, though, things seemed to have gone backwards. It was why she was late getting to Harry's.

Harry was the last of her brothers. Not, perhaps, the one she would have chosen to have been left with – that would have been Alf, the charmer, the one with the smile and the talent for card tricks – but she was grateful to be left with anyone. She had never found her love in life, and her family had been her consolation; first her parents and then, when Dad had died of a stroke, Mum alone, slowly slipping into forgetfulness, requiring care more and more with every day, as she gave affection back less and less with every day. Girlie hadn't minded, though, because she had known that this was her duty; in some sense that she did not – perhaps also could not or dare not – articulate, she felt called to do this.

When Mum had finally died, her breathing heavy and soggy in the cold, dark morning hours while she talked of people Girlie barely remembered, she had turned to her three brothers. Not that she hadn't had suitors of her own, but none of them had stuck with her, either because of circumstance or choice, or perhaps because of God's will; the closest had been Charlie, a farrier's apprentice, short but strong, a young man with large brows but a surprisingly pleasant smile, made the more so perhaps because he shared it so rarely. He had been taken from her by the flu in sixty-nine, his strength of no avail at the end. One by one, all those she had loved had gone, except for Harry, but that was all right, because it had brought them together in a way that wouldn't have happened otherwise. She knew that she was being selfish when she found herself reassured that at least she wouldn't die alone.

She was calling on Harry now not because she expected him to be in – if he wasn't in the pub, he'd be off in the pick-up doing whatever he did to survive – but because she expected an empty house. It would be dirty and messy and there would be several days of washing-up to be done, and the toilet would be disgusting, but that was all right. She would spend a few hours putting it all straight, cleaning and polishing and washing, just as she had done for a succession of family members through fifty years of waiting, never finding, standing still and never arriving. She would feel better at the end of it and, although her brother might not actually express any gratitude, their blood's thickness told her that his thanks did not need to be expressed in anything as fleeting as words.

Receiving no reply to her ring, she felt in her jacket pocket for the key, having trouble because of the arthritis that had twisted her fingers, and because her pockets were crowded with the small but important things of her life – the small handkerchief, her mother's brooch, her own keys, a lip salve. Eventually, though, she succeeded, putting the key in the lock, knowing that her brother would not have double-locked it. She opened it and stepped inside, switching on the bare bulb that hung just above the bottom of the stairs from the switch to her right.

She realized then that she would, indeed, be going to die alone.

TWENTY-FIVE

They had stayed late and were just leaving the pub when her mobile sounded. She had wondered whether she would ask Eisenmenger to take coffee with her at her flat, and whether he would accept. In the narrow side street that ran parallel to the slightly jaded grandeur of the Promenade, they stood while she took it. Lever said without preamble, 'There's been another killing?'

'Where? Who?'

'Chap called Harry Weston. He lives just outside Painswick.'

Painswick? Painswick was rural, middle class, in many ways the epitome of the Cotswolds. 'Any idea when?'

'It's just been reported . . .' She could hear in his voice that there was more. 'It seems he may have had his throat slit.'

Shit. She was at once thrilled that here was another lead, afraid about what it could mean. 'Give me the address. I'll meet you there. Get Sydenham out of his slumber, too.'

She cut the connection and Eisenmenger said sympathetically, 'Work?'

She grimaced, hesitated, then made a decision. 'I need another favour, John.'

'Go on,' he said guardedly. From the High Street there came the sound of laughing and shouting, carrying the connotation of too much drink drunk in too little time.

'I'd like you to come with me.'

'Oh . . .' His head reared back, seemingly genuinely shocked and appalled; perhaps he was.

She could see that he was about to refuse her, but, if she couldn't prolong their meeting at her flat over coffee and a nightcap, then she could at least prolong it over a slit throat, where she would have the added advantage of his opinion on the death. 'Please, John.' She knew that she was good at entreaty and how to use the contrast between her usual sharp, detached persona and the one she reserved for her private life. It worked, too; he was wavering.

'I just need some reassurance that Sydenham isn't missing something . . . or, I suppose, that he isn't talking complete bollocks.'

'Charles won't like it.'

'And that bothers you?' She voiced this as a challenge.

Another pause, and then, 'OK.'

The relief that she felt was just professional; she was just covering all the bases, using belt and braces, making sure that she wasn't making fundamental errors . . .

Their drive back to the wooded area had been uneventful. As it was now dark, there had been little point in attempting to search the undergrowth again, even though they had brought flashlights with them; having parked out of sight of the road, they had therefore walked immediately to the fence that separated the wood from the house. There, standing just under the treeline as Marty had commanded (even though the night was moonless, his training told him to take no chances), they surveyed the fence and the property beyond. The former was a typical stock fence – three rails and posts every three metres; there was stock wiring tacked to it, but the wood was old and rotten, so that in many places it was almost collapsing. Even two seriously ill people could have got over it; she commanded him to help her to examine it carefully along the entire length that marked the edge of the wood and the start of the land around the dwelling. The latter was a typical Victorian Gloucestershire farmhouse, built of brick and square in footprint. There was a low outbuilding opposite – probably a pigsty, she thought – and behind that were two barns.

If Marty thought that it was a waste of time, he didn't say so; he didn't – couldn't – think like that after all his traumas. She had often noticed that, in a way, the military training was all that held him together; it was, she supposed, part of its purpose. Even after the human had been destroyed, had been smeared into a bloody mark on a soldier's forgotten memories, the training remained, even stronger, even more in tune with the martial music that beat constantly in his mind. Yet it proved worthwhile. After a little over ten minutes, she heard a low whistle – one that was anonymous, possibly animal, possibly even the wind through a narrow gap in the trees – that she knew was Marty. She could just see his torchlight to her right and she hurried over to it. It was shining on a part of the fence where the post was almost rotted through and the top two rails had fallen away, bringing the stock wire down with them. The ferns and brambles at this point seemed slightly broken down and they were covered in something dark and slimy in the torchlight; when she bent down towards it, a rank, faecal smell rose into her nostrils.

She straightened up and smiled at the hopeful expression on her son's face; he smiled in relief back at her, and the simplicity of this exchange strained her heart. 'What do we do?' he asked. They looked over the house.

The whole place looks decrepit, she thought.

Plenty of places to hide, he thought.

'Do we go and search it now?' he asked.

She considered, in the same way that an officer would have done, weighing options and priorities against each other; he didn't know it, but he was grateful for this. There was no sign that anyone was living in the house – no lights were on and they had yet to see a vehicle outside – but she didn't think it wise to assume that it was unoccupied. 'We search the outbuildings, but leave the house alone for tonight.'

Given orders, he was content, but only as a computer is satisfied when programmed.

Perhaps it was the time of night, but Beverley doubted it; she was used to working at this hour, battling fatigue and cynicism, paddling in the bloody pool of human evil, the one that seemed to grow wider and deeper by the year; the one, though, that she feared she needed, that she found she had come to live by. No, she decided, her depression was born of something else, yet something allied; she was deflated and saddened to be here, in this kitchen. Ironically, she felt this way not because of a death, but because of a life; this man, Harry Weston (an undistinguished name for a man with an undistinguished life, yet a perversely distinguished death) had seemed to live such a sorry, meaningless life, barely interacting with the world through which he moved, except perhaps to besmirch it or steal it.

Take this room. Once, she judged, it had been homely; now,

that was a term that could not be applied to this place in any sense. It may have been a house, a retreat, a refuge, technically a domicile, but it hadn't been a home for a long time. Harry Weston had gone, but his residence did not miss him, nor ever would. It was as if he had moved stealthily through this place, much as a cat might have done, leaving only some detritus – the unwashed mugs on the unwashed kitchen table, cobwebs that cuddled the torn lampshade above it – and no sense of having been there at all. A spirit, perhaps of a long-dead inhabitant, perhaps of nature herself, would have left more evidence of its existence in that space. The cupboards contained only a few examples of ageing crockery and tins of staple foods that displayed no imagination, no desire for living, merely for existence; under the sink, where there should have been washing-up liquid and bleach and, perhaps, a scourer, there were only demijohns of still cider, looking as if they were skulking, waiting for the coast to clear, the fuss to die down, the house to revert to its customary silence, so that they could breathe a sigh of relief and slowly turn sour.

Why this man, this cipher, this piece of flotsam? The recession, she knew from her own experience, had left in its drying, caked wake many living dead and dying living, but most of them – at least, all the ones she came across – were bewildered, or angry, or depressed, or vengeful, even insane; Harry Weston seemed just to have ceased his existence even while he still breathed, and done so uncaringly, whilst his world around him conspired with this passive exeat. She could not imagine what possible connection he could have had with a dead husband and wife of Pakistani Kashmiri descent, other than proximity (the murder scenes were perhaps ten kilometres apart) and, perhaps, poverty (although even this last did not seem much of a connection, since Harry Weston's had been a poverty of much more than mere money; his had been a poverty of life, of hope, of sheer existence, something that she had not sensed when standing at the site of slaughter that had once been the Maliks' home).

Around her, Lever was directing others in the customs and actions that such a scene, such an act of desecration of societal values, dictated; searching, examining, sampling, deducing. Almost all of it would be at best useless, at worst misleading,

but it had to be done, she knew too well. Better too much than
not enough; the mantra of an age, of a civilization, perhaps one
that was being chanted as the wheels came off the wagon and
the wolves gathered in their envious hunger . . .

What the fuck is wrong with me?

Abruptly, almost jerkily as if moved by someone else in the
dark heights above her, she breathed in deeply and quickly, turned
from the room and its dirty glooms, and went out into the hall.
Eisenmenger was there, to one side of the corpse, whilst others
bustled around him; he was staring at it as if mesmerized. Not
touching, just staring; he might have been trying to will it back
to life, so intense was his stare. She knew him well, but she
found it unnerving in this black night made ineffectually light
by the single naked bulb. What was he seeing? she wondered.
How could he detach himself so completely? It would be all too
easy to imagine that he was entranced by things and places,
shades and wraiths that few others could see, that few others
would dare to see.

She had to make an effort – one she wasn't used to making
– to bring herself once more out of some sort of despond, and
this was a shock. There was a moment of something akin to
vertigo, as if she were momentarily lost, as if she had been
transported into a future where the world no longer made sense,
before normality – as shitty as that was – returned. Perhaps it
had something to do with the arrival through the open front door
of Charles Sydenham. His expression was one to be appreciated
and then treasured always after. In her experience, silences were
forever being described as 'stunned', but this was one that was
probably better filed under 'paralyzed'. Sydenham – a thin, ascetic
man of greyed hair and a look that might have been directly
inherited from the more insane of the autocratic Roman emperors
– for once could not hide what was patently at first surprise, then
astonishment and only slowly indignation.

'Well, well, well,' he said, dragging this repetition out but
slowing as he spoke, so that by the end of what she considered
to be a rather quotidian utterance the sound waves were barely
able to drag themselves over the dirty carpet into anyone's ears.
'Johnny Eisenmenger!' he added, as if he were a game show
host introducing a plebeian contestant, perhaps one that had upset

him in the Green Room prior to broadcast, for his voice did not so much drip as exude venom in a slimed, almost lascivious manner.

Lever had been surprised to be introduced to Eisenmenger. Crime scenes were a temporary but highly exclusive club, open only to a few; not only were outsiders not encouraged, they were actively excluded. For a few hours or days, the club came into existence and the membership was vetted with a degree of dedication that would have impressed the MCC, and what went on inside its transient venue was as sacrosanct as anything that occurred in a Roman Catholic oratory. Everyone knew each other in this place, to the extent that conversation was at a minimum; and what talk there was, was hushed, so adding to the air of a religious rite, a ceremony, a special and exclusive and inimitable occasion. Lever liked that. He found the kudos that came from being a privileged constituent of this thing that few in the world knew about, even fewer would ever experience, a source of empowerment, of pride and of strength; the concept that interlopers were allowed – even if they were interlopers who had knowledge of the rules and sacraments – was to him abhorrent and viscerally unsound.

Yet others did not feel so, it seemed. Others looked on this intruder as an accepted part of the club machinery. They were not surprised by his presence; they even acknowledged him as someone who had endured and passed the initiation rituals. This, to Lever, was difficult to comprehend. This was no place for spectators; everyone had a function and, if no function, then they had no right to be there; admission should have been denied. It would have been, had it been his choice, but it was not; it was Wharton's, and that was of interest to Lever. He thought he saw something in her attitude to Eisenmenger that intrigued him, something that hinted at vulnerability, perhaps at vulnerability he could exploit.

He was most interested, too, to see that he was not the only one to find Eisenmenger's presence a source of discomfort and anger. Charles Sydenham was clearly not a happy man to find that he was not alone in his professional capacity at the crime scene; not happy at all. Lever knew enough about forensic pathologists to know that they tended to be solitary creatures, becoming

aggressive when they met each other, defending in a vicious
and spiteful manner not territory but opinion; as far as he was
concerned, they sought advantage over their colleagues by
quoting scientific shit, but they did so as if they were firing
semi-automatics, except that it sounded like wankers squealing
in mutual pleasure.

Stupid fuckwits.

Still, watching them clash was a welcome diversion from being
given a lot of shit to do by Beverley Wharton . . .

'Could I have a word, Chief Inspector?'

Beverley knew what was going to come, but it was part of the
game to pretend ignorance whilst she and Sydenham went out into
the night; it wasn't quite raining, but it wasn't quite not raining,
either; the wind was cold as it whipped the tops of a conifer hedge
ahead of them. There were six police cars parked out here and
teams of uniformed officers were searching outbuildings, as
instructed. No one paid them any attention. 'Is there a problem,
Dr Sydenham?' she enquired, knowing that it was a question that
could only anger him further; still, nothing wrong with that.

'Is this a new policy of Gloucestershire Constabulary?'

'I don't follow.'

Sydenham waved his hand back towards the house. 'Two
forensic pathologists? What's the matter? Is it that you don't trust
my opinion?'

*Watch it, Charles. Your inferiority complex is hanging too
low . . .*

'Not at all . . .'

'No? Then perhaps you have just got money to fritter? Is the
public purse – contrary to popular opinion – suddenly flush with
funds, so you thought to give employment to two of us? If so,
perhaps I might let my local MP know, so that he can apply
pressure to have your budget cut in the face of such a flagrant
waste of money.'

'Dr Eisenmenger happened to be with me when the call came
through,' she explained.

His expression changed and, she spotted at once, not for the
better. 'Oh, of course,' he said and his words carried foetid
sarcasm. 'No doubt a purely professional consultation.'

She was well used to this hateful man of old, knew his ways and attitudes, yet she still had trouble containing herself; Sydenham had a cut-throat razor for a tongue, the blade coated in hot caustic soda. 'Dr Eisenmenger is not being paid to be here, but I did think that you would welcome a professional colleague.'

He stared at her so intently that he might have been attempting to peer at the back wall of her skull. It was a long time before he said, in a voice that was sweet, much as hemlock in honey might be, 'The last thing we need is an *appendage* contaminating the crime scene, Chief Inspector. Kindly ask Dr Eisenmenger to wait in the car.'

He just stood there after that, looking at her, and she debated the wisdom of entering some sort of professional tussle with him; after all, he had no right to restrict access to the crime scene. Yet she did not, deciding that it would be a battle that even Pyrrhus would probably have considered unwise. She turned and went back into the house.

TWENTY-SIX

Even with torches, it was so dark that she feared it was a hopeless task; she doubted that there was electricity to the outbuildings and, even if there were, she doubted that there would be intact bulbs. It was a meaningless quandary anyway, for they dared not risk the householder – if the house wasn't uninhabited – being alerted to their presence. Had they had time, she would have made Marty do a proper stake-out – he had argued that this was proper procedure – but time was pressing on them. She was vividly aware that the success of their plan was slipping from them and, if they didn't find at least one of the two missing pieces of cargo, they would most likely fail. She couldn't allow that; she owed it to Marty. They had had a small piece of luck when they found evidence of their quarry on the fence line; they had to capitalize on it.

But ill-luck had yet to finish with them. An irruption of barking suddenly surrounded them in the darkness of the old pigsty, pinning them to the cold air in total rigidity, at first seeming to come from all around them; only as it died down did its source become apparent and they saw a faint light shining through the slightly open door at the far end of the building, giving it a shape that darkness had previously stolen from it. In an instant, Marty was down on all fours in God knew what, dragging his mother down with him, causing her to fall awkwardly so that she muttered a soft 'Ow'. His hand came over her mouth – gently – at once, and she smelled dirt and damp and something faecal.

They heard someone – a woman with a broad Gloucestershire accent – talking, although they couldn't hear what was being said. The dog continued barking, though. Eventually, the woman's voice was raised. 'I know you're there, you know.' She should have sounded worried, but she didn't; she sounded confident and aggressive, while the dog sounded large and eager for the chase. 'I'm going to give you a minute, and then I'm going to let Casper go. I suggest you make yourself scarce, because he's not a people dog.'

They heard a door slam, but the dog carried on barking, seeming to do so even more enthusiastically, as if it knew what had been said and was looking forward to some enjoyment. Marty took his large hand away from his mother's mouth. 'Come on.'

She whispered, 'What are you going to do?'

'Kill the dog.' He was surprised to have been asked the question.

'No.'

He looked at her, perplexed. 'Why not?'

'Because then we'll have to kill her, and whoever else is in that house. She's probably on her own, but you never know. Anyway, she might be on the phone even now.' But the answer meant nothing to him, as was plain from the look she saw on his face. She explained, 'We've killed once today. The more we kill, the more likely it is that we'll draw attention to ourselves. We can't afford that; not until we've got what we're looking for.'

There was precious little light in that shed, but she could see that he was disappointed, a look that brought almost complete despair to her; she had lost her son in so many ways, had him taken from her by the authorities. 'What do we do?'

'We leave for now, but we've got to keep the place under observation. We'll get some sleep and come back just after dawn.'

He liked that at least they were going to be doing something; ever since he had come back from his final mission, he had been unable to rest, unable to be not doing something, despite the medication. He crept to the door and peered cautiously around it, his face only just above ground level. Within a second he was back at her side. 'I can only see the dog, and it's a big one – a German Shepherd, I think.'

'The woman's gone?'

'And the door is closed; the windows are curtained, although there's a light on behind them.'

'How are we going to get out of here?' she asked, knowing that, in this situation, he was the one who had to lead, she to follow unquestioningly.

He looked around. At the back of the sty there were three metal-framed, double casement windows set in the wall. Most of the glass was gone from them and they had no window locks. 'We can't risk going out the front with the dog there; it'll bark and maybe bring whoever is in that house back out. We go out through the window.'

He didn't wait for her opinion but moved immediately to the nearest window and grasped the handles to twist them and push open the rusted frames. It made a noise and the dog at once began barking furiously. His response was to move more quickly, throwing the windows wide; he put his large hands on the frame and, from a standing start, vaulted through the gap, then turned and held out his hands to his mother. As she came forward, he grasped her torso, pulling her powerfully forward and then lifting her without obvious effort between the opened windows. As he put her on the ground outside, she saw that they were in a small area of rusted wire fencing, some decrepit garden machinery, mounds of rubble and half-rotted timbers, but she had no more opportunity to examine the details because he grabbed her hand and began to run, almost pulling her off her feet; it was all done despite the stiffness she knew he had in his injured shoulder. The dog was barking even more excitedly, as if it knew that its potential prey was escaping and, as they sprinted away into the darkness, they were aware of the light from the house striking out into the night. They were too far away to hear what, if anything, was said, and hoped that, correspondingly, they were too distant and the night too dark for them to be seen.

'I'm sorry about that,' said Beverley, as she walked with Eisenmenger to the car that she had arranged should take him back home.

'I can't say I'm surprised.'

'I thought he'd behave a little less childishly.'

'I wouldn't put it like that,' he mused.

'How would you put it?'

'He's got a point, you know.'

'You think so? I think he's an arrogant twat.'

He lifted one shoulder in a sort of abortive, half-hearted shrug, tilting his head to one side. 'I think I'd feel pretty much as he did.'

She couldn't believe this. 'You?'

He sighed. 'Why did you invite me, Beverley?'

'I thought another perspective would be useful. "Two heads" and all that.'

He smiled. 'Which might be taken to imply that you don't trust Charles's opinion. He certainly took it that way.'

'I can't help it if he's a sensitive soul,' she snapped.

'But you don't, do you?'

It took a moment for her to find the truth. 'No,' she admitted. They had reached the car; the driver was inside, waiting patiently. 'He's made too many mistakes in the past; mistakes that were potentially crucial. Can I trust him on this one?' she asked. 'Has he missed something?'

'It's rather early to tell,' he pointed out. 'All I could do was observe the body without touching it. And I haven't seen his reports on the first two killings.'

It was her turn to sigh. 'No, I suppose you haven't.'

'Send them to me in the morning. I'll be at the medico-legal complex.'

She readily assented to this. He opened the car door, but before he got in he said, 'One thing that might be significant, though . . .'

'What's that?'

'You said they looked like professional killings.'

'Undoubtedly.'

He pursed his lips. 'I think I'd use a slightly different word to describe them.'

'Which is?'

'Military.'

They looked at each other, she with slow realization. 'A soldier, you mean?'

'Someone like that. Perhaps Special Forces.'

'You're sure?'

'Good God, no. It just struck me as I saw the pattern of injuries; from what you've said, they're exactly the same as the first two deaths. A distinct and unusual modus operandi; someone who is highly trained at killing silently and quickly.'

He got into the car, and she chewed thoughtfully on this new cerebral fodder. As she walked back to the crime scene, she pondered its significance. She pondered, too, her motives for asking Eisenmenger to attend with her. She *had* wanted to know his opinions – this last snippet was proof that she may have been wise to do so – but she knew that there had been other, deeper motives.

TWENTY-SEVEN

Eisenmenger's presence in the dissection room of the medico-legal facility that next morning was because he wanted to see again the body of Arthur Meadows. He was dissatisfied or, rather, he was satisfied that he had yet to see the truth of this death. So far, he felt that all the theories and speculations – both those offered before death by the clinicians, and those after it by himself – were slightly off-target; plausible and possible, but not probable. It would be too soon for the results of his further investigations – the microbiological samples, the histological slides and toxicological analysis – to be available, but Eisenmenger knew of old that sometimes there was no substitute for eyeballing a body.

Sam was sympathetic. 'Not sure about this one?' he enquired

solicitously as Eisenmenger stood in the body store at the head of Arthur Meadows as he lay on a trolley in an opened white plastic body bag. Arthur had purged, as dead people do.

'No.'

'It happens.' Sam was typical of many mortuary technicians. He had a huge inferiority complex and enjoyed witnessing the downfall of pathologists. He believed that he knew far more than he actually did, but, in compensation, he was competent at his job. As far as Eisenmenger was concerned, it was a fair trade.

Eisenmenger was silent for a while. 'Could you turn him over for me, Sam?'

Turning a corpse is no easy manner and, although Sam did the majority of the work, Eisenmenger had to roll up his sleeves and help him. When the back and buttocks were exposed, they both stood back, as if standing before and appreciating a work of art. Eisenmenger found himself beyond perplexity; what the hell kind of a rash was it that affected only the buttocks? The dermatologists – the 'rash doctors' – had been flummoxed, Eisenmenger now equally so. A phone began ringing in the office as Sam said thoughtfully, 'Fucking funny place to get sunburn. Perhaps he's some sort of sun-worshipper.'

Eisenmenger's mind suddenly took a left turn and entered an entirely new avenue of thought, just as Maggie, another mortuary technician came into the body store. 'Chief Inspector Wharton's on the phone for you, Doctor.'

The forensics report on the Maliks' computer had been on Beverley's desk when she had got in. The list of URLs was long and mostly quotidian; Google, of course, as well as Facebook, Genes Reunited and the BBC. The list of 'friends' on Facebook was also long and mostly female, suggesting that they were Parveen Malik's; none of them meant anything to Beverley, but someone would have to check all of them. Nor was there any name on Genes Reunited that jumped out at her – no evidence that either of the deceased had been a distant relative of Osama Bin Laden or Che Guevara. There were three email accounts on Hotmail – one joint one and two individual ones; it was Rashid Malik who proved to have the interesting names in the contacts list, and the interesting communications in the 'trash' folder.

Among the 123 contacts was a name that at first she could not place, although she knew that it was not unknown to her – *Arthur Meadows*. It took only a moment, though, before she recalled that it was the name Eisenmenger had given to her last night; with that recollection came the connection that had escaped her at the time. It was the name that Benny had mentioned that night a few weeks ago, which until then she had completely forgotten . . . *He might be moving livestock . . . And he's not a farmer . . .*

Was that what the 'man with a van' had been into? People-smuggling?

She began to go through the emails that Rashid Malik had exchanged with Arthur Meadows in the weeks before he had died.

Ninety minutes later, Lever came into her office. 'I've got the Maliks' mobile phone records; they're quite interesting.' He hadn't knocked, but she forgave him for that; her head was full of thoughts and wonderings.

She asked, 'Did Rashid Malik make any phone calls to someone called Arthur Meadows in the hours and days before he died?' she asked.

The effect on Lever was satisfying; he almost seemed to jump, as if he had just been goosed by an invisible pervert. 'How the fuck . . .?'

As Lever drove to the medico-legal facility just outside Gloucester, Beverley compared the names on the list of emails with those on the list of telephone calls made and received; Arthur Meadows' name had featured prominently, especially in the days before Rashid Malik's death, and the information supplied told her that he had been in constant contact as Meadows had travelled through the countries of Eastern Europe. Another name on the list of email contacts stuck out, though: Jacqueline21209@AOL.com.

At first, Beverley looked at it, wondering why that one should strike her as potentially important; it wasn't the only female name, and it wasn't the only Western one, but it *was* the only Western female name – always assuming, of course, that the correspondent was, in actuality, what she said she was, that it wasn't an alias. That was the trouble with the modern, digital world; nothing was ever quite as it at first seemed. Perhaps it was her own prejudices leading her astray, but she couldn't imagine Rashid Malik having anything to do with what appeared to be a white Western woman, even in the course of business. There was a high probability that it might be something entirely kosher, but the corollary was that there was a small one that it wasn't, and it was by not ignoring the small probabilities that criminal cases were broken.

Jacqueline had first made contact with Rashid about two months before, requesting help with the transport of a 'fragile pair of objects'. Looked at with an unsuspicious eye, such a description appeared perfectly innocent; read, though, when one was alert for a subtext of people-trafficking and it seemed to be metaphorically underlined and in bold. Bona fides were established through a mutual friend called only Mohammed, which was not on its own a lot of use to Beverley, although a mobile phone number was supplied (and which occurred fairly frequently on the list of calls made and received by Rashid's own phone); at first she was of a mind to make a mental note to find out a little more about Mohammed in due course, but knew it would be a hopeless task with such a common name and nothing else to work from.

The first email was perhaps the most informal, containing the tantalizing phrase, 'I hope that Marty is well'; once again, she noted it mentally, yet knew that, on its own, it was useless. Thereafter, the course of the exchange between the two of them read as what one would expect in the negotiation of business, involving the bargaining about a price – no unit of currency was ever mentioned, but a figure of 22,000 appeared to have been settled upon – and then the arrangements for collection. That the date finally agreed was the day on which Rashid and his wife had been butchered did little to surprise her.

As the car pulled into the car park of the medico-legal centre, she checked for Arthur Meadows' email address on the list, but it wasn't there; perhaps he didn't have one, and all the arrangements had been made by phone. She checked with the list of callers, but no one called Jackie or Jacqueline was on it. Then she phoned Harrison back at the station. She spelled out the email address and told her, 'Dig into it. I want AOL to give us all the traffic in and out of that account in the past year. Find out who it's registered to, and then run that name through the usual databases.'

'AOL won't be keen . . .'

'Tell them how important it is. Tell them that it's a murder investigation and that we need that information. Plead with them.' She knew there was no point in threatening large companies, especially those that weren't based in the UK. Another thought struck her. 'If the names "Marty" or "Mohammed" come up,' she said, spelling them out for clarity, 'pay particular attention.'

Harrison thought that her instruction had finished but, thinking of what Eisenmenger had said the night before, Beverley abruptly added, 'And I want to know if you come across any military connections or references.'

'Military?'

'Just do it, Constable.'

Harrison hesitated and then said cautiously, 'Chief Inspector?'

Beverley asked irritably, 'What now?'

'I think I'm going to need more help with this,' she answered timidly.

For a second, Beverley fought down her anger, then she saw the sense of this. 'OK, take Griffiths and Marks off the building society robbery for the time being; also, you can tell Pippard to stop wasting time interviewing witnesses of the Metz Way stabbing. Satisfied?'

Harrison didn't dare be anything else.

Eisenmenger was waiting and climbed into the back of the car. As Lever pulled out on to the dual carriageway, he asked, 'What's going on?'

'Your man, Meadows, has cropped up in connection with the Barton Street killings.'

Understandably, this news surprised Eisenmenger. 'How?'

'It looks as though he and Rashid Malik were doing business.'

'Drug-trafficking?'

She was non-committal. 'Maybe.'

'Where are we off to?'

'Paul Lynch's yard in Andoversford. Apparently, Mr Lynch asked Arthur Meadows' widow if he could take the lorry back to his compound and store it there; he'd paid Meadows to pick up a consignment of woven linen from Western Turkey and, understandably, he wants it.'

'Do you think he knows what Meadows was up to?'

'We're going to find that out.'

TWENTY-EIGHT

J acqueline had joined her son two hours after sunrise with some coffee and a packet of biscuits; as she watched him wolf them down, a tide of sorrow – one that was now too familiar and too strong to resist, as if it were a rip tide that wanted to take her into the cold depths and kiss her dead – engulfed her. The memories of Marty as a boy – a boy who had been serious and studious, who had refused to weep when, at the age of fifteen, she had told him that his father had been killed in Iraq – drowned her. A boy who had insisted that he should read out his own soliloquy at the funeral and – although he had come close – had still refused to cry. His father's regimental colleagues had stood in solemn remembrance at the funeral, treating Marty as a man, and afterwards writing him letters of support and comradeship that she knew he still kept, that he had never shown her, or anyone else for that matter. She sometimes wondered why none had been written to her.

Up until that moment, he hadn't shown much interest in soldiering, and didn't seem to do so afterwards; his father's profession of bomb disposal had been something that he had never asked about, didn't even seem to appreciate quite what it entailed, that it was (to Jacqueline) an astoundingly brave and reckless thing to do. He hadn't even shown any interest in war comics or guns or anything military, although he had been good at school work and good at games, especially athletics and rugby. He had been in the school's first fifteen, and one of the best at 800 and 1,500 metres. His father's death had deepened his seriousness and academic desires, it seemed, yet that application had also spread to his needs and pleasure in physical activity. He had begun to train incessantly, insatiably . . . religiously.

Her husband, Sean, like many in the military, had believed in God in the traditional, Church of England, pick-and-mix, slightly stolid manner of the Armed Services of Her Majesty Queen Elizabeth. It hadn't been so much deep belief in the existence of God, as deep belief in the belief in the existence of God. She looked back now and she saw that he had played at religion, had used it as a social passport, had dressed in its costume because not to do so would have been not to conform, and not to conform would have been intolerable.

It wasn't as simple as that for her, though. Her childhood experiences meant that she had an altogether more visceral reaction to churches and priests and their regalia. She had kept this to herself at the time for the sake of Sean's career, but the hypocrisy of participation in the Church's antics, its ceremonies and rites – rituals that were, to her, as nauseatingly false as those of druids, satanists and masons – had been hard to bear in silence. She had had to fight to remain composed every time one priest or another had spouted empty phrases in her ears, but she had succeeded, doing so first for Sean, latterly for Marty.

It was not a simple hatred, though. She could not decide in her head whether it was God or the Church that produced such bile within her; she was agnostic in her anger.

'She let the dog out shortly after I arrived, at six fourteen,' he said, unaware that he was intruding on her reverie, unaware too that she was intensely grateful for that.

She knew at once what was coming. Unable to keep anxiety from her voice, she asked, 'What happened?'

'I killed it.' He said it simply, without inflexion, without the expected nuances of expression; without, she had come to accept, humanity. 'She hasn't missed it yet.'

She did not allow any sign of her feelings to show as she asked, 'What else has happened?'

'Two men arrived at six thirty-three. They went into the house for twenty-eight minutes, and then came back out. One of them went off in a tractor he got from the far barn, the other's been in the yard ever since, tinkering with some piece of machinery.'

'Have you seen the woman?'

'Only once, briefly. She brought a mug of something out to the guy in the yard at eight-oh-three; they stood and talked for nineteen minutes, then she went back inside.'

The unnatural precision with which he had timed these happenings might have been impressive – indeed, superficially, it was – but because it was now to him the only way, the natural way, because he was now forever locked into a being a soldier, a killer, it also shredded her heart for the millionth time since he had come back to her. 'No one's gone snooping around?'

'No.'

On the face of it, this was good news. If their presence last night had seriously spooked the woman, she would surely have made arrangements for a search, so presumably her threats of last night had just been bluster. The other thing that reassured her was the absence of any sign of life in the cargo; they must be dead, which would save them a job and reduce the risk of incrimination. 'Good,' she murmured, but it was as much to reassure herself as her son. The killing of the dog worried her, though; it meant that the clock had been started. He asked, 'What do you want me to do?'

She did what commanders on battlefields have done throughout bloodstained, war-torn ages: she made a decision that appeared at the time to be a good one, that proved to be incorrect only later.

'We wait,' she said.

TWENTY-NINE

Paul Lynch had trouble with body odour; or, rather, Eisenmenger had trouble with Paul Lynch's body odour. This appeared to be more of a problem for him, taking no part in the interview, than it appeared to be for Beverley and her sergeant; perhaps, he mused, they were inured to that kind of odour, just as he was inured (more or less) to the stench of decay. They sat in Lynch's office, which was the top of a double-storey

Portakabin; his secretary – a peculiarly vicious-looking late-middle-aged woman of large shoulder pads and distressingly vivid scarlet nail varnish – occupied a small room beyond and, since the door was open, heard their discussions without let or hindrance. On the ground floor was a general office occupied by two more secretaries and a coffee machine next to a huge notice-board on which assignments and schedules were posted. The structure was so inadequate it was highly likely that they, too, were privy to the details of the conversation. Eisenmenger looked out of the opaque window and saw a wide open space, perhaps a hectare in extent, in which there were half a dozen lorries and vans of varying sizes. As he watched, another came in – a big one with lots of axles – slowing to a halt and emitting a loud shriek, then hiss, as the air brakes discharged.

'I needed that cloth,' said Lynch. He was tall and would once have been muscular and powerful, but the summers had done their damage, the life had been lived and gravity had not been denied; now, he was flabby and portly. He retained his anger and his arrogance, though, Eisenmenger saw; he had achieved something, built up a good business, done it without help and with many obstacles, etcetera, etcetera . . .

Beverley saw it, too, and didn't like it; she had come across too many exemplars of this type to believe that here was anything other than evasion, anxiety and guilt. 'You didn't need the lorry, did you?'

'What else was I supposed to do? Unload it by the road in Newent and transfer it then and there?'

She said nothing for a moment, implying that she didn't find that an unreasonable proposition. From the room behind, there came a soft but clearly angry snort. He continued, 'I asked Joan if it would be all right. She didn't object.' Again, Beverley contented herself with no response at all. Eventually, he asked, 'What the hell's it got to do with you anyway?'

'How many lorries do you own, Mr Lynch?'

'Including the vans, fifteen.'

'All sorts of sizes?'

'Right up to forty-four tonnes.' There was an unmistakeable air of pride as he said this; he was on familiar, well-worn turf in describing his business achievements.

'So why did you need Arthur Meadows' lorry? You don't look too busy to me. The recession must be biting the transport business hard.'

Anger, her old friend, flared. 'We're doing all right.'

'Do you often subcontract?'

He hesitated, perhaps a lie about to be born; if so, it was a stillbirth. 'No.'

'Then why Arthur? Why not one of your own drivers?'

He looked uncomfortable, glanced across at the door to the small office next door, then got up to cross the room and shut the door; as he did so, there was the merest hint of a faint, subvocalized 'hiss'. Back at his desk, he leaned forward and kept his voice low. 'Forgive me, but I think it's best if I don't let my wife hear what I'm about to say.'

They waited. Eisenmenger glanced out of the window and saw three men, two of them hands in jeans pockets and one of them gesticulating, standing in a group; he saw them burst into laughter that he could not hear. Paul Lynch said, 'To be truthful, I didn't want to give him the work.'

To be truthful . . .

Now there was a phrase, reflected Beverley, and one she had heard so many times, from so many liars; she looked across at Lever, and even he seemed unimpressed by this admission. 'No?' she asked reasonably. 'Why not?'

Whatever he was feeling, it overcame him; they had the impression that feelings such as this had often overcome him in the past. With a raised voice, he said, 'You said so your-fucking-self!' He was on his feet and at the window by his desk. 'The recession! I haven't got enough business to keep those poor fuckers on full-time, let alone employ anyone else.'

'Except you did,' she pointed out.

He remembered that he might be overheard – probably was being – and calmed himself down. He came back to the desk and sat down again. 'He was my best friend,' he said after a short pause, as if that explained it all. Eisenmenger could see that to him it did, although he was unable to discern that it excused anything.

'He needed the job,' he said. 'He's been in the shit for a couple of years now, and I've been helping where I can.'

'So it was your idea that he should go to Turkey?'

She was used to liars, less used to those who told the truth, but she thought it was possible that Paul Lynch had just wandered into the latter category as he said, 'He asked me if I had a job I could give him that would take him down that way.'

'And you had one?'

'It so happens I did.'

Lever was unimpressed. 'Oh, come on . . .'

In his youth, Lynch could probably have pasted Lever's offal over the rather flimsy walls that surrounded them, but he refrained on that day, contenting himself with a sour glare at the sergeant and a shrug. 'It's the truth.'

'He asks you if there's anything doing in Turkey, and you rummage in your filing cabinet and, hey presto, you find just the thing?'

'He asked if I had anything that could take him down that way, but he didn't specify Turkey.' Lynch looked directly at Lever, his face set, his voice low and harsh. 'He just said somewhere around the eastern Med.'

'Still fucking convenient, though,' Lever persisted.

'I do a lot of business in that area of the world.' This was directed at Beverley, as if he hoped he might find more empathy in that direction.

'What did you think his motive in asking was?' she asked in a voice that swam in lethal curiosity.

Lynch's expression said it all; it was a hard question to answer truthfully, because to do so would potentially incriminate him. 'I didn't ask.'

'No?' She looked and sounded surprised, astonished even, as if Lynch had just confessed to wearing his wife's underwear.

Although she said no more, he clearly felt obliged to offer an explanation. 'Why should I? Perhaps he liked the climate.' Lever sighed loudly and derisively, while Beverley waited. It wasn't long before Lynch added, 'I don't fucking know, do I? I was doing a favour for a mate . . .' And still she said nothing, contenting herself with looking at him expectantly. He finally succumbed; slamming his palms down on the grey plastic-coated surface of his cheap desk, he leaned forward and hissed, 'I thought he had a bit on the side, if you must know.'

Eisenmenger's mind tiptoed around the phrase 'bit on the side', marvelling at the fecundity of the English language as he listened in on this dialogue. He saw that Lever's face held a look of total disbelief and that Beverley's held one that might have told of her amusement at what had just been said; he had to admit that it wasn't in the front rank of the best of lies. He saw Beverley give the smallest shake of her head, so slight it barely disturbed the bottom of her shoulder-length hair.

She asked, 'Does the name "Mohammed" mean anything to you?'

Lynch's face bore its customary unreadable, if slightly citric, expression. 'Not especially.'

'No? You've never heard anyone by that name who was a good friend of Arthur Meadows?'

'No.' Before she could speak again, Lynch asked, 'What the bloody fuck is all this about anyway? Arthur died of some sort of disease. That's what Joan told Angelica.'

Eisenmenger immediately felt a change in the atmosphere, although he could not at first say what had happened; then Beverley, ignoring Lynch's question, asked in a soft, sweet and almost breathy voice, much as she might use in bed to her lover in the dark night, 'Are you absolutely sure you don't know anyone named Mohammed? It's a very common name, yet you're certain Arthur Meadows didn't have any connection with anyone called that? Think again.' He realized what had happened. Lynch had lied – almost certainly not for the first time – but had failed to disguise it; and it was yet more than that, for it seemed to Eisenmenger that Lynch was worried by the lie, that he could foresee that he was potentially making a huge and costly mistake. Beverley had identified this, was working on it.

Lynch's mouth opened before his brain had found the right gear, and for a second no sound either insensate or coherent came forth. Then it closed, his eyes looked from Beverley to the leather of her boots and then back to her face, and at last he said, 'Arthur had got chummy with someone he called "Hammy", but his real name was Mohammed.'

'Mohammed what?'

'Harawi.'

'Why did you lie?'

Lynch's shrug said that it was a stupid question, that lying to the police was what one did, but Beverley wasn't interested. She had her prey and she was not about to let it loose again. 'Is there something I should know about this man Harawi?'

Lynch was torn by two completely opposed and completely unconquerable forces; had he been tied to a rack, and had Beverley been tightening the ropes, he could not have looked more agonized. 'There were rumours . . .' he admitted at last.

'About what?'

Another bout of what looked to Eisenmenger to be the very epitome of soul searching followed before Lynch said, 'That he had some nasty friends . . . nasty, *foreign* friends.'

Eisenmenger saw Lever look up from his notebook at that; he saw Beverley's face remain stubbornly neutral. She asked patiently, 'Would you care to elaborate?'

It seemed that, having started, Lynch now found it easier to talk, for he answered quite easily now. 'Arms smuggling was one rumour.'

'Any others?'

'I heard that some of his friends were "security advisors".'

'Mercenaries?'

'That was what I was given to understand.'

'Who told you this?'

Lynch thought about not telling her, perhaps because giving out names to the police was against his personal credo, but he was wily enough to know that he had gone too far to be afflicted by terminal coyness. 'Arthur was here with Harawi a few months ago. I was just closing a deal with someone who recognized him.'

'Who was that "someone", Mr Lynch?'

'It doesn't matter.'

She smiled just a little. 'Yes,' she assured him quietly, 'it does.'

The answer did not come easily, but it came. 'Chap named Beg. Ulugh Beg. He runs a clothing factory in Leicester. He said Harawi used to work for him.'

If he thought that he might now be given respite, he soon discovered that hope was not a reliable advisor. Beverley merely changed tack, asking, 'Why were you so keen to get your hands on the lorry?'

'I wasn't. It was the cloth I wanted. I've got a contract to fulfil; that cloth was due in London yesterday.'

'Why didn't you take another lorry and transfer the load in Newent?' asked Lever.

Lynch was devastating in his contempt, as was shown by his language. 'Don't be so fucking stupid, sonny. Why waste the diesel? Anyway, Joan wanted the rig put somewhere safer than a muddy field in Newent.'

In Eisenmenger's opinion, it was a good point, well made. Lever seemed to think so, too, because he didn't respond. Beverley enquired, 'Where is it now?'

'The lorry's here.'

'And its contents?'

'That left the yard first thing this morning.'

'Where's it going?'

He had on the corner of his desk a personal computer; it was clearly an old and venerable thing, almost stately in its bearing, although somewhat battered and cosmetically challenged. It became obvious fairly quickly that its performance was on the ebb to the same extent as its appearance. The seconds stretched languidly as Lynch attempted to prod it into action, his fingers stabbing on to keys as if the poor old thing had done particularly spiteful and unforgiveable things to him. It certainly seemed to be getting its own back, though, for its recalcitrance was soon obvious to all. Lynch breathed ominously through his nose as he did hand-to-hand combat with his machinery. He said at last, 'A warehouse in Woolwich. It got there' – a look at his watch – 'two hours and thirteen minutes ago.'

'The address, please.'

He took a deep breath, as if slightly perturbed to be asked so quickly to go into battle yet again. More abuse of the keyboard and then he paused and looked at a laser printer that was on a low table by the desk; it seemed equally tired and emotional, as if slightly abused and bemused by the world in which it found itself. For a moment, Eisenmenger had the feeling that it had perhaps misheard or misunderstood what had been asked of it, but then it staggered into life and wheezily extruded a piece of paper, one that was snatched untimely from its mechanical womb and thrust towards Beverley. This she took from him and, without looking at it, passed it to Lever. 'Contact the Met. Tell them to get off their arses and impound the cloth as soon as possible. They need to make sure that it's what it says on the tin.'

Lever gave her a look. Eisenmenger thought that the hesitation to do as he was told was due to Lever's laziness, but that look suggested otherwise; it was a dark look, one that was not friendly, that whispered that the relationship was built on treacherous foundations. He did as he was told, though.

As Lever left the room to descend the outside steps that led to the tarmac of the yard, Lynch asked, 'Was Arthur into something criminal?'

Beverley's look – one of tired incredulity that such a naive question should have sullied the foetid air in that office – told Lynch that he had made a tactical mistake. Eisenmenger could see him wonder what to say, what not to say, what to give away and what to hide. He added quickly but warily, 'Smuggling, I suppose?'

She wasn't about to make it easy.

'Let's go and look at the lorry,' she said as she stood up.

THIRTY

'There's no need for you to stay here. I can cope if something happens.'

'I know you can, Marty,' she said. 'I've nothing else to do. Anyway, we both need to be here to act at once if the opportunity arises.'

'To do what?'

In truth, she did not really fully know; the words as she spoke them were nearly as new to her as they were to him. 'We look for a chance to complete the task we came for, hopefully in daylight. If they should leave the place unoccupied, then we go in and search properly.'

'What about the dog? Did I do wrong?'

Yes, the dog. That particular unknown worried her. It wouldn't bring the police in, but they might search for it, and in doing so they might stumble upon the precious cargo . . . Still, that couldn't be helped. The worst of all worlds would be to be caught. Almost involuntarily, she glanced across at Marty as she thought this. Prison would destroy whatever was left of her son, as small and pathetic as that was. The bond between them had become strong, but it had been proved into something near adamantine as she had picked him up after that awful time he had experienced on that final assignment, after the army had repaired his body whilst systematically destroying his mind in their search for 'humint' that might help them in their never-ending, ultimately Pyrrhic war with terrorists. Yet she knew that the stronger a bond, the more catastrophic the effects when it broke.

'No, of course not.'

He relaxed, pleased at her assurance. 'What if they find our stuff before we do?'

With confidence spun from the air for the sake of his peace of mind, she replied, 'They won't.'

THIRTY-ONE

Harrison was told to gather as much information on Arthur Meadows, Paul Lynch, Mohammed Harawi and Ulugh Beg as was officially available, to do the same for Paul Lynch's and Ulugh Beg's businesses, especially to check with the UK Borders Agency about any intelligence they might have about any of them, and to find the official records of Arthur Meadows' recent trips abroad. So far, the only vaguely interesting fact that she had unearthed was Arthur Meadows' twenty-five-year-old conviction for receiving stolen goods; he had served two years. It was tedious work with long waits on the phone whilst she doodled on a pad and thought of Lever. She did so idly but with a sense of vague sexual excitement. They had so far been out for a drink on two occasions; on the second, they had both got drunk and he had given her a kiss as they had parted. It hadn't been a peck on the cheek, either; it had been one of those kisses where his tongue had gone into her mouth like a javelin point, before relaxing and curling around behind her teeth, caressing them and . . .

'We've got no alerts on either Arthur Meadows, Paul Lynch or Ulugh Beg, or any of their registered employees.'

'Nothing?' she asked, disappointed. She had hoped to be the one to break the case, even if it were done whilst performing an assigned task.

'Sorry, love.' The voice was female, middle-aged with a Black Country twang, and it sounded to her as if it had guessed what she had been hoping for. 'They're either clean or clever.'

'OK,' she said with an inaudible sigh.

'Harawi's slightly more interesting, though.'

She brightened. 'How's that?'

'He's popped up on the UKBA radar on a couple of occasions, although there's never been anything concrete.'

'What's he been up to?' she asked excitedly.

'Not a lot for a year or two. In fact, he's dropped off the map; disappeared from his usual haunts in Leicester about twelve months ago.'

'Hasn't anyone followed it up?' she enquired, unable to conceal a trace of incredulity.

'Have a heart, Constable. He's not on the FBI's top ten most wanted, you know. Some of his patterns of behaviour have just raised a few red flags. We get false alarms like this all the time.'

'What patterns of behaviour?' she asked impatiently.

'Regular trips to Pakistan, for one thing.'

'Maybe he's got family there.'

'He has. Doesn't mean he's not doing something naughty, though, does it?'

'Where in Pakistan?' she asked, as if she were mentally consulting a small-scale map of the country.

'He flies to Karachi, but then travels on to the town of Quetta.'

'Can you spell that?'

Her informant did so, adding, without sounding at all patronizing, 'It's in the north-west, close to the western end of the Afghanistan border.'

There was a pause before Harrison asked, 'Anything else on him?' She was in truth not a little disappointed at what she had so far been told. It hardly seemed damning.

'The only other thing we've got is a flag from the SIS about fifteen months ago. We were to keep special tabs on him, but he hasn't been heard of since.'

Harrison thought that she had misheard. 'SIS?'

'Yeah.' The voice was matter-of-fact. 'You'll have to ask them why, though. They don't tell us shit.'

'Look, I've been told by my DCI to get that shipment impounded.' Lever knew that he was prone to get excitable and aggressive when he met an obstacle, more especially when he was on the phone, and most especially when he was talking to a prick with a tendency to overuse sarcasm; especially when talking to a *London* prick with such a tendency. 'So, would you please do as we ask?'

The London prick in question was a uniformed inspector; he had tried and failed many years before to get into the investigative branch, and time had failed to heal the wound, many hours of sleep had been unable to knit the ravelled knot of care. He carried on a constant guerrilla campaign against CID whenever he got the chance and, over those years, he had got many such chances; this, for him, was just a minor skirmish, but one in which all the advantages were on his side. A yokel plain-clothes sergeant demanding instant action from him, without proper authorization, without even a pretence at any kind of civility or respect for rank; oh yes, it was as if someone had handed him a bazooka with which to play conkers.

He started explaining to DS Lever why it wasn't going to be quite as easy as he seemed to think. He started slowly and calmly but, as the syllables turned into words, the words into sentences, and those last into paragraphs, he became a tad less tranquil and polite, slightly more – how could he describe it? – incendiary.

To Eisenmenger, the lorry looked exactly as it had the last time he had been introduced to it. Impressive and incomprehensible, an artefact of a universe that impinged only tangentially and lightly on his own; he had known such things existed and that they were socially useful, but they were firmly outwith the set of things about which he understood anything at all. Beverley, however, seemed completely au fait with such mechanical beasts, or at least, he postulated, she was completely au fait with looking

and behaving as if she knew what she was doing and talking
about, no matter what her true feelings. Whilst Lynch stood by
Eisenmenger, she looked first around the entire lorry, then climbed
nimbly and, to all intents and purposes, with practised ease up
into the cab; they watched her looking around it, checking in
various nooks and crannies, paying particular attention to the bed
space behind the seats. With gloved hands, she felt under the
dashboard and around the huge steering wheel. She checked
under both seats, made a note of the dashboard-mounted tacho-
graph readings, and then climbed down. Without explaining what,
if anything, she had discovered, she said to Lynch, 'Let's look
in the rear.'

The lorry was fitted with a rear elevator that Lynch operated,
allowing Beverley to climb on and ascend to the level of the
cargo space. As it rose into the air, she stood with her legs slightly
apart, staring straight ahead into the depths of the lorry; she was
wearing tight jeans and her habitual black leather blouson;
Eisenmenger became aware that Lynch was staring at her and
wondered what Mrs Lynch would make of this intensive scrutiny.
The good lady wife of this rather seedy haulier had not been
amused when he had popped his head around her door to tell
her that he was taking his guests down to the yard. Eisenmenger
had tried to speculate what, precisely, would amuse one such as
she; his imagination totally failed him.

Mind you, a part of his mind mused, he couldn't blame Lynch
for letching . . .

Beverley moved into the darkness of the lorry, her boots
echoing on the floor; a torch splashed its light around for a while
before she came back. He asked, 'Anything?'

'Nothing.'

Whilst she descended to the ground again, he wandered back
around the side of the lorry to the cab, trying not to see the things
that he couldn't fully comprehend but those that he could, those
that perhaps answered questions which he could not escape, that
taunted him, as such things were wont to do. This thing was, in
effect, exactly the same as a horse and cart; the driver sat above
the motive force and in front of the load; that there were several
hundred horses and several tonnes of load was actually irrelevant.
The reins had been transmuted into a large wheel of

plastic-covered metal, the whip replaced by a foot pedal, and the suspension was probably a bloody sight better, but these were peripherals to the essence of the affair; it was about a man sitting atop and commanding the things around him, and thereby achieving feats that were otherwise beyond the weak thing that is the human being . . .

He paused in his musings, backtracking, trying to follow lines of thought that were, by their very nature, ephemeral and unrepeatable. As Beverley and Lynch came from the back of the lorry, he went up to the cab and did something he never thought he would do: he climbed into it. It was, he had to profess to himself as he sat behind the steering wheel, a wonderful place to be; the height gave him a view of the immediate world that, if not exactly breathtaking, was certainly arresting. He could imagine himself enjoying being such a thing as an HGV driver; it would be easy to fall prey to a sense of imperviousness to many of the travails of the world when inside that cab, what with that view and that amount of power and mass at his disposal . . .

'Found something?' called up Beverley.

He asked of Lynch, who was standing beside her, 'Is the driver's seat electrically heated?'

'Yes.'

'How's it operated?'

Clearly puzzled by this line of questioning, Lynch hauled his not inconsiderable bulk up into the doorway and pointed out a switch on the dashboard near the centre console. 'What do you want to know for?'

His proximity, which in turn meant the proximity of his accompanying body odour, was distinctly distressing to Eisenmenger. 'Just an experiment,' he said unhelpfully. 'Would you excuse me?'

Lynch descended and Eisenmenger pointedly shut the door and switched the heater on, then waited. The seat warmed quickly, a discovery which at first pleased him – perhaps here was the answer to his conundrum; but then it remained stubbornly constant – pleasant and undoubtedly doing its job, yet not overdoing it. After ten minutes, with Lynch clearly thinking that Beverley had brought along a window-licker for some work experience, and Beverley herself appearing not surprisingly lost by what he was doing, he switched off the heater, opened the cab door and extracted himself. 'What was that all about? You're surely not cold, are you?' she asked.

'I thought I might have found the answer to one of the PM findings, that's all,' he replied, but his eyes were on the cab, looking at lines and angles.

Lynch was impatient. 'Look, if you've finished . . .'

Beverley rounded on him. 'We haven't even started yet, Mr Lynch. Just because there's nothing superficially wrong with that lorry, doesn't mean a flying fuck. I'm impounding it and we're going to take it to bits.'

Lynch stared at her, his demeanour immediately defensive and guarded. 'Do what you fucking well like. It's not my property, as you've pointed out.'

'Which makes your eagerness to get your hands on it and get rid of its cargo all the more interesting.'

'I told you the reason for that.'

'Which I'll believe when I've made a few checks.'

He tried indignation, but failed; he knew that she knew that he was in a business that had a notoriously seamy side.

Eisenmenger wasn't listening . . . *Fucking funny place to get sunburn* . . . The phrase had not really left his mind since he had first heard it. It was why he had wondered if the electric heating of the seat had malfunctioned, although whilst sitting in that cab he had quickly come to the conclusion that it was a fanciful notion. That phrase, though, recurred again and again . . . The skin had indeed looked burned as if by radiant heat, but the notion that Arthur Meadows had bared his backside in the Mediterranean sun was patently absurd, and would have been even if he hadn't apparently then driven home all the way to England to present himself to hospital; anyway, there were his other symptoms, not to mention the state of his intestines.

A connection flicked through his mind, laughed teasingly and was gone before he hardly had a chance to appreciate its existence; he knew it was a connection because of experience, because such phantoms regularly sought to agonize him, but that was all he knew.

He looked again at the truck, letting his eyes wander over it, trying to see beneath the chrome and the things he did not understand. For a time that he did not appreciate, he was absorbed in his contemplation, oblivious of Lynch's impatience, unaware of Beverley's fascination with his way of operating that was so at odds with normal modern methods of detection. Then he asked, 'Those are the fuel tanks, right?'

Both Eisenmenger and Beverley looked at Lynch for an answer. 'Yes,' he admitted cautiously, as if scenting traps.

'Carol Meadows said that he'd had extra fuel tanks fitted a while ago.'

Lynch became even more cautious. There was a pause before he said, 'So he told me.'

'She couldn't understand why.'

The pause this time was even longer. 'I don't know. To give him extra range, I suppose.'

Beverley walked purposefully to the lorry and began to examine it closely. Eisenmenger noted that Lynch became slightly agitated. She looked carefully around it, squatting down and feeling with her hand, even, at one point, getting down on her hands and knees to look up at the underside; she felt around the huge wheel arches on either side, and knocked at various points on the hide of the beast. Eventually, she came back to Eisenmenger. 'If you're right, it's been done well.'

'It would have to be, I suppose, given the sophistication of border agencies these days,' he said ruminatively.

'All that means is that the smugglers are getting more sophisticated,' she pointed out.

'Your cynicism is showing,' he murmured.

She went back to the lorry, this time climbing into the cab; perhaps, she reasoned, there was some sort of release mechanism controlled from the driving position. The dash was an impressive array of switches, buttons, LEDs and backlit dials, but, as far as she could tell, they were all legitimate. She felt under the dash, around the steering column, in the door pockets, under the seats and under the mattress in the bunk behind. She met with no success.

Climbing down again, she was almost ready to admit that she had been defeated. She knew that she couldn't spend too much time searching the lorry, yet she was loathe to abandon the hunt; she could get the lorry impounded, it was true, but what happened thereafter would be out of her hands because she knew that others

– her superiors, for a start – might see it as a distraction from the main investigation of the slaughter of the Maliks and the subsequent murder of Harry Weston; although she only had Joan Meadows' word that her husband was home at the time the Maliks were killed, she was as sure as shit that Arthur Meadows hadn't sliced and diced Weston, since he had predeceased him. Gloucestershire Constabulary's resources were in a parlous state, and she feared that, unless she could bring forth more evidence than she had, her request to have the lorry forensically examined would be turned down.

At which point, she caught sight of Lynch's expression; it might have been triumphant, it might have been relieved, but either way it was significant. At once, she turned again to the lorry and, almost without cogitation, she climbed back up again, this time stopping halfway, so that her head was only just above the floor of the cab and she could look directly first under the dash and then under the driver's seat. Perhaps it was her imagination, but she thought she detected an increase in tension behind her, yet still she could see little that brought her satisfaction. She could see no hidden buttons, no odd wires leading down into the floor . . .

The only thing was that one of the nuts on the chassis of the seat was surrounded by circular scores in the black paint, as if it had been turned; none of the others had such marks around them, though . . . She reached out and put the tips of her fingers on it, expecting it to be too tight to turn, but she was wrong; it twisted with only a small amount of resistance, and from somewhere around the level of her hips, there came a soft 'click', and then a hiss, as of escaping gas. Not long after that, there was an intolerable stench of decay.

THIRTY-TWO

'Now's our chance,' she said.

The two men had been gone for half an hour. The woman had spent the intervening time searching the farmyard, calling out a name that Jacqueline thought might have been

'Duke', although she couldn't be sure; clearly, though, it was the dog she was searching for. The woman didn't seem to be too bothered when it didn't come bounding up to her, which was a relief; probably she was used to the thing disappearing for long periods. She had gone back into the house, then re-emerged ten minutes later, got into an old Volvo estate and, after several minutes of trying to get it started, driven off. They both stood and made their way back down to the farmyard; Marty didn't say anything because, she knew, he didn't think he needed to.

As soon as they reached the farmyard, the line of authority between them switched soundlessly and completely; he first assessed the situation, for a moment just standing there while looking and listening; when she started to speak, he held up his hand immediately to silence her, and she obeyed this soldier who had once been her only son, who would never again be such. Then he said in a low voice, as if he feared that the shadows in the buildings around them hid enemies that wanted to know their secrets, 'You do the pigsties again, make sure we didn't miss anything last night. I'll do that barn; you join me when you're sure you've missed nothing.'

So she did as she was ordered, happy to help him, suppressing her distress that she should have been forced to do this thing, that she had been so cruelly robbed of a child, that he had had his humanity ripped from him. There was nothing to find in the sties, but there was so much rubbish in there that it took her ten minutes to kick it aside, or turn it over. She coughed more than once because of the dust that billowed in the dank air around her.

When she joined Marty in the barn, he said, 'I heard you coughing.' His voice was flat, without accusation, but she still knew that he was reprimanding her.

'Sorry.'

It was a big barn, with walls and roof made of corrugated iron supported by a metal skeleton painted dark red. It had room for a large trailer, a bright green and yellow tractor and several pieces of incomprehensible farm equipment that were rusting badly. Even with these, there was a large number of straw bales piled up the back. While she hunted around the corners, under piles of paper sacks, reels of plastic binding wire and what she could only describe as rubbish, Marty climbed the straw bales, looking for signs that they were close to their quarry.

'I've got something,' he called suddenly. His voice was low, but it carried through the dust of the shed. She had been slowly dragging crates of ancient, rusting metal shelving brackets away from the corrugated iron wall of the barn; at his words, she came hurrying over. He was about halfway up the pile of bales, perhaps two metres off the ground. She began to climb, and the smell of organic dusty sweetness – pervasive in the barn from the moment they entered it – became overwhelming. At her age, it wasn't easy to climb, but Marty came down and helped her to the spot where he had stopped, to the spot where the straw was stained in a dark-brown crusted blood. He was staring at her intently as she bent down to study it closely, careful not to touch it. When she straightened, she nodded to him.

'Can I help you?'

The woman they had been observing for so many hours was now standing in the entrance to the barn. She was scrutinizing them with her hands balled and resting on her hips, her jean-clad legs wide and solidly planted; it was difficult to make out the details of her face because the light was at her back, but she seemed to be confident, certainly not in any way scared. Jacqueline knew instinctively that the responsibility for action had flipped again to her, that Marty would do what she required and only what she required. She said, 'I'm sorry. You must wonder what we're doing.'

'It looks to me like you're trespassing,' said the woman, a broad, slow, Gloucestershire drawl giving the impression of extreme insouciance. 'Maybe even looking to thieve from me.'

'No, no. Not at all. We're looking for something . . . Let me explain.'

With Marty's help, she climbed down the straw bales and then approached the woman, Marty just slightly behind her. She held out her hand, 'My name's Jackie. This is my son, Marty.'

The woman didn't take the hand, didn't even look at it. She asked, 'What did you think to find in my barn, in the middle of my straw?' she asked. She was perhaps fifty-five or sixty, had weathered features and faded grey eyes that were watering slightly, as if she were forever saddened by something, perhaps something in her past. Jackie knew that look, because she saw it in every mirror she glanced at.

It was a good question, but Jackie had an answer. 'Your dog.'

That made the woman change her attitude. Clearly surprised, she said, 'Duke? What do you know about Duke?'

'He's missing, isn't he?'

The woman, already suspicious, grew even more cautious. Her eyes flicked to Marty who was standing exactly behind his mother. 'What have you done?' she asked.

Jackie knew, as if this were a rehearsed manoeuvre, perhaps a piece of choreography, what was going to happen as she stood to one side and that cruel knife, with its curved gutters to let the blood run and its so-soft handle, was in Marty's hand. She turned away before she saw it go into the woman's belly, but she could not escape the sound of the shocked, agonized scream, as short as it was. She told herself that she was sorry to have done it – for she knew that Marty might have delivered the thrust, but it was she who had brought about the death – and she did feel some remorse, but it was at once subsumed and then consumed by the single overweening urge that had filled her life for the past two years, the urge of vengeance.

It was, she had come to appreciate, a good feeling, one that would sustain her until the day she died.

THIRTY-THREE

'I am arresting you on suspicion of conspiracy to facilitate the entry of illegal aliens into the United Kingdom, in contravention of the Immigration and Asylum Act of 1999. You do not have to say anything but it may harm your defence if you do not mention when questioned something you later rely on in court. Anything you say may be given in evidence.' Lever had sounded bored as he had read through the litany, much as an ageing priest might when invoking call and response in the ten-thousandth ceremony over which he has presided, the ten-thousandth time that God has remained stubbornly unresponsive, as perhaps befits an omnipotent, omniscient but ultimately mysterious Being.

Lynch, though, made a contrasting study for the psychologist, whether professional or amateur; he was exercised and, watching him from afar, Eisenmenger had the feeling that he was used to such a state; it did not, Eisenmenger suspected, help the man's nerves that the goodly Mrs Lynch had somehow, possibly magically, arrived on the scene and was adding her not inconsiderable twopenn'orth to the proceedings. It was clear that she had reserves of ire and venom that even her appearance, formidable as it was, underestimated; she was not happy that her husband should be so treated, and she made damned sure that Sergeant Lever knew it. It was clear to Eisenmenger, too, that Beverley did not give a proverbial toss that her junior was getting it in the similarly proverbial neck. It made him once more wonder about the nature of that relationship.

To be fair to her, he could see that she was having problems fitting the pieces of the problem together in a way that was even remotely logical; as he saw this, a pang of something – perhaps guilt, perhaps commiseration, more probably a delicate, crystalline compound of the two – passed through him, for he very much feared that he was only going to make matters worse. They were waiting for a forensics team to turn up; there were already six uniformed officers there, who were taking the details of everyone who worked for Lynch, in preparation for interviewing them. The near intolerable reek of faeces and old blood hung around the scene, colouring it for all.

The 'fuel tanks' had not given up their secrets easily. It had required some minutes of careful examination of the spaces around them – all passing in an indescribable miasma – to discover on each side a small lever deep in the mechanical beast's recesses – before they opened fully.

Eisenmenger could see that the open 'fuel tanks' would once have been quite comfortable for those not prone to claustrophobia. Padded, with an oxygen supply, he supposed that, of all the many ways people had tried to cross national borders illegally, this was conceivably one of the more tolerable. That the inhabitants of the tanks on Arthur Meadows' last trip had clearly been extremely ill, with what appeared to be foul, bloody diarrhoea and vomiting, was unfortunate and might, he surmised, put others off travelling in such a style.

'Amaze me,' suggested Beverley, interrupting his reverie.

He thought that perhaps he heard an acerbic edge to this imperative. It perhaps said much about the type of mind that was housed in Eisenmenger's cranium that he conjectured, with a spark that was intense, albeit brief, that she was demanding some sort of conjuring trick. Perhaps for the best, he said only, 'How do you mean?'

'I know you, John. You know something that I don't.'

He did – that he could not deny – but he didn't yet have the ability to incorporate it into anything that made sense to him; what he knew was crazy, and it was so crazy that his brain had yet to integrate it into anything resembling a story that was not incredible. He might have a different perspective to Beverley, but it was as fractured as hers. He said carefully, 'Perhaps you should tell me what you know, and I'll be able to help you with some of the gaps.'

She ought to have been used to Eisenmenger's caution, but it still aggravated her. It was, accordingly, only after a sustained effort to suppress her irritation that she started. 'Rashid Malik negotiated with Arthur Meadows to bring in some illegal immigrants; presumably two in number. Meadows had been doing this for some time; we're still running checks on Meadows' phone and email contacts, but there's one name that keeps cropping up as the middle man in these negotiations – a man by the name of Mohammed Harawi. It's a common name, which is making the job hard, but we hope to have pinned him down in a short while. Interestingly, Malik was also in contact, through the same man, with an online presence that we know only by an email address – Jacqueline21209@AOL.com. She – presuming it was a "she" – initiated this particular shipment. She specified a contact in Turkey and an approximate time window in which they were to be picked up.'

She stopped. 'Anything you want to add at this point?'

He smiled and shook his head. 'Not yet, but it's most interesting.'

Mrs Lynch's protestations rose in volume and ferocity, and he could see that Lever was losing the battle and beginning to abandon his temper; Beverley called a statuesque female uniform over and suggested that she might like to take Mrs Lynch away for a cup of tea. 'Point out to her that she's fucking close to being arrested for obstructing us in the course of our investigation.' The officer complied, although her expression suggested that, had it been her choice, discretion would most definitely have been the best part of valour. Beverley and Eisenmenger moved away from what otherwise might have been an entertaining fracas.

'So Meadows arranged with Lynch to undertake a job that would take him close to Turkey,' she resumed.

'Do you think Lynch knew what was going on?'

She laughed scornfully. 'People like Lynch always know what's going on; it's just that they're cunning enough to make sure that it's fucking difficult to prove. As things look at the moment, I'd say that he knew what Meadows was doing and wasn't about to impede him, but I doubt that money ever actually changed hands. It was an "old pals" thing; muckers sticking together and all that kind of crap. It doesn't matter, though; the way the law stands at the moment, he'll be dragged in and dragged down; Mrs Lynch knows it too, which is why she's wailing like a berserking banshee.'

'And you've no idea who this "Jacqueline21209@AOL.com" is?'

'Not at the moment. If they're clever, it can be fucking difficult to trace online identities; if they've used totally false details to register the address, and if they only use internet cafes, or stolen laptops, you haven't got a hope in hell of finding out who they are unless they accidentally include personal information or other identifiers in the emails.'

'But presumably that person is the one you think is the killer?' he suggested.

'It makes sense. They arrange for Malik to bring over the illegals, using Arthur Meadows' specially modified lorry. Malik picks them up from Meadows – I'd lay down a lot of hard-earned money that it was done here, considering that Andoversford is nicely situated on the eastern side of the county and this would be wonderfully private in the dead of night – then takes them back to his place in Gloucestershire. Things only go a bit shit-shaped for him when "Jacqueline" turns up and proves to be very handy with a carving knife.'

'What about Harry Weston?'

'I haven't the faintest fucking idea.' She stopped. 'No, that's not entirely true. It's clearly the same killer. I don't know precisely why he was killed, but my guess would be that it might be telling us something about the base of the killer. Nothing's been uncovered to suggest that Weston knew the Maliks or Meadows, either socially or through any other kind of contact. If he was killed, it probably wasn't part of the original plan; he presumably saw something or knew something. The import of this is in where it happened; it narrows the geographical area.'

Murders have their uses, even to the righteous. He suggested, 'The two immigrants seem to be somehow central to all this.'

'They're valuable.'

'Maybe,' he said distractedly.

She looked at him, catching something in his tone. 'Isn't it about time you told me what you know about this, John?' she asked.

But then she was hailed by Lever, who had extracted himself from the altercation with the Lynches and had just put Paul into the back of a police car, while his female colleague had taken Mrs Lynch back to the office on the pretext of taking a statement; he sounded excited. They hurried over to him. 'There's been another killing.'

THIRTY-FOUR

'Who's doing this?' Beverley asked everyone and no one, both of whom failed to give an answer. She was sitting in the front passenger seat of the car, with Lever and Eisenmenger in the back, a uniformed constable driving. 'Some sort of deranged serial killer?' she prompted.

Eisenmenger had his head back against the rest, eyes closed, thinking. 'It started out as very well planned,' he said thoughtfully.

'It doesn't look fucking well planned to me,' opined Lever in characteristically blunt fashion. 'It looks like the work of a loony-tunes.'

Eisenmenger persisted. 'It begins as a well-executed operation. You might almost say that it's designed and carried out with something like military precision . . .' Beverley glanced around at him sharply, but he didn't see her. He continued, 'It only goes wrong with the murder of Harry Weston; I would suggest that this killing is a ripple effect from the Weston killing.'

'But what's it all for?' she implored him. If he knew, though, he wasn't ready to confide.

The farm was quite close to Upton St Leonard, a sprawling village to the south of Gloucester. It was set well back from the road, reached by an unmade track and overlooked by a wooded hill. A square, typical West Country farmhouse stood with a small garden at the front, the farmyard at the rear; there was a row of low pigsties opposite the back of the house, a large barn at the far end. In the doorway of the barn was a body, around which a temporary plastic fence had been erected. The drive ended at the side of the house; as they got out of the car, they could see also an elderly man in dirty jeans and dark green shirt sitting on a chair just by the back door of the farmhouse, clearly in some distress; sitting with him was a policewoman. They walked to the open barn, in front of which they were met by Sergeant Henry, a man who struck Eisenmenger as being impossibly young for a member of the police force, let alone a sergeant therein. Just inside the building behind him, the collapsed body of a woman lay in the dust; her clothing was bloodstained and, spreading into the shadow at her head, there was in that same dust a drying spray of blood.

Sergeant Henry was, at least, to the point. 'Her name's Amelia Stark. She's the owner of this place; widowed four years ago and not really coping, but struggling on.'

The information came forth like the lukewarm drops of a poorly functioning shower; they were annoying rather than useful. Their only use was to make Sergeant Henry feel better about himself, a tiny flywheel in the huge machine that was his exist-ence. Eisenmenger even fancied that he saw a smile being suppressed on those downy cheeks as they went past this custodian of the law to survey the deceased. The body was that of a short, stocky woman of late middle age. It was immediately obvious that she had been killed in the now familiar way: stabbed and her throat slit. Eisenmenger stepped over the fence and squatted by her side. He carefully reached out and lightly touched her throat with the back of his hand. As he stood up, he said, 'She's still quite warm. I'd say she's been dead less than two hours, maybe less than one.'

Beverley said to Lever, 'Get more men here. I want an immediate search of the area for a radius of one mile.'

Lever said, 'We haven't got the manpower. There are six officers still at Lynch's yard, don't forget.'

'Pull them. Get them over here. And see if you can rustle some more up from Cirencester.'

'That'll need authorization.'

'I'm fucking giving you authorization, Sergeant.' Overhearing this, Sergeant Henry's face suggested that he wasn't used to hearing such language emanating from the lips of female detective chief inspectors, and thereby showed his innocence.

There was a moment when Eisenmenger saw a dilemma; perhaps Lever was going to argue, perhaps not. The question was never going to be answered because there came a shout from the back of the barn. A couple of enterprising constables had begun a search of the building, and one of them had climbed up the straw bales; it was he who had shouted. He was standing near the top and pointing. 'I've got two more bodies here.'

Before anyone could say or do anything, Eisenmenger stepped forward and said urgently, 'For God's sake, don't go anywhere near them.'

THIRTY-FIVE

Jackie could not describe her emotions, for they were legion and they were contrasting and they were swirling, whirling in her head as she and Marty had hurried back through the wood. Relief that they had at last retrieved their goods, that the plan was back on track; joy that she was going to have her revenge on those who had done so much to rob her; the continuing, slow-burning yet agonizingly hot anger that she had been forced to do this; the huge sorrow, so deep and wide that it was without bound, that she was shortly going to die; the amelioration that Marty's pain would end at the same time.

She was at last truly on the road to some sort of fulfilment; already, she knew, their deaths were coming to meet them, hurrying ever faster with every further moment that she and Marty carried the small yet surprisingly heavy metal cylinders that he had retrieved from the bodies hidden among the straw bales, while she kept watch. They had only just escaped the farm to take refuge in the wood when the two men they had seen earlier came back to the farm. She felt her heart not just pulsing in her chest, but ever-expanding and growing, as if all her blood were being forced into it; she was light-headed and dizzy, although whether that was a result of running so hard, or elation, or both, she could not say. Marty was younger and far fitter than she was and had pulled well ahead of her; fear drove her on but could only do so for so long. When anxiety that she had not run far enough was overcome by exhaustion, she dropped to the floor of the woodland, almost falling into a bed of nettles. She tried to call out to her son, but he was too far ahead and she was too breathless. Consciousness left her . . .

Her father stood just behind her, as he had so often in her memory. She was doing her homework – resolving quadratic equations, she remembered – and he was looking at what she had done, pointing out where she had gone wrong. It was a wonderful paternal thing to do . . .

Except for his hand that nestled between her thighs . . .

THIRTY-SIX

The woman at America Online had proved surprisingly cooperative with Constable Harrison's request when it had been explained to her that it was part of a double murder investigation. True, she had had to hold the line for nearly twenty-five minutes, but in that time the request had passed rapidly up line management until it reached someone who felt themselves to be of sufficient seniority to weigh the demands of the Data Protection Act and those of giving assistance to the police in investigating one of the most serious of crimes, and to decide which was the lesser of the two misdemeanours.

Jacqueline21209@AOL.com, it transpired, was registered to Jacqueline Hoyle. Harrison asked for all the data they had to be emailed to her; she also asked for all the email traffic in and out of the account to be sent to her, but was told that such data were not immediately available and that it would take probably forty-eight hours to get it. Very well, then, she said, could they please send it as soon as possible.

The email giving the account details arrived ten minutes later. She checked the address, which didn't exist. The mobile phone number was registered to someone delighting in the name of Melvyn Bell; when she rang it, a man who sounded elderly and possibly slightly confused, answered. When she asked to speak to Mr Bell, he told her that she was already speaking to him; when she asked to speak to Jacqueline Hoyle, he said that he didn't know anyone by that name. He was starting to sound peevish, so she apologized and rang off before he could go any further.

She wondered then what to do. She could, she knew, merely pass this information on to her superiors and she would escape criticism, because she was only a relatively inexperienced constable, and nobody expected anything more of her. She, however, felt capable of more; she had ambitions, did Constable Harrison, and she intended to end her professional career looking down from a far greater height than was possible in her present lowly position on the greasy pole of UK policing.

'Turn right up here,' she said calmly.

Marty looked across at her. 'What?'

'Turn right at the next junction . . . there.'

She knew enough to speak calmly yet commandingly; the look on his face was one of incomprehension, but he did as he was told; Marty was now nothing if not the good soldier. Their diversion took them down a route towards Gloucester. 'Why are we going this way?' he asked.

'We have a drop-off to make.'

'What?'

She hadn't let Marty know all the details of the negotiations and planning that she and Hammy had gone through: how their part in the plan was to kill the Maliks, take the girls, extract the material and then pass it on to Hammy for his own ends; she did not know what those ends were – it was important that she should not, she appreciated – but she could guess. She said now only, 'I have to fulfil a promise to Hammy.'

'What promise?'

But she could not face explaining the reasons and deceits, the plans and hopes, the plots, subplots, texts and subtexts. 'I'll explain later.'

The object of their labours over the past few days was in the glove compartment and she now got them out. They were cylinders about ten centimetres long and two in diameter; they had originally been gunmetal grey in colour but were now covered in streaks of coagulated blood as a testament to Marty's hurried surgery; as she handled them, they felt slightly hot. She knew that she was being irradiated as she held them, that invisible rays or something were doing terrible things to her flesh, and wondered if the impression of warmth was her imagination. They had each had a screw cap and were about two-thirds full with white ash-like powder. She had brought with her two tin boxes; one was empty, the other full of grey cinders that she had taken from the wood burner and then sieved. As Marty drove, she emptied the contents of the two cylinders into the empty box, then mixed these with approximately the same quantity of cinders, discarding the rest. She refilled the two cylinders to their previous levels, then screwed the tops back on them. She then put them into a padded envelope.

'What are you doing?'

She didn't answer; said only, 'Turn next right.'

'That's a cul-de-sac.'

'I know. Just do as I say.'

The cul-de-sac was short; at its end was a terrace of four small houses; they had been built perhaps thirty years before and begun to decay even as the last ugly tile had been put on the roof and the first council tenant had moved in. Jacqueline told her son to stop just outside the one on the far right; it might have been empty, but, then, so might all of them. She got swiftly out of the van, walked quickly up the drive, careful not to look around, and dropped the envelope through the letter box; she made sure that she made no sound. Then she moved hurriedly back to the van. 'Drive on,' she said. 'Don't speed.'

As he did as she commanded, he asked, 'What is all this about?'

'I'm just doing as I promised Hammy I would.'

He didn't understand. 'Hammy? I thought it was all for us.'

And Hammy had thought it was all for him, she thought tiredly. She had persuaded him that she was willing to be a soldier in his Jihad, and that she and Marty were compliant in his schemes. Such was the way her life had always been; she had been forever surrounded by people who had used her in their own plots and stories. Everyone she had known – her parents, her husband, her friends, her superiors, her inferiors, her church, the state – had assumed that she was little better than fodder.

Not any more, though.

THIRTY-SEVEN

'Arthur Meadows died of multi-organ failure, but that means nothing. To a certain extent, everyone dies of multi-organ failure.' Eisenmenger was talking more rapidly than usual and Beverley didn't miss that fact. He was, she realized, worried; which was, in itself, worrying.

'And?' she prompted.

'The assumption was that he had contracted an infection abroad. It's a reasonable supposition, because it's the likeliest. Everything told them that he had overwhelming sepsis; all the blood markers – CRP, WBC, ESR . . .'

'We get the picture, Doctor.' Lever's interruption served only to delay the exposition and aggravate Beverley, but, before she could say anything in reprimand, Eisenmenger went on. 'Of course. Nobody could find any evidence of a bug; however, that doesn't necessarily mean that it wasn't an organism. Some viruses can be devilishly difficult . . .'

'John,' warned Beverley before Lever could interfere.

'Sure.' Eisenmenger nodded a bit, before, 'The point is the peculiar rash that Arthur Meadows had on his buttocks.'

Lever began to speak. 'Oh, for fuck's . . .'

'What about it?' Beverley asked this whilst looking meaningfully at her sergeant.

They were standing at the far end of the farmyard, whilst they waited for a team from the Health Protection Agency to arrive from Chilton, and whilst Sergeant Henry organized a search of the surrounding area with the available personnel. He explained, 'It was exactly like sunburn, except that it clearly wasn't. But sunburn is just a radiation burn, really.'

Lever was one for shortcuts; it was, Beverley knew from personal experience that was not so much bitter as acrid, a tendency that would get him into seven shades of deep dung, but, she also recognized, it was also potentially the thing he required to become a good policeman. He said now, 'So you think he got radiation burns after sitting on top of these two?'

Even Beverley had to admit that he had got to the nub. Eisenmenger took this edit in his dialogue without comment. 'He was irradiated right through the axial skeleton, which meant that the two organs most sensitive to radiation – the gut and the bone marrow – were exposed. No wonder he got diarrhoea and pneumonia.'

Lever glanced across at the barn, now empty, the whole area cordoned off. 'I don't get it. You're saying they were radioactive?'

'They were carrying something radioactive; something intensely radioactive.'

Lever considered this. 'You mean some sort of atomic material?'

Eisenmenger nodded.

'And that's what killed them?'

But Eisenmenger was never going to allow that sort of loose thinking. 'We don't yet know exactly what killed them . . .' he prevaricated.

Lever clearly couldn't get his cranium around this basic concept, though. 'Why would they do something as fucking stupid as that? Everyone knows you don't go near radiation; even fucking Blacks know that.'

'Shut up, Sergeant.' Beverley's voice was like a blast from the tundra.

'Maybe,' Eisenmenger pointed out mildly, 'they didn't know what they were carrying.'

Beverley said slowly, 'It wouldn't be the first time.' Lever shook his closely cropped head of hair, but said nothing. She went on, 'If you're desperate to get out of somewhere, you'll be quite happy to do a bit of smuggling at the same time. Usually it's drugs, though.'

'Exactly,' persisted Lever. 'No one would be desperate enough to carry something radioactive.'

'Perhaps they didn't know,' Eisenmenger suggested. 'Perhaps they were merely told that they were going to be drugs mules.'

Beverley nodded. 'Which adds a layer of security to the whole thing; whoever organized it would be able to use the mules and the man carrying them without either of them knowing the true purpose of the operation; probably even Rashid Malik didn't know the truth. Arthur Meadows carried them thinking they were just a couple of illegal aliens; or maybe he knew that they were smuggling something, but he didn't appreciate what it was; he probably just thought it was heroin, given the place he picked them up in. Then Rashid Malik took over and he didn't know the reality of things, either. He took them back to his house where he and his wife were killed for their trouble, presumably by whoever is behind the "Jacqueline" email address.'

Lever seemed unconvinced, at least to judge by his body language and his tone of incredulity. 'Why all these shenanigans, then? Why didn't these two just hand over the stuff – whatever it was – to the murderer? How did they end up here? And why kill Harry Weston and this woman?'

Beverley said simply and dismissively, 'I don't know, but it doesn't really matter, does it? We've potentially got a serious radioactive hazard around here.'

Eisenmenger, as was his way, wouldn't let the problem lie. 'Something happened that meant that Harry Weston – until then, apparently nothing to do with the plan – had to die. Maybe that's when the mules escaped, and they made their way here, where Amelia Stark also got in the way.'

Lever had one more objection. 'Why didn't they just throw whatever it was away when they escaped, then? Even a couple of fuckwits would have realized it was the cause of their problems.'

In truth, that had been bothering Eisenmenger, but Beverley had an answer. 'It wouldn't surprise me if they couldn't get rid of it. I would suggest that it could well have been sewn into them.'

THIRTY-EIGHT

'**M**arty?' The room was in darkness, the heavy curtains drawn so that the afternoon sunlight, strong as it was, could not penetrate the bedroom, and she could not see him for certain, but she could sense his presence.

'I'm here.'

He sounded distressed. It was a sound that she was too familiar with since that fateful day in early 2008 when he had gone missing whilst on duty in she knew not precisely where. She had never known either what he had been doing, or even who he had been working for, although she guessed the Special Air Service. He had joined the army as a tribute to his father and, perhaps as the result of a cosmic irony, had found an aptitude for the life that had – at the time at least – delighted both of them. He had been welcomed by the Parachute Regiment but, too soon, he had become secretive; it had been, she now believed, the first step in what had proved an irreparable separation. The army had taken her son from her.

'Are you all right, Marty?'

'I don't know.' He sounded agonized; it was a sound she knew too well.

She was careful not to take liberties, not when he was in this mood, not knowing what he was capable of. 'May I come in?'

'Yes.'

He was lying on top of the bed, fully clothed, just staring at the ceiling where there was a ring of damp because the roof leaked; not that he was seeing it, though. She sat on the edge of the bed, but kept her hands on her lap and was careful to keep apart from him. He looked tranquil, but that was only an appearance. She waited, looking not at him but at her hands clasped in her lap. They tingled slightly and she wondered if that was the start, if other symptoms of radiation poisoning would soon start.

As far as she could work out, he had been taken by freelance fighters working for whoever paid them. Seven months or so later, he had been found purely by chance in his own filth at the top of an apartment block in Chechnya. She still didn't know most of the details of what had happened thereafter, let alone what he had undergone in getting there, but it was clear that he had been tortured on more than one occasion, that he had been sold and resold. Hammy had filled in some of the details, for which she was grateful. He had pointed out that, to the people Marty had come to kill, it was her son who was the criminal, that he had come in the night to do murder; his quiet, insistent explanations had gradually worked on her, and she had come to appreciate that it was more appropriate to condemn those who had sent him on the mission in the first place.

She had not even been told that Marty was missing in the first place; by then, she was used to prolonged periods in which she would not hear from her son, knew nothing of what he had done or what had been done to him. Then, unexpectedly, a colonel from an unspecified regiment had turned up at her house in Tewkesbury to inform her, in slightly patronizing language, that her son was in a hospital in Edgbaston, assuring her that he was physically sound. In her memory, he now sounded, to her ears, to have been supercilious, dispensing alms to a commoner, as if somehow gifted by God. She had indeed been overcome with joy as he had dropped the words of this news into her ears, but it had not survived the first, over-anticipated visit to see Marty.

'What's wrong?'

Marty looked across at her; it was, she knew, her imagination, but she had trouble seeing her son in the eyes that were looking at her. 'Is what we're doing *right*?' His voice was that of someone lost, someone completely without anchors.

Once upon a time, she might have stopped to consider that question, might have been brought up short by it, but that was a long, long time ago. 'Yes.' To her, it was as simple as that – a single syllable from behind her lips, as much a sigh as a word, yet she could not stop it sounding as much aspiration as affirmation. He turned his head back to the ceiling, but didn't reply. She asked, 'Don't you believe me?'

Silence, so that she was on the point of repeating the plea when he said, 'Would Dad approve?'

She was aware that Marty's father had never really left them and, at times like this, he was as incarnate as he had ever been. 'Yes,' she said, and she sounded in her own ears resolute and certain, as a mother should be; her conscience had long been subjugated to her desire for vengeance, yet she could not resist adding, almost as if she felt guilty, 'He would have been as shocked as I was to learn how they treated his only son.'

He did not move, but she could sense that he was assured by her answer; she wondered if she herself could find similar assurance in her utterance, deciding only with difficulty that she could. She knew before he spoke what his next question would be. 'Are we going to do it tomorrow?'

'We are.' It would be Sunday – a special day for her and for her God. When better? When he didn't respond, she asked, 'Are you OK with that?'

He didn't reply directly, instead asking, 'We'll do it together, yes?'

She found that her throat was too tight, her eyes too liquid, her chest paralyzed, so that it took her some seconds to frame the words so that he would not know that she was crying. 'You bet, Marty.'

There was a longer silence than ever. She asked, 'Would you like me to stay with you?'

His answer was barely more than sibilance.

'Yes.'

THIRTY-NINE

The Police Service was not officially able to contact the Secret Intelligence Service directly; all requests for information had to be routed through Special Branch, which was fine by Melanie Harrison, because she had spent six months on secondment to Special Branch and had got to know Chief Superintendent Thomson, its operational head, fairly well.

'Hello, lovely,' he said in what she knew was his idea of an alluring voice. 'How are you doing with Chief Inspector Wharton?' His intonation changed subtly as he said Beverley's name.

'Not bad.'

'That's good.' She thought it might be her imagination, although she doubted it, but she suspected he was mocking her. She said, 'She's not as bad as people say.'

'Neither is the pox.'

I'll take your word for that. The thought remained unspoken as she said, 'I need a small favour, Raymond.'

'Perhaps it's about time you started to explain, Doctor.' Eisenmenger heard the anger in Beverley's suggestion; everyone there did. He had heard it before in Beverley's voice, but never until then directed at him.

'I think they might represent a health risk.'

The man on the hay bales began to climb down, looking scared.

'You think they're carrying some sort of disease?'

He hesitated because, even at this point, he was unwilling to produce an opinion that was not yet quite certain; he did give an answer, though. Shaking his head, he said, 'No. I think there is a serious risk of significant radiation exposure.'

FORTY

'They're clean.'

The man from the Health Protection Agency was short and stout, and laboured under the given name of Hubert, the family name of Boyle; his rimless glasses covered rimless eyes; his beard was grey, only just greyer than his skin. In his heavy radiological protection suit – a less than appealing shade of puce – he looked liked a clown without the garish make-up. It didn't help his case that he was sweating enthusiastically, though whether that was through fear or the heaviness of his apparel was not clear; *probably both*, thought Beverley. He looked sick, too, and his voice was strained; she guessed he was not used to such sights. He put down his equipment and breathed deeply; they heard him say beneath his breath, 'My God . . .'

Lever's perpetual look of low-level exasperation bloomed. 'Nothing at all?' he asked in a voice that, to the initiated at least, could have been faintly incredulous.

Dr Boyle said, 'Nothing at all. It's perfectly safe.'

'But they've supposedly been transporting highly radioactive materials.'

Dr Boyle frowned. 'Yes, I know. Most disturbing.' He shook his head, as if saddened at this state of affairs.

Lever persisted. 'But surely there'd be some residual trace?' Beverley had the distinct impression that Lever's enthusiasm was not purely to find the truth, was perhaps due in part to a desire to find holes in Eisenmenger's theory. Dr Boyle, innocent of such base suspicions, replied easily, 'Not if the substance – whatever it was – didn't spill. Do we know what it is?'

'No,' admitted Beverley.

'But we're supposed to believe that they've been irradiated for days now,' persisted Lever.

Beverley was about to slice him into small constable-sized chunks of gristle, but Boyle obliviously forestalled her. 'It's a common misconception that radiation always makes other things radioactive, which is very far from the truth. Of the common types of radiation – alpha, beta, electromagnetic and neutron – it's only the last that causes that particular effect, and neutron irradiation is relatively rare outside of nuclear reactors, thank goodness.'

Eisenmenger said, 'I'll get on with the examination, then.'

'Where is the substance now?' asked Boyle.

It was a good question; it was the only good question at that particular moment. Beverley replied, 'We don't know.' Slowly, Boyle's face began almost to explode as the significance of her words drew down upon him. Before he could speak, though, Beverley added, 'Don't worry. I don't even know if there is one.'

21209's a date.

It had taken the comely Constable Harrison a long time to come to this epiphany but when it came, as with all such moments, it transformed her thinking so that she could only wonder how she had not seen this truth before.

Jesus, they're young.

Eisenmenger suspected that they had probably not even entered their twenties, perhaps had not even been sixteen. Now, though, they looked old; not old as in possessed of too many years, but old as in decrepit, broken down, distressed; the world had taken their youth and their beauty and traduced them. He had always found autopsies of the young difficult, as did so many pathologists; a post-mortem examination of an adult – especially an older adult – in his mind was somehow part of a normal process, a component of the story of human existence; an autopsy on a child or adolescent was the rudest of reminders that life was not fair, death even less so. It was, no matter how hard he tried to rationalize the process, an *unnatural* thing to do. It would never be anything but a distressing experience for him.

The bodies had been transported to the county medico-legal centre. At his back, behind a transparent barrier, Beverley and her sergeant watched him and the police photographer; he spoke out loud for their benefit, but this also allowed him to think through his conclusions as he worked.

It had been immediately obvious from his first inspection in the barn that Beverley had been right; each of the girls had had an incision made in the lower part of the left buttock, at the top of the thigh; it had been done crudely, then stitched up with thick black sutures, the residuals of which still poked from the dirtied, bloodied flesh. The handiwork might have been crude but it had been done effectively; it would have taken a sharp knife and an unbelievably high pain threshold to have got the contents out. The compartments in the fascia that had been thus made had become infected and were pus-crusted; even if their contents had not been intensely radioactive as he suspected, the amount of sepsis would have been disabling enough. The muscles of the buttock and upper thigh were almost necrotic, decayed and burned to an extent he had never before seen in such recently deceased bodies, especially in such a localized manner.

'The pelvic organs are affected, too,' he told his audience. 'The abdominal organs less so, the chest organs to a certain extent. They've got a lot of superadded changes because, like Mr Meadows, the radiation probably killed the bone marrow – it's exquisitely sensitive to such an insult – and right from the start they were prone to infection and anaemia.' He pointed to the opened cranial cavity of the girl on his left. 'She suffered a massive subdural haemorrhage, which was probably the final insult, as a result of lack of platelets.'

'What about the other one?'

'Well, both their gastrointestinal tracts are almost falling to bits, but I think it was most probably a chest infection that killed her. Certainly both her lungs are fairly well consolidated.'

Lever had yet to lose his air of unbelief. 'Look, what precisely do you think is going on here?'

It was a good question, even if it did come couched in words that were coloured with a faint hue of insubordination. Beverley looked to Eisenmenger who shrugged and smiled. 'Somebody's been smuggling something radioactive, using two innocent girls as mules, and using an innocent people-trafficker – if that isn't an oxymoron – to transport them. It's a good plan, allowing the real criminals to hide behind multiple veils; we'd be none the wiser if things hadn't gone slightly awry.'

Beverley asked, 'But I am right, though, aren't I? This stuff couldn't be used to make a nuclear bomb, could it?'

Eisenmenger had never been known to show undue confidence. 'As far as I recall, the only common fissionable materials are plutonium and uranium . . .'

'Meaning?' demanded Lever.

'By "fissionable", I mean that they might potentially go "critical" in a chain reaction; the huge majority of radioactive substances will never do that . . .'

Lever breathed, 'Hoo-fucking-rah . . .' and earned himself a venomous glare from his superior.

'. . . and both plutonium and uranium are alpha-emitters.'

Before Lever could speak again, Beverley intervened. 'What does that mean, John? To the uninitiated, I mean.'

'Alpha particles are heavy,' he explained. 'They do a lot of damage, but they don't go far – no more than a few centimetres. Beta particles – electrons, by another name – are lighter, go further and do less immediate damage. Electromagnetic radiation – gamma rays – go a long way, but are highly energetic. Whatever this stuff emitted, I would say there was a high proportion of gamma rays. I doubt that it was destined for a nuclear bomb.'

'So what's the point of smuggling it in?' asked Lever.

It was Beverley who answered before Eisenmenger could explain. 'To make a dirty bomb.'

FORTY-ONE

'So we're not talking about a pukka nuclear bomb?' Lever sounded almost disappointed to Beverley's ears. They were in an office near the dissection room; Eisenmenger had just joined them after a shower.

Eisenmenger shook his head. 'Nothing like. It wouldn't have to have much explosive force at all.'

'So what are we worrying about?'

Beverley fought to retain some control of her aggravation. 'Contamination. The idea of a "dirty" bomb is just to spread radioactive materials over a wide area. Depending on wind conditions, even a small explosion could contaminate a huge acreage.'

'You'd need a lot of it, though,' opined Lever. 'How much stuff could those girls have had sewn into them? Not much, I bet.'

Eisenmenger explained, 'That doesn't matter. It's about the psychological effects of doing it. Radioactivity terrifies people in a way that few other things do. If word gets around that there's radioactive dust on surfaces and in the atmosphere, they'll panic. Imagine if someone triggered a dirty bomb in Trafalgar Square; not only would you kill some people, but you'd achieve huge publicity, almost as much as a bona fide nuclear blast. The rolling news stations all around the world would hammer it home to almost everyone on the planet, hour after hour. The alarm would be colossal. Whatever cause you espoused would go straight to number one in the worldwide terrorist charts. If you could do that same and hit a nationally important target, you'd achieve the perfect score.'

'The "oxygen of publicity",' quoted Beverley bleakly.

Harrison was learning that a secular epiphany was something completely unlike the religious type, that it was not an absolute thing, that it was probably merely the first checkpoint along a potentially long road. She and her team had been searching databases on the internet now for several long hours – hours that seemed to have been composed of more than the usual sixty minutes – and had discovered in this aeon that there had been a huge number of 'news events' on the date in question, but she could not imagine that the death of Socks, the White House cat, or some accidental damage to the FA cup were likely to be of great significance in the present investigation.

It was at this point that Beverley returned to her office and called Harrison in. 'What have you found on that email address?' Lever and Eisenmenger were also present. Harrison took a deep breath; she was really rather proud of the progress she had made, and she wanted to tell everyone about it. 'Not much on that . . .' she began.

'What the fuck does that mean?' Beverley looked at the clock on the wall: eight seventeen.

Flustered, Harrison stuttered and, much as a lioness will pounce should the antelope hesitate, Beverley moved in. 'What the fuck have you been doing, Harrison? I need to know whose address that is.'

Defensively, the constable said, 'I think the numbers might be a date.'

Lever nodded, commenting, 'That's a good idea.'

Beverley scribbled the number on a pad of writing paper, then scrutinized it for a while. 'So . . . what? You looked up February the twenty-first, 2009?'

'Yes . . .'

'It could be December the second,' she pointed out.

Harrison frowned. 'No, it couldn't.'

Eisenmenger was sitting in a chair to one side of this exchange, the best seat in the stands. He saw that Constable Harrison had made what is known in sporting circles as a 'complete fuck-up' in saying this, as was immediately apparent from the further deterioration in climatic conditions in that small and somewhat cramped office. Beverley gave her subordinate a look that masqueraded as interest, but to Eisenmenger it was conceivably something a little more menacing. She asked, 'No?' Her voice was curious. Then he decided that, no, it was *curiously* curious.

'It would start with a zero, wouldn't it? It would be zero-two, twelve, zero-nine.'

Beverley appeared to consider this deeply and there was relative silence in that space; it took some courage for Eisenmenger to point out, 'Or perhaps "Jacqueline" is American, and the month comes first, so we should be looking at February the twelfth . . .'

It was undoubtedly a coincidence that all extraneous noise ceased at that moment, so that the silence became quite profound, almost significant, certainly somehow uneasy. It was Lever who broke into this void. 'Maybe it isn't a date at all.'

'We can't afford to exclude any possibility,' was Beverley's immediate response. 'We need to check all possible combinations of that date . . . *including* the ones we've discussed.'

Lever pointed out, not unreasonably, 'We're going to need help, you know.'

Beverley's reaction had more than a touch of Oscar Wilde about it in Eisenmenger's unvoiced opinion as she asked incredulously, '*More* staff?'

'Do you have any idea how many possibilities you're asking them to chase down?'

Lever's question bordered on impertinence, but only bordered on it; it had its effect on his superior. Her glance would have made Joseph Stalin think about giving up the dictating game for a living, but Eisenmenger saw that Lever took it, and took it well. Without taking her eyes from her sergeant, she said, 'I'll go and see the Superintendent, see what can be rustled up.'

There was the briefest of smiles on Lever's face which had Eisenmenger puzzled for a moment; it had seemed almost triumphant and he wondered why. Then he understood; Beverley was committing a huge amount of scant and overstretched resources and, if she were wrong to do so, she would be damaged by the act. He wasn't exactly laying a trap, more making sure that the hurdle in the path before her was high enough to break her professional neck should she trip over it; he was also making sure, by loudly and repeatedly voicing doubts, that he – Lever – would come out of it looking relatively pristine, or even the bright boy of the neighbourhood.

'There's something else,' put in Harrison quickly, keen to restore some belief in her investigatory powers.

'What?'

She told them of her progress in looking at the backgrounds of Lynch, Meadows, Beg and Hawari, in particular of Mohammed Hawari. She mentioned that she had contacted Special Branch to get the information, at which Beverley looked at her sharply. 'Who do you know in Special Branch?'

'Chief Superintendent Thomson.'

'Oh, yes?' said Beverley. 'How do you know him?'

Harrison explained, and Beverley's expression became one of realization; she had history with Thomson, episodes that gave her deeply buried regret and also understanding of the true state of affairs about Melanie Harrison's time at Special Branch. Thinking that she ought to be grateful to have a contact in Special Branch, that she was not the person to judge Harrison's behaviour, she asked only, 'What did he say?'

'Harawi's name popped up because he attended a wedding in Quetta at which' – she consulted the sheet of paper in her hand – 'Kamaloddin Jenab was also present.'

She had trouble pronouncing the name and handed the paper to Beverley for her to see; it was passed in turn to Lever and then Eisenmenger before being returned to Beverley. Lever's expression strongly suggested that his thoughts mainly consisted of the expression *whoopi-fucking-do*. Beverley asked, 'What significance is that?'

'He's apparently a scientist. He's very high up in the Iranian nuclear development programme.'

She had hoped that her news would prove to be of interest; she had failed to foresee that it would be devastating.

Jacqueline couldn't sleep and didn't feel the need to; her time on earth was running short and she was spending what was left to her with her son; for the first time in many years, she was as close to contentment as she considered it possible to come. Everything was in train. Her world in the last few years had shrunk down to this and, until now, this contraction had terrified her; yet at this time, just before the end, she found in it calm. Perhaps it was the expectation that tomorrow she would at last be heard and, in that hearing, she would find satisfaction; she would never remember that moment of satisfaction but it would somehow live with her, even if she herself was no longer aware of it.

She thought once more of her husband and tried not to wonder if he would approve of what she had come to, what she was bringing their son to. He still *was* their son, she reminded herself viciously. Every word of that sentence rang with implication, each one a bell that struck with sonorous vibration in her soul. This man, this killer, this weapon of the state, had been born of her womb; changed almost beyond all recognition, he was now perhaps only visible as the same person who had been placed in her arms so many years ago to her and to her alone. To all others who had come to know him during his life, she suspected that he would be a stranger, and most probably a frightening one.

It was growing cold in that room but she did not mind this. The heat of her mother love warmed her enough.

FORTY-TWO

'You do realize this could be a complete waste of time, don't you?'

Eisenmenger could see that Lever was nothing if not direct. He could see that Beverley was making an effort to restrain her temper – one born of exhaustion and frustration as much as dislike – as she said, 'Explain.'

'We have no definite evidence that this theory about smuggling radioactive material is anywhere near the truth; nothing we've got is radioactive, and all we've got is one pathologist's opinion.' He didn't exactly sound contemptuous, but Eisenmenger could hear the beginnings of it in Lever's last three words, a few steps on the downward slope towards it.

'We have the connection from Meadows to Hawari to the Iranian nuclear physicist,' she pointed out.

'Connection?' Lever almost laughed, certainly made it plain that it was only polite restraint that stopped him splitting a couple of sides due to hilarity in the presence of such imbecility. 'He once went to the same wedding?'

'And repeated trips to the region, which is very close to the Iran–Pakistan border.'

'Which is why there was an Iranian there, presumably.'

Eisenmenger enquired, 'Was this scientist connected in some way to either of the families?'

Beverley consulted the paper that Harrison had left with them. 'Good friend of the groom's uncle.'

'And Hawari's connection?'

'Cousin of the bride.'

Lever said, 'There we are, then. Just coincidence.'

'And at least three murders,' murmured Eisenmenger.

'This is all about smuggling drugs or sex workers; that's a far more likely explanation.'

'If that's so, what killed the lorry driver and the two young girls?'

'Some sort of disease. Meadows picked them up in Turkey or somewhere, didn't he?'

He makes it sound as if the place is rife with sickness and degradation, Eisenmenger thought. Beverley, he could see, was trying hard to remain objective and reasonable. She asked him, 'How certain are you that they all died of radiation poisoning?'

Eisenmenger had been practising autopsy pathology for a quarter of a century and, with every year that had passed, he had become less and less certain about causes of death, and ever more loathe to let the police believe that he was infallible. 'I can't think of a more likely explanation for the post-mortem findings,' he said cautiously.

Lever made a noise from the back of his throat, clearly advancing quite purposefully down the slope towards outright contempt; Eisenmenger was well used to the type, for police officers who dealt only in absolutes, who failed to recognize fractions and shades of belief, who did not believe that pathology was as much a medical opinion as any other clinical diagnosis, were not at all rare. Lever said, 'If they escaped from imprisonment and were on the run in fear of their lives, why didn't they hand themselves in?'

'They're illegal immigrants, Lever. They end up going straight back to where they started from.'

He hadn't finished raising objections. 'Why didn't they just pull this hypothetical radioactive stuff out, then? If it was hurting that much, it would be the sensible thing to do.'

Eisenmenger replied, 'It was buried deep and someone had gone to a lot of trouble to ensure that they *couldn't* get it out.'

Lever came back yet again. 'And why the military thing?'

Eisenmenger explained the reasoning behind his deduction, to which the sergeant responded, 'Not a lot to go on, then.'

Beverley felt utterly lost, and couldn't remember ever feeling so far from the answer and so near to disaster. She said to Lever, 'Why don't you get us some coffee and sandwiches from somewhere, Sergeant?'

There was a moment when he might have been about to refuse, for his face fleetingly bore an expression of incredulous anger at being relegated to tea-boy, but he did at last do as he was asked.

As soon as he had left the room, Beverley said, 'It's fucking important, you know, John.'

'I never thought otherwise.'

'He's got a point. We have a lot of lighter-than-air supposition – most of it yours – and absolutely no facts to support it.'

'I know that.'

She suddenly exploded, an ignition born of anger, fear and tiredness. 'Jesus-fucking-Christ, John! It *is* rather important, you know! If you're right, this isn't just a few tawdry deaths done by a fuckwit murderer.'

If Beverley was under stress, so too was Eisenmenger. His normal role was to provide a cause of death, perhaps replete with details that might help trap the killer or exclude an innocent suspect, but, in this case, his conclusions were leading to consequences and suppositions that were expanding into something that might result in a huge husk of hares set running; the consequences of being wrong were potentially professionally disastrous.

Yet, he somehow knew, he *wasn't* wrong . . .

Was he?

He drew deep breaths, as if he had been holding his chest totally still for a long time, which, perhaps, he had. He said in a controlled voice, 'Radiation poisoning is the only single explanation that takes account of all the post-mortem findings in all three deaths.'

'"Only single"? What does that mean?'

'Things in medicine aren't always clear-cut.'

'Explain, John.'

'It's possible there's more than one thing going on here.'

'What the fuck does that mean?'

'I'm looking for a single thing that caused all three deaths. Maybe Arthur Meadows *did* die of something different to the two girls.'

She looked intently at him, shouting at him wordlessly, *Now, you tell me!* 'How likely is that?'

His voice held the shrug that his body didn't quite manage. 'It's the nightmare that every doctor dreads, whichever way you play it; either you see two diseases where there's only one, or you're so intent on finding a single cause for the symptoms that you don't spot that there are, in fact, two.'

'You're not helping me, John.'

The answer she received was no answer at all; he remained silent for a long time and, if she hadn't known him so well, she would have interrupted him long before he finally spoke. 'It's the lesions that Arthur Meadows had that I can't explain any other way. Something blasted him through his buttocks and anus, and there isn't anything else that could have done it except ionizing radiation; the two girls had tissue changes that were entirely consistent with the same pathogenesis.'

'Meaning?'

'We're looking for something intensely radioactive.'

She allowed herself to relax just a fraction. 'What about the military thing? How certain are you about that?'

'It was just an idea.'

Which response earned him a long stare; Eisenmenger had ideas like other people had babies.

At ten fifty-three, Lever came back, bearing a tray on which were packed sandwiches and cups of coffee from a large machine that played reserve when the restaurant was closed; his face bore an expression that might have rotted the food.

Jacqueline began to type at her laptop. She was not a writer and never had been; never now would be. She had much to say, though, and the hour was growing late with not much time to say it. On the bed by her side, Marty slept as peacefully as he ever did now; it was the rest of the damned, an uneasy thing, like that of a scarred beast.

This is the testament of Jacqueline Millikan, written shortly before her death.

Eisenmenger remained as unnoticeable as he could during Beverley's telephone conversation with Superintendent Greene; he could only hear half of it, but it didn't require much in the way of intellect to fill in the unheard side of the conversation. At its end, she said tiredly, 'We've got reinforcements, but only until seven. After that, no more help. They're stretched too thin as it is, apparently.'

FORTY-THREE

Because she had been staring at the screen for so long, Harrison's eyes felt so sore they might have been bleeding; she began to regret her bright idea, which she didn't think was a good idea any more. Her neck ached, too, and she should have been back in her flat five hours before; not that the bitch queen Wharton cared. Nat had told her all about Chief Inspector Beverley Wharton over a dinner and, in the process, shocked her profoundly. There had always been rumours about her, of course, but she wasn't stupid; she knew that the profession of policing was steeped in gossip, because the detection of most crime and the apprehension of most criminals were based not on clinical deduction but on listening to what people had to say; it wasn't a particularly clean or clever way to fight wrongdoing – not the kind of thing that was likely to appeal to the screenwriters and authors who made a living out of writing about the lives of the police, and even less to their readers – but it was the most effective method they had. The trouble was that the mindset thus entrained seeped pervasively and inevitably into working life *within* the station, into the way that police officers viewed each other; gossip became something like a turgid sea through which they all swam.

Thus, until now, the talk about what Beverley Wharton had done to achieve her rank had, to Harrison at least, merely been a swirl of pollution in the waters that surrounded them, the usual scuttlebutt about senior – especially female senior – officers. Lever, and the two bottles of wine with vodka chasers, had persuaded her that there was some truth in the stories, that Beverley Wharton had really used her body to achieve her rank, that she had frequently manufactured evidence, or just as frequently 'mislaid' it, that she had on more than one occasion betrayed her colleagues and subordinates.

At first, Melanie had been suspicious of Nat Lever. He had seemed superficial, brash and aggressive, but she was now coming to appreciate that maybe he wasn't as bad as she had first believed. He was, after all, certainly good-looking, and she had enjoyed being with him and being touched by him; his attitude, too, she now realized, was not totally unpleasant. In fact, he had demonstrated a funny, almost playful side when out of the confines of police hierarchy and in a more normal social setting. Now, she was starting to wonder if her allegiances might be best made with him rather than Beverley Wharton, because it was entirely possible that she, Melanie Harrison, would go the same way as most other lieutenants of the chief inspector. She had learned a lot in her relatively short time as a police officer, but the most useful component of her education had been studies in the political arts: when to make allegiances and, more significantly, when to break them.

The outer door from the corridor – the one on which someone had scratched in small letters, *Fuck BW*, under which somebody else had scratched in even smaller ones, *Why not? Most people have* – opened and the rather naive visage of PC William Hubble came in, followed by the rest of his body. 'I've been sent to help you.'

FORTY-FOUR

I wish I could say that I regret the things I am about to do, but I do not. Nobody deserves what I am about to do to them, but I now know that nobody gets what they deserve and that, sooner or later, everybody gets what they don't. They are merely 'collateral damage', just as I am, just as every civilian ever killed in war has been. When my family went to war for you, they knew that they might pay a price for their decisions, perhaps would even pay 'the ultimate price', and each of us – both those who went and those who stayed behind – signed up willingly to this contract; yet I and my family discovered that this contract had small print that we had not read, that we had not thought we needed to read. This is my universe. I am merely about to leave it and I wish, for the first time in too long, to take with me a small degree of contentment.

I lost my husband for the state and I accepted it.

Would that I had lost my son in so simple a manner.

Had he died – shot or torn apart by a roadside bomb – that would have been something to have found pride in. I would have accepted my side of that bargain and allowed my grief to be contained. I could have participated in the ceremonies of national mourning and celebration with a sense of completion; I could have lived by drawing on a sense that he was being in some way acknowledged. Nothing has been given to me for sustenance, though; I have been left alone, unregarded and ignored. At first I accepted this. My son had been engaged in secret work, and it was right that it should not be publicly avowed; I did not feel anger when the laurels were laid on the graves of others as they flew back, for I thought that there was solace to be found in the esteem in which he was held by his government. It was so when my husband died, and I thought that this second, harder blow would be softened by similar approbation.

I was wrong.

He had not died, nor lost a limb, nor his sight; he was not photogenic, nor could he ever be allowed into the public's theatre, for he was damaged, *and damaged in a way that made him at least an embarrassment, potentially, even, a national security risk. He had been told too much, seen even more, and did not now appreciate what was 'right'; he was made into a child – with a child's amorality, a child's ingenuousness, a child's lack of interest in or knowledge of consequences – and he became a liability. He was, unlike his fallen and injured comrades, not something that could be used as a tool to rally support in a cold, cynical attempt to engender approval, to manipulate the sentiments of people too nice or, perhaps, too jaded to wonder if their leaders were at all interested in other agendas.*

And yet, more than that, he was under suspicion; without evidence, he was considered to have somehow 'gone rogue', to have betrayed a trust. They could not prove it, but they could not disprove it, either, and that seemed to be enough.

But he was still my son, although he was both more and less than that; he had become a macabre mix of blamelessness and total corruption; only man could make a man like that.

*   *   *

Harrison came to with a start as Lever walked out of Beverley Wharton's office and sat down heavily beside her. Her watch – the one her parents had given her when she had finally passed out as a police officer – told her it was just after midnight. He hadn't bothered to close the office door quietly, but she knew at once that he was angry; his normal walk was something of a slouch – as if he enjoyed the world's adoration whether or not it was looking at him – but now it was something close to the heavy feet of an adolescent deprived of internet access. His expression, too, was thunderous. When he sat down next to her, it was as if the pilot had made a bad mistake on touchdown. By now, there were eleven uniformed police officers at desks in the darkness of the room, all intent on computer monitors; not a few of them looked up at Lever's emphatic entrance.

'What's wrong?' she asked.

'That bitch.'

She hadn't known him well for long, but it was already a familiar refrain, although not one that bred resentment. 'That bitch' was Beverley Wharton.

'What's she done now?'

'She's so fucking stupid.'

'Why?'

A brief look of incredulity crossed his face and was then gone, much as a breeze disturbs and then is no more. 'She's going completely wrong on this one.'

'You don't believe she's on to something?'

'Do you?'

Constables were not encouraged to disbelieve; courage, dependability, stoicism and the ability to follow orders unquestioningly were actively promoted by the higher ranks of the police force, and those in command were, on the whole, quite happy with a state of unquestioning obedience. She was savvy enough to suspect that the whole edifice might disintegrate if the people at the bottom of it actually began to do something about their grumbling discontent. 'I haven't thought about it.'

He did just not quite enough to hide his contemptuous despair. 'Look, Mel . . .' She hated that nickname – her father had used it too many times when full of remorse about hitting her mother – and she had told Lever this, but perhaps he hadn't heard. 'She's plain fucking *wrong*.'

'About what?'

'About the whole thing. This has always been about people-smuggling.'

She considered what she had just been told. 'Why were the Maliks killed?'

'To cover the trail; eliminate the witnesses.'

This struck her as slightly wasteful. 'Just because they helped bring in a couple of illegals?'

'We don't know that there haven't been a whole lot more before them.'

Which made sense, she supposed. 'Why were the girls killed, then?'

He had to pause. 'Because they ran away,' he decided.

'Wouldn't that be a bit harsh?' she asked. 'And it would be a waste of money, too.'

This did not disrupt his theorizing for long. 'I don't know . . . Maybe they saw something they shouldn't have, someone who was afraid that he'd be recognized in the future.'

'What about Harry Weston? Where does he fit in?'

'He must have seen something, too.' It was a glib answer but, like all such, it was convincing as well.

'But I don't understand why the girls were killed. What was the point of that? They couldn't have been any sort of danger, could they?'

'They were damaged goods,' he said with a touch of impatience. 'Look at the fucking state of them. They had some God-awful tropical lurgy. Who would have wanted to shag someone like that?'

She said nothing in direct response. 'I thought there was something about radiation.'

'What about it?' She didn't know and had to shrug. He said, 'Nobody's shown me any believable evidence at all that there's anything radioactive within half a world of this case.'

'Doctor Eisenmenger seems to think there is.'

'So?'

'He's a pathologist . . .'

'Doesn't mean he's always fucking right.'

'No, I suppose not,' she conceded, because she was at heart a reasonable person.

'Anyway, Wharton's smitten.'

'What do you mean?'

'She's got the hots for him.'

'You reckon?'

'It's obvious.' He then added, perhaps because she looked less than convinced, 'Haven't you noticed?'

Now that he mentioned it, she thought that perhaps she had noticed something between the two of them, although she found Eisenmenger such an odd fish, it was difficult to tell what he was thinking. 'I suppose . . .'

'Poor fucker's head is too far up his own arse to realize his own luck, though.'

'What does that mean?'

He heard her suspicion. 'Just that he's clearly smitten.'

Melanie Harrison had come to consider her chief inspector to be a slightly scary mix of irascibility, jealousy, brains and leather; she had never before thought that anyone might find her attractive, let alone that Nat might find her so. 'You're joking.'

He shrugged. 'That's what I reckon.'

'So what's the plan?'

He didn't know, but he wasn't about to tell Constable Melanie Harrison that. 'You carry on as you were. I'll just follow my nose.'

'What do you think?' asked Eisenmenger.

Her face said it all. *How the fuck should I know?*

She took a breath that was deep enough to suck out an ocean trench. 'To be honest, I don't know, John. I've managed to get extra help temporarily, but if I start seriously screaming about international smuggling of radioactive materials with the intention of someone making a dirty bomb and we're wrong, the shit storm will bury me under a million metric tonnes; mind you, if I don't, and we're right, I'll be buried under a billion tonnes of the fucking stuff.'

'Tricky decision.'

She managed a smile. 'No shit, Sherlock.'

'Which doesn't answer my question,' he pointed out.

'There isn't an answer, is there? How am I supposed to decide if it's better being buried under a million or a billion tonnes of shit? You're buried; end of.'

'There's a royal do at Highgrove next weekend,' he pointed out. 'Perfect target, I'd have thought.'

She stared at him as if she couldn't believe what he was saying. 'So you think I should ring the alarm bell?'

He found it difficult to judge from her tone what answer he should give. 'I'm just thinking out loud.'

'Well, fucking don't,' she hissed. 'There's always going to be a potential target, no matter what day it is, or where in the UK we are. The question is whether or not I've got enough information to risk making a public idiot of myself.'

He said nothing, didn't even show a reaction, except by remaining unnaturally passive; had he screamed obscenities at her, the effect would have been no less dramatic. 'Well?' she demanded aggressively after little more than ten – albeit ten *long* – seconds.

He took a long time to answer. Eventually, he said, 'I understand,' his voice modulated with sympathy. He knew at once it had been a mistake. Beverley Wharton did not do 'understanding'. She rarely gave it and she most definitely never accepted it; he might just as well have offered her the dust from her father's grave. 'No, you fucking don't, Doctor Eisenmenger,' she hissed, rounding on him. He suddenly realized that he was once more in her sights, tracking radar locked on, missiles armed and away; 'lock and load' had been and gone, and it was not comfortable to be in the centre of the head-up display that CI Wharton was presently intent on. 'You're not the one who has to hit the red "fire" button, or turn the key, or pull the trigger. You just think, and advise, and *pontificate*; you're just a back-room boy, a boffin, one who sits on his arse and comes up with wonderful theories that make oh-so-perfect sense, when all that matters is that the Bunsen burner might go out, or the milk for the tea might be a teeny-weeny bit off. You've got absolutely no fucking idea of the magnitude of the decision I have to make.'

He was not, by nature, someone who relished a fight; indeed, he tended to make complex semantic, even semiological detours in order to avoid them. There was, though, a limit. 'Is that what you think?'

She heard the tone of the question, that it was different to his usual one, that it wasn't merely a question, and that it carried with it challenge. Her hearing of these things made her stop before she responded with an answer that was too easy. She said slightly more diplomatically, 'What you're telling me has consequences . . .'

'And I don't realize that? I live in that famed "Ivory Tower", do I, and just emit my judgements through some sort of loudspeaker system, then go back to the laboratory?'

Her surprise that he should have reacted thus did not outlive her habitual reaction to fight back when an aggressor – any aggressor – challenged her. 'Most of the time, *yes*, John.' This had something in its pitch that could have been heard as a hiss, especially when the penultimate word worried its way between her teeth. He had no rational answer, his arsenal empty, a feeling of hopelessness within him as he realized, yet again, that normal, human arguments were not like scientific or other kinds of academic debate; fact as a basis for logical deduction and intellectual argument as a method of moving from one proposition to another had no place when emotion took hold.

'I'm not totally remote from the world,' he countered, hearing in his words only a rather pathetic and automatic gainsaying of what he had just been told. 'I've been doing this for over twenty years, Beverley, and every time I give you or one of your colleagues a report, I am fully aware that what I say may be instrumental in convicting someone, or in allowing another to go free, or even in saving someone's life. I am also aware that I get things wrong, that pathologists give only an opinion, not gospel, that someone else might look at the same set of findings and come to a different – perhaps even the opposite – conclusion.' And he found, as he went on through this testament, that he discovered anger again, and that its passion gradually increased as it came out, so that by the end he was almost as sibilant as she had been. He had moved closer to her, as well, an act that spoke as loudly to her as his words and voice had done.

There was then a moment – an ephemeral and insubstantial

thing that was at the same time as hard and potent as a brick wall, and that existed by the very reason of its absence – when the row might really have escalated, when all the pressures of making the wrong decision might have welled up and flooded all else. Beverley paused, though; she felt the moment, felt its importance, and hence did not respond. Instead, she said in a low, angry yet restrained voice, 'If we don't find anything by sunrise, I suppose we assume that this is all a flight of your fancy, and start all over again.'

It was one thirty-one.

FORTY-FIVE

'What have you done so far?'

'We're working our way through the archives of the nationals. We've been through the BBC, ITN and Sky. We've still got to cover the international news agencies such as AFP and Reuters, though.'

'And what are you searching for?'

'Well, we start with references to "Jacqueline" on all the possible date permutations.'

Lever couldn't stop himself from pointing out, 'There must be millions of those.'

'I know that,' she said patiently. 'But then we're searching through those for references to certain other keywords.'

'Which ones?'

'*Radioactive, radioactivity, bomb, military, army, weapon . . .*'

She was quite pleased with herself; before starting in her present post, she had just completed an advanced computer skills course of which database searching had been a large component; she had come up with this search algorithm herself.

'And?'

'Well . . .' She opened the computer window that held the results of the search thus far. 'We've accumulated a total of five hundred and sixty-three references involving "Jacqueline" and "army" . . .' The pride with which she said this did not last until the second half of the sentence as she added, 'but we haven't got any for "Jacqueline" and "radioactive" or "radioactivity".'

Lever sighed. 'You need to look at the days that follow the dates in her email address.'

'Why?'

'Because the events you're looking at won't have been reported on the day they happened, will they?' He asked the question with something that she recognized and did not like, even as she recognized its truth. He went on with a touch of cruelty, 'You'll have to tell everyone to go back and do the search on at least three more days after the ones you've already done.'

She sighed and kept a profanity to herself; before she could do as she been advised, she discovered that Sergeant Lever hadn't finished his critique of his colleagues' performance. 'Anyway, I reckon you've got jack shit.'

'Why?' She was affronted.

'Even if we assume that Eisenmenger isn't broadcasting out of his A-hole when he talks about a military dimension to the killings, it's all a red herring.'

'I think it sounds very convincing,' she interjected in an effort to assert herself, one that was condemned to receive only further disparagement.

'So the murderer was once in an army? What does that matter? He's working for some sort of gang of people-traffickers; of course they're going to employ someone who can use a knife. They're not going to call on the Hairdressers' Fucking Federation to find an enforcer, are they?'

'No . . .' she said uncertainly. What he said made some sort of sense.

'As I see it, it's all perfectly simple. Meadows was employed to smuggle the girls into the country for Malik; in doing so, he trod on somebody's toes. Presumably, he got a bit big for his boots and he was taught an appropriate lesson. Some hired muscle was brought in; it doesn't matter what kind of training he had.'

'What about the connection with the Iranian scientist?'

Lever's scorn could have unblocked a drain. 'What connection?' he demanded. 'They attended the same wedding *once*. Talk about being damned by coincidence.'

Harrison continued to resist what seemed to her to be a nearly unquenchable desire to demolish Beverley's case. 'How do you explain the death of Weston?'

'He was a loose end.'

'Dr Eisenmenger said they'd had something implanted into them.'

'Drugs. They do that to dogs, you know.'

She made a face of disgust, unable to believe that anyone could be that cruel to another human being. 'But that's different,' she said.

'They do it to humans, too, Constable. We're dealing with fucking savages.'

She considered what he had just told her; it seemed at that moment to make as much sense as the theory about dirty bombs and radioactive materials. 'What should I search on, then?' she asked.

'"Jacqueline" – as you did – and then refine the search on terms related to sex-trafficking, people-smuggling, all that kind of thing.'

He was a man full of confidence.

FORTY-SIX

I was stupid; it took me too long to realize that Marty wasn't just like any other wounded soldier. Of course, I'd known that he was in some sort of special unit, but he had never told me any of the details – not the name of his unit, and certainly not where he had been or where he was going, or what he had done – and I accepted that ignorance, even embraced it with pride; I was already a military widow, a military mother, and I knew how to behave now that I was to become a military carer.

They count on that, of course. They use it for their own purposes; I now see all too clearly.

I was told that he was in hospital at the Queen Elizabeth Hospital, Edgbaston; it's new and expensive, standing like a thing from the future on a hill, and it has a section for the military. I took a long time trying to find my way in, feeling small. When I discovered it – 'The Royal Centre for Defence Medicine' – they told me he had been shot; which he had – in the shoulder – and I thought his mental state was merely shock because of this. I didn't know then, you see, when he had been shot, how long ago it had actually been; I assumed at the time that all the surgery had been done in a base abroad – probably in Germany – prior to repatriation for rehabilitation. Before I could see him, though, I was surprised to be ushered in to see the same colonel who had first contacted me. He was still in uniform, and uniforms are rare in military hospitals, so I should have known that there was a problem. I never found out his name; he was tall and young, and he smiled too much, as if he were selling me something I didn't want.

He wanted to let me know why Marty – 'Corporal Millikan', he said, of course – had a guard outside his room. He said that it was because of Marty's special service, that the man was there to protect him. I believed him, because that's what you do, especially if you're an army wife, or an army widow, or an army mother. I thought no more about it at the time.

I soon saw that Marty's wound, though, was totally healed. An ugly scar twisted and puckered the skin over his collar bone; I was once in a road accident and was cut down my thigh; I watched it heal over time and it only came to look like Marty's shoulder after months of scrutiny. When I questioned the doctors, they were non-committal; doctors always are when you ask them too many questions that are too close to making them lose the power they gain from superior wisdom.

And all the time there was that guard, although I soon recognized that there were six of them in rotation, and they never showed a sign that they recognized me as anything other than a stranger.

The doctors said that they didn't know when it had happened. So I asked who would know, but they said Marty's unit wasn't recorded; it didn't matter to them, they pointed out, which was true, I suppose, but they knew more than they were ever going to tell me. I made a bit of a fuss then. I demanded to see the colonel again, although he was always too busy, or so they said. It was so frustrating, because the more I demanded to know what had happened to Marty, the more kind they became, and the more they sighed and the more reasonably they behaved towards me, as if I was just a stupid, naughty girl who was best handled by patience and forbearance.

The guards just guarded; I started to appreciate that they weren't keeping him safe: they were keeping him in.

You see, it was obvious even to me that his shoulder wasn't the problem; his whole arm was stiff and he had trouble dressing and washing, but that wasn't the reason he was still in hospital. The problem was that he wasn't normal any more; he frightened me, in fact. He looked like my son, and he sometimes sounded like a faint, inhuman echo of him, but most of the time he was a stranger to me. There was something awful in the back of his eyes, living there and seeking to impersonate him, but it wasn't Marty, not any more. I think it actually thought it was Marty, because I could hear a sort of pleading in its words when it spoke to me of Marty's childhood and his memories. I think Marty was still in there, too; he was still occupying a small part of the head that looked so much like my beautiful son, but he was unable to get out, unable to be himself any more.

By this time, I had moved into a rented bedsit in Edgbaston to be as close to Marty as I could get. I was working as a shelf-stacker in Tesco's and, when I wasn't sleeping, I was with Marty. The cost of the flat was breaking me, but I didn't have a car and I wanted to be as near as possible to my son. I continued to pester the doctors, and they continued to be vague about his problems. When I asked if it was post-traumatic stress, they said that, yes, it was partly that, but I could tell from the voices that they were lying, if not through commission, then through omission at least. I asked if he'd had a mental breakdown; they were more certain in their medical opinion that he'd definitely had one of those, but again I got the impression I was being steered away from something. Whenever I was left alone with Marty, I would ask him questions about what he knew; once, the thought of asking him to reveal what he had done for his country would have been impossible for me to do, because I would have considered it as bad as treason, but by then I was becoming more than confused, more than anxious, far more than accepting of the fate of a military son and his mother; I was becoming angry. Something had happened to Marty and nobody was willing to tell me what; he had been smuggled back into the country, had received no recognition for his service and had clearly been severely wounded at some point. When I asked them directly if he was accused of something, I was met only with blank looks and declarations of ignorance that were eloquently evasive. I began to realize then that something bad had happened, and they thought Marty had done it.

It slowly became clearer and clearer that I might not get him back, that he was not a patient, but a prisoner. He wasn't even free within the confines of the hospital, for the room was the limit of his liberty. I asked why he could not leave, but I was met only with vague explanations about his mental state, how they were concerned for his welfare, how they could not say precisely when he might be well enough to leave. I could not understand what was going on; Marty was clearly ill, but he was being treated as someone in custody, although no one would tell me why. Again I ranted, again I made loud noises and again I got no reaction. I wrote to my MP, to the Prime Minister, to the Archbishop of Canterbury, all without answer. Eventually, I went to the television, but not just any television channel; I picked one that would get their notice. It worked, too.

The reaction, though, was not in the form that I was expecting. I had just got back to the flat after a shift at the supermarket, and I was tired; it was four in the morning and wintery cold had allowed cruel, dank air into the pores of my bones. I was tired, too, tired because it had been hard work that night, and tired because exhaustion was now not just a reaction but also a comfort, a thing from which I could draw succour; the only thing I had left from which I could draw succour. There were two men waiting for me in a car outside, although they did not make their presence known until five minutes after I had shut my front door and I was in the middle of making myself hot milk to take to bed to make me believe that it might help me sleep. One was short and perhaps sixty or sixty-five; the other was a decade or so younger and slightly taller, although it was the short one that had the authority.

'Mrs Millikan?' he asked. I said that yes, I was. He smiled, although it was a thing that left me afraid. 'May we come in?

I'm sorry for the lateness of the hour, but we felt that it was of the utmost importance that we talk to you.'

I let them in to my room, where we sat at the small cheap dining table with its rickety legs and gatefold flaps, and its scratched, wine-stained laminate top. I didn't offer them refreshment and they didn't ask for it. They ignored the bed in the corner of the room as if it were a smelly, sleeping tramp, although it was made up and covered in a throw. The shorter, older one said, 'Mrs Millikan, I am the Private Secretary to the Minister of State for Armed Forces; this gentleman is the Second Permanent Under-Secretary of State.'

They didn't offer me their names, their titles apparently enough to know them by; to be frank, I was too much at a loss to ask what their mothers called them. I couldn't understand what was going on, only that it was something to do with Marty; I knew then, too, I think, that it was going to be bad. 'What can I do for you?' I asked, because I am an army widow and an army mother, and such people are unfailingly polite.

'We're here to talk about your son, Martin.'

They called him 'Martin', not 'Marty', note, and in doing so they showed me that they did not know him and did not care about him. Army widows and army mothers may be polite, but they are not stupid. I did not correct them. I did not even speak, which, I think, disconcerted them a little. The man – the same one as who spoke before – said, 'We're here to explain the situation.'

'Thank you,' I said.

'You've been a little concerned, and I can understand that.'

I doubted that; I doubted that he understood my feelings at all. I said nothing.

'The circumstances are somewhat unusual.'

And when I still said nothing, he looked, I think (I hope), disconcerted; when he continued, there was almost pleading in his voice. 'I'm sure you'll appreciate that there is much we cannot tell you about what has happened.'

I should have remained in silence, but I couldn't stop myself from saying, 'I just want to know what's happened to him. I want my son back.'

He nodded, perhaps relieved that he was no longer alone in the dialogue; his companion nodded, but it was he who said, 'We understand that, and it is the reason for our presence here.'

If he hoped that he was now into a conversation, my return to silence soon told him otherwise. There was a glance at his companion – not that he seemed to receive any response from that quarter, either – before he said, 'Martin was on an assignment that went wrong.'

My son was almost catatonic in the hospital, there was a healed wound in his shoulder, and there were months missing from his life; this man hadn't yet told me anything new. 'But you can't say where,' I suggested.

'No.'

'And you can't say what the assignment was?'

'That is clearly impossible.'

'Or when it happened.'

'I'm sorry.'

But he wasn't sorry and perhaps he was slightly hard of hearing, because he didn't seem to detect the sarcasm in my voice. 'What can you tell me?'

'Martin is highly trained and has done many fine and brave things for his country. It is the nature of his work that his service cannot be openly acknowledged but, rest assured, it is appreciated.'

I heard earnestness in his words, but I also heard a man who was well used to being earnest, when it was required. 'What's wrong with him?' I asked.

But he still wasn't about to answer any question directly; perhaps that ability had been ground out of him by the wheels of government. 'As I say, something went wrong. We thought at the time that everyone had been' – he hesitated slightly, eyes suddenly interested in my face – 'killed.'

There, he had said it and I didn't give him the satisfaction of showing my reaction; I had lived with the possibility of my son dying as my husband had done, yet to hear that he had apparently come close – albeit with the details and circumstances hidden from me – was still hard. I was not as tempered as I thought I was. Instead, I said, 'But he wasn't.'

He acknowledged this truism. 'No. He was found, some several months later.'

'*Found?*'

A gesture with his hands to tell me that he was bound by forces greater and mightier than him. '*I can't be more specific.*'

I knew that he would say that; you don't have to be a genius to work out how people like him and organizations like his go about their business.

'*What had happened to him?*'

He looked uncomfortable but answered. '*He was found in an apartment.*'

'*An apartment? Where?*'

He said, '*Chechnya.' The younger one glanced sharply at him, as if surprised I had been allowed to know even that; as if it were a breach of security, or something.*

I think he thought I wouldn't know where that was, but I did. '*How did he get there?*' *I waited for an answer, but he wasn't going to give it to me, so I asked,* '*Did you make him like he is?*'

'*Most assuredly not.' I obviously didn't look convinced because he went on,* '*Mrs Millikan, I understand your concern, but please be assured that we have done nothing to Martin to harm him.*'

'*But you've questioned him, haven't you?*'

'*We need to find out what happened,*' *he conceded.*

'*He's in no fit state to be interrogated.*'

Suddenly, the younger man spoke for the first time. His voice was more imperious than the other's. '*Three of his colleagues died, as did a family of civilians – including some children. There were no witnesses, as far as we can tell.*'

I suddenly understood. '*You think he did it,*' *I said, full of wonder.*

The younger one replied. '*It seems the likeliest explanation.*'

'*What other evidence have you got?*'

They had no answer or, at least, they would not tell me of it.

I was momentarily silenced by the shock of this. How could they think that, after all Marty had done for them, for his country? '*Has he confessed?*' *I asked.*

They looked at each other. The older one said, '*No. The doctors tell us he is too traumatized; he seems to have completely and totally blotted out the experience.*'

'*There you are, then. Innocent until proven guilty.*'

The smile of the younger was crushingly condescending. 'It's not as simple as that.' I was fearful, but I said nothing. He explained, 'We accept that there is not enough evidence to convict him and, even if there were, a general court martial would not be in anyone's interest . . .'

I knew what he was saying; they wanted their secrets kept under the stone, but there was something else that was bothering me, as ravenous for sleep as I was. 'Why did you tell me he was back at all? Why wasn't he just listed as missing and then made to disappear?' I tried to put sarcasm into that last word, a wasted effort on those two.

They exchanged glances, and I felt that somehow I had scored a small victory. After a small pause, the younger one said, 'Her Majesty's Government does not go about its business in that way.'

The older one said more gently, 'It was hoped that your reunion might bring about a change in his condition and help him remember precisely what happened. Unfortunately, that proved not to be the case.'

I nearly laughed. 'So why are you here?'

The older one said, 'We are not unreasonable, Mrs Millikan. We appreciate that this situation should not last . . .'

The younger one took an envelope out of his inside breast pocket and gave it to me. The envelope was expensive, I could see; it was the kind of thing that wills are put in, but this didn't contain a testament. It held three printed pages, covered mostly in small type, all carefully set out in sections and subsections, all of these with reference numbers. Across the top of the first page, under the royal coat of arms, were the words 'OFFICIAL SECRETS ACT 1989'; under that were the words '1989 Chapter Six'. Before I could speak, he said, 'If you sign that and solemnly agree to be bound by its authority, we will release Martin into your care.'

'An honourable discharge?'

His response was quick and snaked down his long nose with a sneer. 'I hardly think that would be appropriate, given the circumstances.'

I think it was at that moment that I took the first steps of the journey that ends tonight. The older one explained, 'Martin will remain a member of Her Majesty's Armed Forces, albeit not on

active service and with no duties. He will continue to receive his
salary so that you will not be destitute.' He made it out to be an
unreasonably generous package.

His colleague, though, wanted to make things perfectly clear.
Again fishing in his breast pocket, he pulled out this time a folded
piece of A4 paper. I knew what it was, of course. He unfolded it
and then handed it to me. It was a still picture, somewhat blurred
because it was a freeze frame taken from a television programme,
the one in which I had been interviewed by an Arab journalist,
the one in which I had told the world what the British Army was
doing to my son.

'This must never happen again. Only if we leave here assured
on that point will we allow your son to depart the hospital.'

FORTY-SEVEN

I ronically, Lever made the breakthrough. He had been searching
for references to people-trafficking, drug-trafficking and illegal
arms trading, each cross-referenced to the name 'Jacqueline',
going through the normal news databases, when it occurred to
him to do likewise using slightly more obscure news archives
and sources. He soon discovered a rich – and therefore depress-
ingly large – selection, but he reckoned to reduce the scope of
his trawl to those based in the Near and Middle East, since that
was the place that the girls had been picked up by Meadows. In
Turkey alone, there were four – the Anatolian Agency, Anka
News Agency, Cihan News Agency and Ihlas News Agency; none
had news stories that involved two or more of his search terms.
He accordingly widened his search. It was when his questing
reached Qatar that he came across the independent current affairs
television channel, Al Jazeera. When he searched their archives,
he hit blisteringly bright gold.

Beverley's nerves were screaming with the tension when Lever
came in. The abruptness and loudness of his entry woke Eisenmenger
who had dropped off in his chair, his head lolling back against a

memo from the Chief Superintendant warning staff to be vigilant because there had recently been a spate of thefts of money and credit cards from the station. Lever didn't bother knocking, but Beverley didn't have time to bollock him before he began.

'We may have something.'

Was it Eisenmenger's imagination, or did Lever sound disappointed?

Beverley's words of coruscation remained on her tongue. 'What?' she asked instead, unable to stop relief and excitement fighting to fill her.

By way of answer, he said, 'It's on my computer.'

They followed him out; everyone had stopped work to look at Melanie Harrison who was leaning over Lever's terminal; she stood aside as they approached. It was a YouTube video of a studio interview between a portly man in late middle age, with tightly curled, greying hair and a bushy moustache, and a small, slightly built woman with large, luminous eyes. Lever said, 'This is an interview on the Al Jazeera satellite television channel.'

'What of it?'

'Her name is Jacqueline Millikan.'

'Is that it?' asked Beverley; she knew that it wasn't.

'The interview took place in early 2009.' Beverley closed her eyes, but Lever hadn't finished yet. 'She's an army widow and, it would seem from the interview that her son's also in the forces. She's got some beef about the way he's being treated; seems he was injured on a secret mission that went wrong, but she claims he's being made a scapegoat.' He saved himself from immolation by saying, 'Her son's name is "Marty".'

They watched the video, listened to a woman who gave the impression of normality undercut by desperation, trying without hope to maintain dignity. She kept repeating how her husband had died for the UK, how her son had willingly joined up and how he had done whatever had been asked of him. And now he had been wounded on some sort of mission – she couldn't, or so she said, give the details – that had gone wrong, and he was being blamed for it; he was being made a scapegoat, she thought, but he was disturbed and couldn't defend himself. He was being unfairly imprisoned, held without trial by the very people for whom he had risked his life and for whom *she* had given everything. How she felt she had been forsaken by those in whom she had placed her trust. No one, it seemed – not even her Church – would help her. She said that she felt betrayed. At its end, Beverley looked at Eisenmenger. 'Well?'

As ever, he could not just give a short and straight answer. 'There are points of concurrence,' he conceded.

She gave him a cold, almost contemptuous stare, which he failed to spot, and turned on the spot to go back to her office, calling over her shoulder, 'Lever? Harrison? In here, now.'

They followed, Eisenmenger at their backs, leaving a room full of uniformed police personnel wondering what they should do. In the office, Beverley said, 'I've only got the extra personnel until daybreak. We concentrate on finding references and traces to Jacqueline Millikan and her family. The usual searches; in particular, I want a geographic location for her.'

Harrison asked, 'How do we do that?'

Before she could be incinerated for ignorance by her chief inspector, Lever said in a neutral voice, 'We interrogate the mobile phone companies for signal traces, the banks for cash machine withdrawals; there may be a registered address for benefit, that kind of thing.'

Beverley nodded and, with what was obviously deliberate restraint, she asked, 'Are you clear?'

Lever assured her that they were. When they had left the office, she turned to Eisenmenger. 'I could do with something more certain than "there are concurrences", John.'

It took him a moment, but he finally committed. 'It's her,' he decided at last.

FORTY-EIGHT

Jacqueline was down in the kitchen, making coffee, feeling tired but anything but sleepy; her fatigue was more than just a desire to sleep, for it was an amalgam of disgust and bitter, acrid anger. She had read that the desire for vengeance consumed and was as destructive to its possessor as to those at whom it was aimed; she could believe that. She had also heard that revenge was an act of passion, vengeance one of justice; she wasn't sure about that, for she knew that she was hoping for a release of emotion as much as she was seeking justice. Upstairs, Marty groaned in his sleep, as he did so often. She knew now something of what he was seeing, because at last, a few months ago, she had found the truth.

'What's wrong?'

Beverley sounded almost shrill. Eisenmenger was startled by the tone, shot through as it was by something that could have been mistaken for paranoia. 'I was just thinking,' he replied, perplexed as to why he felt almost guilty.

'Tell me, John.'

Just how much pressure did she feel she was under? 'I was just wondering,' he replied, feeling unaccountably defensive.

'Well, tell me what you were wondering.'

He was seeing a side to her that before had bypassed him; he found that he was almost humouring her as he said, 'I was wondering how easy it is in this day and age to be invisible to the state.'

He saw clearly that his musings were anything but a source of comfort to her, for she clamped her jaws tight, accentuating her already sharp cheek bones, and said in a low, dangerous voice, 'I hope to God I don't find out.'

Jacqueline had hoped that in getting back her son – or the thing that had become her son – some of the smouldering shame and resentment would begin to dissipate, and for a few weeks it did. She felt she had won a victory, that she could move on, begin to help Marty, but it was not to be that simple. She soon realized that she was being watched, and none too subtly, either; her post was clearly being tampered with, vans would sit outside the small maisonette they had moved into, and at the same time the internet connection would unaccountably slow every now and then. They had moved to Leicester by this time and she had a job working in a clothing factory on the western outskirts, along Humberstone Road; Marty would spend the days she was working doing Airfix kits or watching the television, seeming to be no different to when she had first seen him back in hospital; he slept a lot, but he slept badly. Even then, things might have been different but for the incident of the mugging.

They were returning through the early winter evening from the fish and chip shop, heads down against driving rain, hurrying both because of this and because they did not want the food to cool too much. They were about a kilometre from home, cutting through a narrow alley when suddenly, silhouetted against the glare of a neon orange street lamp that lit the rain like showering sparks, there reared up the figures of two young men. They stood in front of them, blocking the way, about three metres distant. One was *huge,* perhaps two metres tall and a metre wide, dressed in a dark hoodie and jeans, wicked-looking knife held high for them to see; the other was smaller but similarly dressed, less showy with his knife. It was he who spoke.

'Cash and cards. Now.' It seemed to Jacqueline that no time at all passed before they moved a metre closer and the smaller one shouted, 'NOW!'

In her memory, there was a pause filled only by the sound and feel of cold rain, but she doubted that it really ever existed. Completely from nowhere, Marty reacted. He had been standing slightly behind his mother's right shoulder, but as the mugger shouted, he seemed to move forward without effort or sound or even *sentience.* Only in the moments after it had happened could she make sense of what Marty did; only in memory was there any form of understanding of what happened. The smaller mugger's knife had barely moved in response to Marty's forward movement when Marty's fist shot out into his neck; he had no time to collapse from this before Marty had plucked the knife from his hand and thrust it into his stomach. The big one was too surprised and too bulky to do anything other than gape as the knife was withdrawn from his colleague and the body pushed to the floor by Marty's hand on its shoulder; Marty moved forward with that same automatic, mindless grace and stabbed him twice, each done quickly and with a twist of the blade. He uttered a low, agonized groan – almost a mewl – and collapsed heavily to the wet pavement.

Only then did Jacqueline gasp. Only then did she start to appreciate just exactly what her son had become.

At two forty-five, Beverley had come out into the general office and was prowling around the room, looking over the shoulders of everyone and anyone, saying nothing but not needing to; Eisenmenger, watching from the doorway to her office, thought that she bore an uncanny resemblance to a prowling carnivore, perhaps one irritated by hunger and ready to pounce. It was Lever who was chosen.

'Well?'

If he thought himself in danger, he hid it well. 'Martin Lawrence Millikan was born in 1988, on April the twenty-second.' He sounded as ever; cocksure and insolent. He had a plastic folder from which he produced a dozen photographs of varying size and technical quality. They portrayed a boy ageing spasmodically into a man; he was tall, with wide, slightly too large eyes and a generous mouth; it was difficult to tell how tall he was in most, except for one in which he was framed in a doorway and appeared to be nearly two metres tall. In another, he had his arm around a much smaller woman in perhaps her fifties; she had greyed blonde hair and too many lines around the corners of her eyes and mouth, but her eyes were strikingly piercing. She was the woman from the television interview, but somehow this image captured something altogether more intriguing, more preternatural. Her look into the lens saw not just the lens, nor yet just the camera, but maybe even the soul of the photographer; for a moment, Eisenmenger had the uncanny feeling that she was perhaps even aware of his. Lever produced more photographs of this woman.

'Millikan's father was a lieutenant in the Royal Engineers, thirty-three regiment, serving in both the Falklands and Iraq.'

'Is this relevant?' There was, Eisenmenger deduced, a degree of testiness in this enquiry.

'He was in bomb disposal. He was blown to bits in late 2003, when Martin was just fifteen. The son joined the army at the age of seventeen, applying almost immediately after basic training to join the Third Battalion, Parachute Regiment; after two years, he transferred into the First Battalion. He was there less than six months before all official trace of him seems to have vanished.'

'What do you mean?' she demanded.

Lever shrugged, and it was left to Eisenmenger to answer. 'I would guess he was swallowed up by the SFSG.'

'Which is what when it's at home?'

'The Special Forces Support Group; it's the loose structure in which the SAS, the SBS and all that lot operate.'

Harrison murmured, 'Black ops.'

Eisenmenger smiled faintly. 'I'm not sure they'd thank you for that term but, yes, "Black ops".'

'And, if we're to believe his mother, he goes on a mission following which he is illegally detained by the Army.'

Lever asked, 'Why go to Al Jazeera? Why not *The Sun* or the BBC?'

'Maybe she thought it would be a good way to get attention,' Eisenmenger suggested. 'Al Jazeera isn't much liked in certain Western political circles.'

'What have we got on the mother?'

Constable Hubble said, 'Jacqueline Esther Millikan; born on the fourteenth of March 1947, the only child of a Church of England priest – John James Hooke – and a legal secretary, Elizabeth Anne Hooke. They lived in the south of Gloucestershire, in Stroud. He was parish priest in Stroud and apparently highly regarded – he preached regularly at the Cathedral – but there were clearly family problems, and that hindered his career.'

'Such as?'

'At the age of fifteen, Jacqueline made allegations of sexual abuse against her father.'

'Not a particularly good reference for a vicar,' was Lever's comment, sour and dry as might be expected from an atheist.

'What happened?'

'Nothing. The police said that there was insufficient evidence; the Church's own investigation also found nothing to incriminate her father.'

'So do we believe that she was just a fantasist?' asked Beverley.

'The Reverend John Hooke's career never recovered. He hanged himself in the crypt of Gloucester Cathedral fourteen months later.'

Momentarily, Beverley found herself wondering if there was anyone in human society who had a happy family. She said, 'Go on.'

'Elizabeth Hooke developed Alzheimer's disease in the mid-seventies and her only daughter nursed her to the end; she met Sean Alan Millikan through a dating agency and they married in 1985. He was at the time a corporal, although he received a commission in 1999 and was a lieutenant at the time of his death.' He stopped, but it was obvious that he had something else to say. 'I don't know how relevant this is . . .'

'Tell me,' advised Beverley immediately.

'It wasn't a happy marriage. There were numerous reports of arguments between them, including two occasions on which Sean Millikan was charged with assault on his wife, although she later retracted the accusation on both occasions.'

It was detailed information but, as with much of this case, none of it was apparently relevant, whilst any or all of it was conceivably very important indeed.

'What about recent sightings of the Millikans?'

Another uniformed constable – one that Beverley didn't know – said, 'At the time of the interview, Jacqueline Millikan was living in a small flat in Edgbaston—'

Eisenmenger interrupted, 'The main military receiving hospital is there, a ward in the new Queen Elizabeth Hospital.'

'—but she cancelled the direct debit for the rent one month after the TV interview. She then started paying rent on a house in Leicester.'

Where Mohammed Harawi was from. Eisenmenger saw his own thought echoed in Beverley's face. She asked, 'Then what?'

'Direct debit payments were made for five months, until October 2009, then they stopped. We also have numerous uses of a debit card in her name in and around the city, and we're just trawling through mobile phone records made at that time, but there's nothing obviously suspicious so far.'

'And after October 2009?' she asked testily.

There was silence. They had, it seems, just dropped off the world into oblivion. Eisenmenger saw Beverley's mouth form the single fricative: *fuck.* 'Nothing? Nothing at all?'

Nothing at all. Lever filled the silence in. 'They had

accumulated over sixteen thousand pounds in unspent earnings and benefits; over the course of that October they gradually withdrew the lot . . . in cash . . . and then closed both their current accounts. We have a record from the Department of Transport that they used two thousand eight hundred pounds of cash to purchase a rusty, yellow Renault van, registration number GN51 GYW. It was taxed for six months but never insured. It has dropped off the radar.'

Was there, Eisenmenger wondered, now a hint of hysteria in Beverley's demand as she said, 'Keep trying.' Then another thought occurred to her. 'Get someone round to the house she grew up in Stroud, just in case.'

Careful, Beverley. You're close to losing it . . .

She swung round to Harrison. 'We need to find out what happened between Martin Millikan's recruitment in the Special Forces and his mother's appearance on television in 2009. You're "friendly" with Special Branch; see what you can do.'

Lever bristled. 'You can't ask her to do that . . .'

Beverley seemed to have trouble controlling herself, and there seemed a real possibility that she might hit him, but then Melanie Harrison said timidly, 'I'll see what I can do.'

FORTY-NINE

I know now, when I am here at the end of my life, that I have been manipulated, but I do not mind that; at the time, I was just grateful to be given a chance to make my voice heard, to right some of the wrongs that have been done to Marty and to me. Yes, to me as well. I have unsettled debts, too; I have a sense of injustice not just because of what the state did and is doing to Marty, but also because of what it allowed to be done to me. Anyway, people such as us are born to be manipulated; the only choice we may hope to have is to choose by whom. Hammy was my choice and will be my final choice. I am grateful to him for being given this chance, although I do not think he will thank me.

He was working as a cleaner in the clothing factory in Leicester. I don't recall how we struck up a conversation, but it happened and it seemed natural enough at the time, although it is now clear it was all arranged, all scripted and all entirely make-believe on his part. He presented himself to me as pleasant and funny, and he was careful to appear compassionate and considerate of me and Marty at all times. Our relationship was never sexual, and maybe it was all the stronger for that. It was based on mutual understanding.

There were several small parks not far from where Marty and I were living and, one Saturday afternoon, the three of us went for a walk to one of them – Rushey Fields. Marty loved walks, would have walked for hours, and I used to go out with him as often as I could; sometimes, when I could afford the petrol, we would take the car out of the city to Rutland Water, something of a treat for him. I had initially been terrified to let him out of my sight after the incident with the muggers, but, with time, I was seeing more and more that Marty was not mad or irrational; he had seen two men threatening us, and he had reacted as he had been trained to do. He would not be dangerous to anyone who did not threaten him with violence.

Later, Hammy and I drank tea in the sitting room while Marty rested in his room; he rested a lot now, I noticed. Of course, Hammy had had to be told something of what had happened to Marty but, in my head, I was still an army widow and army mother, and so I had told him only vaguely that Marty was suffering from severe post-traumatic shock. He had seemed content with that explanation, had never shown anything other than concern for us.

Out of nowhere, as I sat back down on the sofa with a fresh cup of tea, he said quietly, 'I have seen the interview.'

Through the surprise, I knew at once what he meant, but could only utter, 'Have you?' He nodded but did nothing more other than look at me intently. I could say only, 'Well, that was in the past.'

His smile was wide, his eyes understanding. 'I understand.'

But, of course, I could not leave it at that and it was not long before I asked, 'How did you come to see it?'

'Al Jazeera is very popular in my community.'

And I thought, 'Of course.' I thought, too – deeper down, where you don't really think things, you just assume them, because thinking is a luxury that most animals can't afford – that it was an explanation that was reasonable. I said, 'I can't talk about it, Hammy. They've told me it's secret.'

He understood. 'As long as you're now content.'

I was.

Except I wasn't; the thinking part of me was, but the deeper-down part wasn't. I can't remember how long it was before the subject came up again, and I can't remember precisely why, but somehow it came about that he suggested he might be able to find out more about what had happened to Marty.

I asked, 'How can you do that?'

'I don't know if I can . . . but I can try.'

'How?'

'Through friends and relatives.'

I didn't understand. 'But I don't even know which country Marty was in.'

His smile was wide and the shake of his head soft; I know he was a man who had secrets, although at the time I was dazzled by the desire to find out more about what had broken my son, made him something other than the boy I had raised. He said, 'I have a great many friends and relatives, Jacqueline.'

FIFTY

'Is that it?' asked Beverley incredulously.

Melanie Harrison felt that she had failed. She was forced to nod sadly in acknowledgement of her woeful performance. Her relationship with Chief Superintendent Thomson might have been close, but it had proved not to be of sufficient proximity for him to disclose state secrets. 'He said he wasn't at liberty to divulge any more information.'

'Or he doesn't know at all,' suggested Lever.

'Possibly,' agreed Beverley.

All that Thomson had been willing – or able – to say was that

Martin Millikan had been on a special mission that had gone
wrong. He wasn't able to say which country or precisely when;
the only survivor of the unit had been Marty, but he had been
rendered unfit for active service. His mother had misunderstood
how matters stood when she had gone on television and claimed
that her son was being 'imprisoned'. He had been discharged
from hospital care shortly afterwards, purely coincidentally.

When Constable Harrison had asked if Special Branch had
any idea where Martin Millikan and his mother might be now,
he had replied, 'No. Why should we?'

'Do you believe him?' asked Beverley.

She considered. 'I'm not sure . . .' she said hesitantly, then
changed her mind. 'No . . . actually, I think he probably *was* lying.'
She had thought of his phone calls to his wife, made when they
had interrupted Thomson's furtive fumbling in the car or at the pub,
how his voice had carried similar notes to those she had heard that
early morning on the phone; and it had been strange that he had
known immediately what she had been asking about, as if they had
stumbled across an unfortunate mess left by the state, one which
nobody was supposed to talk about. 'There is one thing, though.'

'Tell me.'

'I don't think he was in bed.'

'What does that mean?'

'It's the early hours of the morning, but he didn't sound sleepy.'

'You rang his mobile?'

She nodded.

Beverley knew that she had just been told something significant, but the nature of that significance was obscure; she felt lost,
almost concussed by events, and she was still totally unsure of
whether to escalate things or to rein things back; either way, if
she were wrong, she risked professional obliteration, perhaps
even a nuclear disaster. She looked at Eisenmenger despairingly;
she didn't have to ask a question, because it was luminously
large in her wide eyes that she didn't know what to do.

She didn't know that Constable William Hubble had just had
a brainwave.

*Hammy warned me that I would be upset by what he had to
show me. He sounded convincingly concerned, but I suspect his*

acting fooled me. It was video footage of Marty. He was in a plain room that looked cold, the walls of grey brick; the perspective was of a camera high in a corner facing him; we could see that he was sitting on a wooden chair at a plain wooden table and that, facing him, with his back to the lens, was a man in a pale brown suit. The contrast was painfully sharp and the image was fuzzy, but it was plainly Marty, and his shoulder was heavily bandaged; his face was difficult to discern, but I thought that I could see soreness in it. His speech was slow, his tone agonized.

'What is your name?'

'Martin Edward Millikan.'

'To what organization do you belong?'

'The British Army.'

Each question was perfectly modulated. 'Which part of the British Army?'

'First Battalion, Parachute Regiment.' She thought Marty sounded proud as he said this.

The man facing Marty had an accent, but his words were clear; he sounded old and he sounded gentle. 'Why did you come to our country?'

Marty took a moment to answer and, when he did, he seemed to be a whisper's breath from tears. 'I was told to.'

'What were you told to do here?'

'Kill a man.'

The camera only offered me an oblique rear view of the man who was asking Marty questions, from which I could see that he was thin, with heavy black glasses and neatly trimmed hair and beard. Although accented, he sounded cultured, which, to my ear, made Marty's Gloucestershire accent come across as crude. He asked in a quiet, apparently sad, almost distraught voice, 'Why?'

Marty did not know. He shrugged and said, 'Because we were told to.'

A nod, as if of understanding. 'How many of you?'

'Four.'

'Who was in charge?'

'Lieutenant Charles.'

'How did you come?'

'By helicopter to . . . Sharbarjak . . .' Marty looked, I think, confused.

'*Char Borjak?*'

'*That's it,*' *he agreed too readily.*

'*In Afghanistan?*' *But Marty did not know. He looked apologetic when he shrugged his shoulders, as if he felt he had let people down.* '*And from there?*'

By car, it seemed.

'*And when you arrived at the house of your target?*'

'*We did what we'd been trained to do. We moved in and reconnoitred the area. We'd been told there'd be eight guards, and there were.*'

'*What were you told about the "target"?*'

'*That he was some sort of Pakistani atomic scientist.*'

'*Anything else?*'

Marty shook his head but said nothing. He was staring intently at his questioner, his hands lying passively on his lap. I thought that he looked almost eager.

'*Were you told his name?*'

'*No.*'

There was an abrupt change of direction. The bearded man asked, '*Have you been tortured, Marty?*'

I caught the use of his preferred name and it hit me in the midriff and left me winded, although I could not say why. On the screen, Marty shook his head and I believed him when he said, '*No.*'

I looked across at Hammy, and he was looking at me; I could not read his expression, for it could have been sympathy, or could have been calculation.

The bearded man nodded. There was nothing on the table between the two of them other than stains, scores and reflections. He leaned forward and, for the first time, put his arms on its surface, clasping his hands; I saw that he had a large golden signet ring on each little finger. He said, '*And after you reconnoitred?*'

'*We had a final conflab, then launched into the operation.*'

He paused for so long that the man facing him had to say, '*Go on.*'

I could see that Marty was becoming agitated; I had seen such behaviour a lot since he had been returned to me. Were he not my son, his next words would have chilled me. He said, '*We moved in as we had planned. We killed the guards with knives, then entered the house through a side door; it all went as we had practised. I found the man we were looking for in a room at the back on the ground floor.'*

'How did you know it was him?'

'They'd shown us photographs.'

'What did you do?'

Marty seemed taken aback by the question. 'I killed him,' he said, as if his questioner were being stupid.

'How?'

'I shot him.'

'A single shot?'

Another stupid question. 'Not with a Heckler.'

'Heckler?'

'It's the gun we use.'

The man nodded, as if he understood and, for all I know, he did. 'And then?'

Marty paused, but it wasn't a pause for effect; he began to sob. The bearded man, who was so refined and so apparently understanding, waited. The camera waited, too; all the sounds in the room were those that my son made as he wept. Eventually, 'I went back into the body of the house; there was a lot of shouting and screaming, and there were intermittent sprays of rifle fire from various rooms. I remember thinking that there were a fuck of a lot of people in that house.'

Another pause before I heard the man suggest in a reasonably toned, calm, even pleading voice, 'Please, Marty, tell me more. Tell me what was happening.'

But Marty's words were caught and muffled by the sobs, so that it wasn't immediately obvious what he was saying, and the man had to ask him to stop and take a deep breath, and then begin again. Even then, it was hard to hear what he had to say; I managed, though, to catch the words, 'The lieutenant was killing everyone . . .'

'Those were your orders.'

Marty was angry. 'No! The rules of engagement were quite explicit; we were empowered to kill the target, his guards if armed, and anyone who threatened us with violence. No one else.'

'But he was killing others as well?'

'He'd gone berserk. I'd heard about that happening – rumours about people who get some sort of red frenzy about them – but I'd never seen it up close. The lieutenant had it, though. I could see that in his eyes; they were dead and yet he looked somehow gleeful as he shot down everyone in his way; I saw him kill three women – one of them must have been over seventy – at the end of the hallway by the front entrance, then start up the stairs. I called to him, but he didn't respond. I sprinted to the bottom of the stairs, but what I saw in the front room brought me to a stop.'

'What was that?'

Marty breathed deeply. At the back of my mind, his description of the lieutenant's eyes resounded; it was eerily similar to the look I see so often in Marty's gaze. On the screen, he said, 'The other members of the squad were in there; they were dead, shot in the face and chest.'

'By the lieutenant?'

'Must have been. I don't think there was anyone else left alive with a gun.'

The man nodded slowly and was languid in asking, 'What then?'

Another pause from Marty; one more sob was wrung from him. 'There were three more bursts of gunfire from the floor above.'

'What did you do?'

'I ran upstairs. I called his name, although I knew he wasn't going to hear it, let alone answer. There were only three rooms upstairs and I saw him at once . . .' Marty came to a halt, his spirit seeming almost to sigh and die. The man, though, saying nothing, just waited. Marty was hyperventilating now. 'He was standing in the nursery . . .'

The silence now stretched and, as it did so, it screamed. The man with the beard looked at Marty constantly but refused to speak, whilst Marty writhed. At long last, Marty broke; he began to cry uncontrollably, only able to speak after a further long moment. 'He'd killed the children,' he explained, and his tone was completely despairing. 'He'd shot two babies in their cot . . .'

I looked again at Hammy. His stare was now directed solely

at the screen; he seemed to be trembling. On the screen, my son cried; he cried as Judas perhaps did, although we are not allowed to know. 'Lieutenant Charles killed two babies?'

'And a small boy in his bed.'

The bearded man moved then, although it was only to bow his head briefly. Marty was suddenly shaking, as though the footage had been edited, although there was no suggestion of this in the movements of the man opposite, who made no sudden or jerking motion that I could detect. He said dreamily through cloying tears, 'They were just babies . . . they were in romper suits . . .'

The man just looked at him, for so long he might have been asleep or paralyzed, or perhaps incredulous at what he was being told; I had the feeling he knew it already, though. I had the feeling that Marty had told his story many times before; this was not for the sake of the man who was asking the questions, but for mine . . .

Suddenly, Marty blurted out in a voice that I hadn't heard since he was nine, 'I am so SORRY!' He resorted to blubbing and rocking, muttering things that might have been prayers, might have been gibberish, were probably both.

Yet the man said nothing for a full minute longer, perhaps not even then. When he did, he sounded bored, as if the important bit was over and we were coasting to a finale. He asked, 'What did you do then?'

It was Marty's turn to be silent, not that his questioner minded; he was a man who had time and a world to waste. Marty eventually explained simply, 'I killed him. I looked at what he had done and I looked at his face and I saw only deadness in his eyes; I think I was screaming, although I don't remember much about it.'

He spoke as if his life had ended then. I think perhaps it had.

The recording finished and I said nothing, because there was nothing I could say and no way that I could have said it anyway. There was nothing but silence for a time that was countable in pounding heartbeats, until Hammy said quietly, 'Lieutenant Charles comes from a distinguished military family. His father is a Lieutenant-General, no less.'

I frowned, momentarily unable to understand what he meant

by that; when its importance occurred to me, it was like a blow to my stomach.

FIFTY-ONE

'Why here?' asked Eisenmenger of the darkness beyond the window.

'Is that a metaphysical question?' asked Beverley irritably. She was tired, and Eisenmenger was quite capable of such irrelevancies, she knew.

'Why Gloucestershire?'

'It's the place she knows, I guess. She grew up here, after all. It explains why everything seems to be happening around there.'

Jacqueline Millikan's parents' house in Stroud was under observation, but all the evidence suggested that it was a dead end; it had been turned into a residential home for the elderly in the nineties. Eisenmenger said nothing; Beverley knew well enough that silence from John Eisenmenger was often a prelude to some insight and she waited expectantly. Instead of proffering a pearl of precious prudence, he said suddenly, 'I need to look at the interview again.'

She brought it up on the computer on her desk and stood aside to let him view it – stare at it; when it ended, he played it again. He did this three times. Eventually, perhaps stretched into intolerability by the quietude that entrapped her, she sighed, 'I can't wait any longer.' She sounded so wretched that even Eisenmenger heard her from the depths of his reverie.

'What are you going to do?'

'Push the button.' Did she mean that as a joke, some part of his brain wondered? She continued, 'I'm going to have to go upstairs with this and recommend we bring in the security services.'

When he said nothing, she demanded, 'Well?'

'It's a risk,' he opined cautiously. 'If we're wrong . . .'

'As we've discussed, if we're wrong, they'll never forgive me and I might as well stick the business end of a shotgun in my mouth, at least from a professional point of view; but, if we're right and I do nothing, I'll never forgive myself.'

She only just caught his voice, low as it was, as he said, 'What's the target?'

It made her pause. She had been so wrapped up in trying to work out what was going on and who was doing it that she had neglected that obvious question. She sat down in a chair by the window and said, 'Given his training, a military target, presumably.'

'That Highgrove do is the obvious one,' he said.

'Presumably . . . although there are plenty of other potential targets, especially if you consider high-ranking military, barracks in the county, GCHQ . . .'

He nodded. 'All very appealing if you're a disgruntled soldier.'

She could see that he was saying and thinking different things, as if holding some sort of half-internalized, half-externalized debate. She said, 'We'll never get anywhere by trying to work out where he's planning to attack. It doesn't even have to be important to the state – we're only assuming that because of his military background. He would make just as big an impact by letting off a dirty bomb in the middle of a major town or city; or just poisoning a reservoir.'

She picked up the handset to set in train a series of events that she knew would be unstoppable.

There was a knock on the door and Lever came in, followed by Constable Hubble. 'Hubble's got something.'

Beverley immediately demanded, 'What?'

Hubble began to explain his reasoning. 'I'm usually in the traffic division.' No one said anything to this. He continued, 'We've been piloting some state-of-the-art number plate recognition software for the Department of Transport.' He began to make an impression on the assembled company. Beverley went from bored to interested instantaneously; Eisenmenger sat forward. 'It records and stores all the numbers from every camera in the county . . .'

Lever couldn't wait and cut him short. 'We've found traces of Millikan's van. It seems to have been based somewhere in the Painswick area.'

*   *   *

Jacqueline came to with a start. She had heard a voice she knew well; it couldn't have been there, because it was her father's, and he was dead by his own hand . . . She knew that it was just a random memory thrown up by her subconscious mind, perhaps to taunt her, to let her know that there were parts of her mind that still argued about the rightness of her actions, that she could not take equanimity for granted. She did not believe in ghosts, at least not the type that inhabited physical space, that moved curtains in dead air, that flung bric-a-brac around the room; ghosts that lurked in the deeper parts of the mind – those she could understand, though. The voice had been soft and kind, had assured her that she was loved by her father and by God. It had been close to her ear, just as it had been in her childhood . . . She found tears in her eyes and her face hot with embarrassment as the remembrance of his fingers' actions came to her.

She sucked in cold, mouldy air harshly and painfully, as if to explode the memory, shivered, shook her head violently, then finished the document she had been writing as she fell asleep. She saved it to disk and put the laptop on the kitchen table. She then went upstairs to snatch some sleep. Her hands were sore and, she now noticed, beginning to blister; there was an ache in her lungs, too; one that was getting worse, one that was enticing a desiccated cough to start torturing her throat.

It didn't prove the breakthrough Beverley had been hoping for. Traffic cameras had picked up the van on numerous occasions in the past week – the farthest back that the data were stored for – but this information did not actually tell them anything more than they already knew; the computer generated a map of the area on which were superimposed hundreds of pinpoints, each with a date and a time; it was far too busy and complex to make any sense out of it. Beverley sighed angrily. Eisenmenger said, 'It's a quiet area; presumably you'd want that if you were planning a terrorist attack. Maybe that's the only reason for choosing it.'

'It's a large, hilly and wooded area. It's going to require a large force to search it,' pointed out Lever, mercilessly. Beverley's nerves were now so stretched, Eisenmenger noted, that she didn't notice what her sergeant was doing. In any case, it was at that moment that Melanie Harrison knocked and entered. 'Over the past five months, there have been three separate thefts of nitrogen-based fertilizer in the area, totalling five hundred kilos.'

Eisenmenger saw Beverley form the word *fuck*, heard it loudly in his head. She bowed her head briefly and then said, 'I'd better go and raise the alarm.'

The phone on her desk rang. Somehow, they all knew that it was no ordinary phone call. Beverley picked it up with what seemed to Eisenmenger almost to be a sense of resignation. There was a silence. Her face didn't change. She put the handset back in its cradle. 'It appears I don't have to. I've been summoned upstairs,' she said bleakly.

He wondered what the expression that crossed Lever's face meant as she left the room; it was unreadable to him, as if in a foreign language. It was a language, though, that seemed to Eisenmenger to be a harsh, unforgiving thing.

The clock on the wall told them in jerky, silent movements that it was seven minutes past three.

FIFTY-TWO

Acquiring the components of the bomb had been easy; the difficult part had been doing so in a manner that didn't attract official attention. Patience had been the answer, of course; Jacqueline had acquired the art of patience over the course of her childhood, her lost adolescence, her marriage and its end, her son's long trips away from her life. They had stolen nitrogen-based fertilizer from scattered farms and had siphoned enough petrol from cars in the dark of the winter nights to fill a fifty-litre drum, never taking it all, just a few litres at a time and, as far as she knew, never being detected. The greatest hurdle had been the Semtex, but in this they were helped, ironically, by the army's training; Marty had stolen it from a large quarry in southern Dorset; it had required him to scale two three-metre chain-link fences topped by razor wire, and evade the alarm systems in the fortified storeroom, but he had done so without difficulty. That had been several months ago, the first thing they had done when they had arrived in Gloucestershire, to allow time for the theft to be forgotten. He had stolen an electronic detonation fuse with a Bluetooth link to a hand-held control at the same time, one which could give them up to twelve hours' grace before detonation. Over the past few weeks they had slowly constructed their bomb in the back of the Renault van, Marty doing most of the heavy lifting and, she had to admit, the design of the bomb; now the back of the van was crammed with the bags of fertilizer, the drum of fuel at the centre, the Semtex and detonator strapped to its side. Last night, after they had arrived back from retrieving the cargo from the girls, they had opened the tin box and scattered the fine grey-white powder over the top of the drums and the bags of fertilizer. Inevitably, it had gone on to their hands and their clothing; they had probably even breathed some of it in, although the dust and stench of the ferti-lizer made it impossible to know for certain.

It doesn't matter, she had thought.

And then she had thought again. *As long as it doesn't kill me before tomorrow morning . . .*

When Beverley returned to the room, she looked pale, might even have been trembling, Lever thought with arcane, unvoiced and otherwise undisclosed amusement. 'What happened?' he asked, using a tone that was offensively neutral.

She was perhaps too shaken up by the experience to notice his passive taunting. 'It's being escalated to the MOD and Home Office, all the way to ministerial and senior army level. It won't be long before the alarm bells are being rung in Number Ten, NATO, the SIS and every other fucking testosterone pond in the Western world. Even as we speak, they're setting up Gold Command Headquarters at Quedgeley. We're not invited, though.' She sighed and sat down in the chair that Eisenmenger vacated. 'Basically, if ever there was a big red button, I've just pressed it.'

In the same tone he had used before, Lever asked, 'How did they take the news?'

For the first time, the significance of his words and how he was using them penetrated what seemed to Eisenmenger to be something akin to shock. She looked at her sergeant and said simply, 'Get out. Stand them all down. Everyone goes back to normal duties or home.'

He left without argument, either verbal or non-verbal; indeed, Eisenmenger thought he saw an exemplar of *Schadenfreude* behind those pale eyes and beneath that aggressive, bullet head. At once, Beverley said, 'They roasted me, John. They completely and utterly incinerated me. I'm history.'

'Why?' he asked, aware that it was the question of a man who did not, and perhaps could not, understand.

'Because as soon as we suspected radioactive materials were involved, I should have let the Special Branch know what was going on. It was made worse by Harrison's cosy chats with Thomson – he's been hoisting a few red flags because of that – and by the little cunt from the Public Health people, who's also been making worried phone calls.'

'We still don't know for certain that this business has anything to do with radioactivity, or even any form of terrorism,' he pointed out.

'That, I have been told in words that were short, sharp and interspersed with numerous and diverse profanities, is no excuse. It was not my decision to make and . . .' She stopped, seeming almost to deflate. She could only manage a whisper as she admitted, 'I am suspended.'

All he could say was 'Oh, shit,' and that only after a shocked pause. He knew how worthless and inadequate that particular gift of sympathy probably was. She said nothing in reply, just sat at her desk, resting her face against clasped hands, looking presumably at her impending immolation, and he thought that she was about to cry, a possibility he found profoundly shocking, almost impossible to grasp. But she suddenly spoke. 'We had no need to make a list of likely targets – there's one in existence already – but that's not the point.'

'No? Why not?'

'We've been idiots, John . . . no, *I've* been an idiot. I was stupid enough to think the security services wouldn't have a fucking good idea of what's been going on.'

'They knew about this?' he asked incredulously.

'They knew all about Mohammed Harawi; he's recently

become fucking red hot, apparently. He's always been something of a wannabe revolutionary, but he's lately become closely linked with anti-Western groups in northern Pakistan, especially those unhappy with the UK's stance on Iran.'

'But nobody said anything like that to Constable Harrison.'

She laughed. 'Melanie Harrison, like me, is "plod". She's stupid and doesn't need to be told anything, let alone everything. It was enough that her phone calls began ringing all sorts of fucking loud bells; no wonder Thomson seemed to be clued up on things – he is. They've known for some time that Harawi is planning something big, but they didn't know what and they didn't know how. They knew about Harawi's contacts with the Millikans, although they had the grace to admit that they'd lost track of the two of them in Leicester; we've filled in some of the blanks for them – not that we'll get any thanks. Anything but.'

'What's the target?'

'Next weekend, the Prince of Wales and Duchess of Cornwall are hosting a gardening show at Highgrove, organized by the Royal Horticultural Society. There's a VIP list as long as an elephant's trunk.'

'How they can be so sure?'

'Because on that VIP list there is a certain Lieutenant-General Roderick Charles; his son was the officer in charge of the mission on which Martin Millikan was wounded.' Eisenmenger thought back to the television interview with Jacqueline Millikan; she had talked of something going wrong and her son being made a scapegoat for it. Were she and her son extracting some sort of revenge for that? His mind was split by this possibility; it was perfectly feasible and seemed to fit the facts. Beverley said, 'They've been tracking Harawi for months but never had anything concrete on which to act.'

There was a silence like no other he had known. 'What are you going to do?' he asked at last.

Her reply was bleak. 'Go home and get some sleep. There's nothing else I can do.'

She sounded so desperate and without hope that he felt alarm. He was momentarily lost for words, then asked timidly, 'Would you like some company?'

Whatever went through her mind, he saw on her face only what was at first surprise, quickly becoming gratitude. He fancied she might even have had tears in her eyes as she nodded and whispered, 'That would be good.'

FIFTY-THREE

Jacqueline and Marty sat and ate breakfast – just white toast and butter and Marmite, because that had always been Marty's favourite; she felt sick, although of what cause she could not say. Marty's hands, she saw, were even worse than hers – they looked as if they had been scrubbed in caustic soda – and he left smudges of blood on the knife and the handle of the mug, but he didn't seem to notice and she was too distraught to mention this. She didn't see much point in doing anything other than tidying the used plates and cutlery into piles on the draining board; let the ones who came afterwards wash them when they had taken their useless forensic evidence from them. She said then, 'I'll be back in half an hour.'

'Where are you going?'

'Just into the village.'

He frowned; he didn't understand. 'What for?' he demanded, and there was a now familiar petulance in his voice, the reaction of a small boy of uncertain moral framework.

She smiled reassuringly. 'I just have something to do.' He began to argue, demanding that he should go with her, but she reached across and ruffled his hair with her sore fingers. 'Please, Marty. I just need to be alone for a short while. I won't be long, Marty. Promise.'

Of course, Marty acquiesced, but he did so angrily. He watched her walk away, wondering what this could mean, and, as he did so, he scratched his hands; they were itching intolerably, and he had scored so deeply through the skin of his palms that they now bled freely. He felt pain as he had always done, but now he felt it differently. He could not – and would not – express how his experience was different, but he dimly appreciated that pain did not worry him any more; it was merely a sensation, as emotive as feeling the damp sweat of his shirt on his back, no more. His guts ached, too; that did disturb him, but only on a deep level, one that barely reached the thoughts that now filled his head, the thoughts that were almost exclusively occupied at this present time with his mother's absence. It was inexplicable that she should desert him at this moment.

He had awoken in hospital in Germany and he had been born at that moment; *born*, not reborn. They told him that he had a past, but it meant nothing to him on an emotional level; it was true that he had memories, but they did not constitute a past. It was all just a story that had been told to him, that he owned only by dint of being given it, not because he had lived it. He had been neonatal and motherless in that airless, high and sterile place, until the woman that he now regarded as his mother had come in. He had seen documentaries of how birds were programmed to bond perfectly with the first face they saw after emergence from the egg, and he could understand that. He felt as if a similar process had enveloped him when she had walked tentatively into his room. He had memories of someone who looked and sounded more or less like this woman, but there was a dislocation within him, so that he could not bring himself to believe that she had been his mother, not as he was convinced that *this* woman – Jacqueline Millikan – was.

Over the months, the bond had strengthened, until all his emotion rested within its fibres; he had found no ability to do anything other than what she told him, but this did not matter, because he had no desire, either. In that way, he was in perfect equilibrium, a *tabula rasa*, an embryo. He was unquestioning; as long as she provided him with maternalism, he was satisfied and he did not take issue with what she asked of him or what she did. Her friendship with Hammy had, to him, been beyond query, because it was being done by his parent and, as a child, he could not conceive of arguing against it, or even of the idea that it was anything of his business.

Yet, perplexingly and worryingly, she had left him alone at this time.

He felt frightened and lost, almost let down; she should not have done this to him.

FIFTY-FOUR

Had she expected them to go to bed? In truth, Beverley didn't know; in any case, she didn't mind. She felt too traumatized; she could see only tatters where just a day or so ago her career had seemed to be so energized and, at long last, growing. She had spent a long time trying to escape the mistakes and practices of her younger days, trying to accumulate something that looked out through her eyes into a mirror's reflection, and that did not see there something tainted, and she really thought that she had done it. The irony was that the metamorphosis into something that she did not find morally flawed – if not downright repugnant – had not brought with it immunity from error, or retribution. Was this just? Was it in any way earned? No, of course it wasn't. It was just fucking life.

The first thing they did when they had reached her flat was go to sleep; he on the sofa, she on top of her own bed. At some point, though, he had come to her and she found she had been weeping. They stayed holding each other until dawn. Then she had risen and, completely uncharacteristically, she had poured two large drinks – a vodka for her, a Glenfiddich for him. Then she went for a long shower. Eisenmenger had asked if he could have access to her internet connection and she obliged without asking why; this was John Eisenmenger, after all, a man who seemed sometimes to operate outside the normal physical universe.

Eisenmenger felt eroded into skeletal remorse. He should have confided his hypothesis about the cause of Arthur Meadows' death earlier; even an hour or two would possibly have made all the difference, if not to the investigation, then at least to Beverley's career. He hadn't, though. He had done what he always did, which was to stand outside and construct a wall of objective, scientific excuses not to get too involved; he knew enough about himself to appreciate that he was terrified of being wrong; better, then, to remain silent than to commit the intellectual crime of failure of reason. He had been right this time, it appeared, and look where that had got him. Look where it had got Beverley.

After a full half-hour in the shower, she came out of the bathroom in fresh clothes and poured them each another drink. Eisenmenger was still at the computer; he was watching Jacqueline Millikan's interview yet again, as he had been when she had left him. Something was still wrong, though. All the way through, someone – perhaps more than one – had been pulling strings, making a shadow dance, feint and disappear, dart and then reappear. He could not believe that they had yet reached the kernel of what was going on. He thought that perhaps he knew, though, that this whole business had not necessarily been about anything as simple and vulnerable as terrorist lunacy. And the answer lay in that interview.

At last, Jacqueline came back down the short cul-de-sac that led from the village high street to the house. She looked ill, he could see, something that made him feel terror inside, even in the knowledge of what they were about to do. He came forward. 'Are you all right?' he asked.

Her face suggested that she was in pain, although he was too naive to know whether that was physical or emotional, or both. She nodded, lips so tightly drawn they were merely a darker shade of grey against the ghostly white skin of her face. Her hands were deep in the pockets of her parka, pulling it down and taught against her thin body. Had she been crying? He could not say and dared not ask. They hugged awkwardly, as they had always done; it was something that saddened both of them, although neither could acknowledge it, not even to themselves. 'Come on,' she said. 'We need to go.'

He obeyed, of course, but not without first asking, 'Why did you leave me? Where did you go?'

'Just for a walk.' She smiled, but it wasn't reassuring; it was a gesture that was too tired, too ill, and even her damaged son could see that; he began to argue again, but she was his mother and she cut him short with a curt, 'Please, Marty. No more.'

She couldn't tell him that she had just made a phone call to the police.

*   *   *

Lever put the phone down, his head almost spinning. He was elated, puzzled, wondering and slightly frightened; he knew exactly what to do, though. He picked up the handset again and asked to be put through to Gold Command; his voice was trembling.

FIFTY-FIVE

B everley had not been asleep when the phone rang, but she might just as well have been. She had been sunk into contemplation of something that felt like oblivion, that looked like hell, that sucked her towards it every time she closed her tired eyes. She was on the sofa, the third vodka in her hand: Eisenmenger was on his second whisky. She looked first at the clock on the wall above the television. It said that it was twenty past ten; still morning, and she had a hangover, and she didn't give a flying fuck; she had been completely unmoving for twenty minutes now. 'Yes?'

She listened. The silence called loudly enough to attract Eisenmenger; he looked at her expression, saw impossibly that it seemed to become even more desolate. She cut off the call without a word, put it carefully down on the glass surface of the coffee table and lay back on the sofa, looking up at the pale blue ceiling. He was about to asked tentatively what the call had been about when she said, 'An hour ago, Lever took a phone call from Jacqueline Millikan. She said that she had left the radioactive materials at an address in Abbeymead; she said it was a safe house that Mohammed Harawi had told her to use. They've just raided it and picked up Harawi and three others; they've also taken possession of the radioactive materials.'

He said quietly, 'Oh . . .'

He turned back to the computer and Beverley just stared at the ceiling, thinking that another vodka seemed to be a fucking good idea. She said, 'At least they've stopped the attack. I got that much right, I guess.'

Eisenmenger carried on tapping away at the keyboard and staring at the computer screen, saying only distractedly, 'I suppose . . .'

'What the hell is so interesting on that screen, John?'

His back was to the clock and he suddenly whirled around in his chair to look urgently at it; the movement was violent enough to bring Beverley out of her morose contemplation. 'What's wrong?'

'It's just about to start,' he said.

'What is?'

He stood up suddenly. 'We must go. We'll get there before anyone else.'

'Where?'

He found that he was slightly drunk. 'Gloucester Cathedral.'

'Why the fuck should we want to go there?' She sounded aggressive even to herself.

'Because the Archbishop of Canterbury is celebrating Holy Communion there.'

'And how is that significant?'

'We've only stopped one attack. There's going to be a second.'

FIFTY-SIX

Marty said, 'We're going to be late. The service will have started.' They had had to take a roundabout route to get into Gloucester because Jacqueline had thought it wise to avoid the Abbeymead area.

She said, 'It doesn't matter. As long as we get there before its end. The effect will be the same.' She was speaking through clenched teeth as she fought down wave after crashing wave of nausea; her guts ached and her chest was on fire. She asked anxiously, 'Are you all right, Marty?' The last thing she needed now was for Marty to be unable to get the van into the city centre, perhaps even to crash it. That wouldn't do at all. Jacqueline didn't want to do random damage; she had very specific targets in mind.

'Fine.'

She could see easily that he wasn't, that he was just as sick as she, but she knew also that he was soldier enough to overcome it. Now that was all she had left to ask of her son.

'I should ring this in.'

They were sprinting down the staircase of the apartment block, and Beverley had to shout over their clattering footsteps. Eisenmenger called back over his shoulder, 'No point. We're only a few minutes from the Cathedral. There'll be security there; if we've got time, we can brief them.'

'Would you mind telling me what this is all about?' She felt sick and more than a little inebriated.

They reached the bottom of the staircase in the underground car park. They ran to her car at its far end; only as they reached it did Eisenmenger have the breath to say, 'This has never been about him; it's always been about her.'

'What do you mean?'

She unlocked the doors and they climbed in. As she started the engine, he said, 'The interview she did tells the whole story. Martin Millikan was broken by something that happened on one of his assignments. Initially, Jacqueline Millikan lost her husband, in effect first to the military and then to death; she then lost her son in the same way. Only this time it was worse, not just because it was the second time but because he was somehow damaged and, at the same time, he was seen as the one in the wrong. She has an injured son – one who reminds her of her loss on a daily basis – and the organization that took both him and her husband says that he has committed some sort of unspecified crime.'

'Which means she wants revenge for him.'

She sped out of the garage, slowing just enough to gain clearance of the barrier. 'No. If you analyze what she says in that interview, it's all about her. She sees *herself* as the one who's lost out.'

They were on the road. Even though it was Sunday, the road was busy. 'OK, so she's pissed off. There's a long journey from being pissed off at the government to an act of terrorism.'

'All her life, the authority figures, the big institutions, have taken from her and not even – at least in her opinion – said "please" or "thank you".'

'My point stands.'

Eisenmenger was having trouble hanging on as they accelerated; Beverley's car was not equipped with a siren or lights, although she was driving as if she had both. She was not proving popular, especially when she twice jumped red traffic lights. They sped along by the River Severn, then, before Eisenmenger could respond, swung sharply right across the oncoming traffic into the bottom part of Westgate Street. They were only two hundred metres or so from the lower part of the pedestrian zone; it was just beyond this point that Shire Hall, the seat of the county government, resided; opposite this there was a short street leading off to the left, and at the end of that was Gloucester Cathedral.

There were large crowds in the street, and Beverley had to sound the horn continually to make any progress. As they edged forward, they looked around for any vehicle that might be the Millikans'. Because there was nothing to say that it was an official car, they earned a lot of hostility from the crowds. 'I fucking hope you're right about this,' muttered Beverley.

'I've been right all along,' he pointed out. 'It's just that I've been too slow.'

At last, they reached the point where the pedestrian zone began; here the crowd was three deep. They got out of the car and pushed through to the front; at least now she could wave her ID and tell everyone that she was police. She was met at the temporary barriers on the corner of Shire Hall by a constable, one who knew her and let her through. Out of the crowds, they looked around. Another row of temporary barriers at the top end of Westgate Street held back another crowd of onlookers. They could see at least twenty-five uniformed police; six along each row of barriers, another dozen or so just standing around in the weak sunshine. As they looked towards the Cathedral, there were many more. They could just see that around the huge front doors of the distant Cathedral there were settled two black limousines and a whole host of other lesser cars of different colours, including two black BMW all-terrain vehicles. There was no sign of anything untoward. They began walking towards the Cathedral.

After a hundred metres or so, a uniformed woman police inspector came up to them. 'Can I help you, Chief Inspector?'

Beverley asked, 'Has the service begun?'

'Yes.'

'Have you noticed anything suspicious?' She felt lameness exuding from her skin as the question limped forth from her lips.

'No. Should I have done?' The inspector clearly did not like Beverley; she had intelligent eyes above a sharp nose and lips that formed a supercilious line to underscore everything. She was taller than Beverley, almost to Eisenmenger's height. Her question was posed in a tone that was just the acceptable side of impudent. 'We've increased precautions, in view of the events at Abbeymead.'

Eisenmenger asked, 'Are there any armed police here?'

The gaze flicked to him with a sign of vague recognition. 'Doctor Eisenmenger, isn't it?'

'Yes . . .'

'Why do you want to know?'

'Just answer the fucking question, Inspector Harber. I can see there probably are.' She indicated the BMWs.

Taken aback, the uniformed officer said in a tight, angry voice, 'They're here in reserve, yes.'

'Get them here,' ordered Eisenmenger.

The unorthodoxy of the situation gave Inspector Harber indigestion. She was certainly not about to do as . . .

Beverley barked, 'Do as he says, Harber. Now.'

It worked, but only just. She turned and walked in an official, dignified gait into the cathedral grounds; every muscle and movement radiated a spectrum that ranged from anger, through resentment to humiliation. Beverley turned to Eisenmenger. 'You have perhaps two minutes to explain what you have got me into.'

Marty turned left into Westgate Street and drove about halfway along the road. The road ahead of them was partially blocked by people milling about. He pulled into the side. 'What do we do?'

Jacqueline looked at her watch. It was ten forty-three. The service would be well underway. 'We drive on.'

'What about the people?'

She did not want to kill innocent people, she told herself;

yet she could not come so close and fail. She had to make this one last statement, this one last attempt at true and proper vengeance . . .

Her answer was no answer at all. 'I love you, Marty.'

He didn't know quite what to say; his answer was almost automatic. 'I love you, too.'

She heard the words and could not help but find them unsupported by emotion; he was reciting a ritual, nothing more. It seemed to her then to be the final encouragement she needed.

'Yes, Jacqueline grieves for the loss of her husband and the near destruction of her son, and, yes, she blames the government, but that's not who her major beef is with.'

'The fucking Archbishop of Canterbury?' Beverley sounded as though she were close to hysteria. 'You think she's got it in for the head of the bloody Church of England?'

'They were the first and the major offenders against her. She was the daughter of an Anglican priest who sexually abused her . . .'

'So she said.'

Eisenmenger talked calmly but insistently. 'Yes, so she said; and the authorities in the Church of England, specifically the Diocese of Gloucester said, "No". I can understand a huge sense of injustice being generated by that.'

'What if she imagined it?'

'To a certain extent, that doesn't matter; if she's convinced it really happened, her motive remains just as powerful. And her father committed suicide, don't forget.'

'Which means fuck all, as you well know.'

Inspector Harber was returning with two uniformed and heavily armoured police officers; they each carried a submachine gun slung over their right shoulder and had at their waist some sort of pistol. A car started sounding its horn somewhere in the background. Eisenmenger went on, 'Everything that happened after that just added to her sense of being wronged by authority figures. With her father dead, when her mother became ill, she had to look after her; I should imagine that was a thankless task. This leads to her meeting with a military man, but even that may not have been a very happy marriage; when he's blown to bits, she loses whatever little emotional support she had from him.'

Inspector Harber listened to Eisenmenger, much as bored shoppers stop and listen to inept buskers. The armed policemen kept looking around; the sound of the horn was getting louder and more insistent. Harber's radio suddenly began talking to her and she turned away to listen. Eisenmenger said to Beverley, 'What happened to her son was the final insult. Not only was he mentally scarred, he was accused of being the one responsible for the mess that was his final mission; effectively, he's been judged, found guilty and sentenced for it, too. Once again, she got nothing but misery from the most powerful figures in her world. She wants revenge . . .'

'They won't get out of the way,' complained Marty.

Jacqueline ordered calmly. 'Just drive them down.'

Harber joined the group and said imperiously, 'I've just been contacted by Gold Command. They tell me, Chief Inspector, that you've been suspended from operational duty. As such, I must ask you to . . .'

Suddenly, not far from where Beverley and Eisenmenger had made their way through the crowds to the barrier, there came a scream. Almost instantaneously, it spread as if borne on the slight but cold breeze that the morning had brought with it. The horn began to sound continuously and an engine began to roar; the policemen on that side began to move to the point that seemed to be the epicentre of the disturbance when, shockingly abruptly, an old yellow van erupted through the crowd, pushing people forwards, running them down, bumping up and down on their bodies; it shoved the barriers out of the way, catching and hurling aside five of the six police officers as it did so, nearly a perfect score. There was blood and worse on the brick surface of the road behind the van as it swung around to face the Cathedral. Through the reflections of sun and cloud on the windscreen, Beverley saw the dim and distant faces of Jacqueline Millikan and her son. The van stopped, as if surprised by the view of the Cathedral in front of it, or, perhaps, by their little group that stood in its way.

'Shoot them,' said Beverley loudly. 'Shoot them both and do it quick.'

No one seemed to respond. Eisenmenger said, 'If I'm not mistaken, that van's full of explosives and highly radioactive material.' His voice trembled. A lot of the crowd had pulled away, although some were trying to tend to the half-dozen people that lay in the wake of the van. The initial shock of its appearance had dissipated and police officers were starting to approach the van; its engine again roared and it began to move forward. Eisenmenger heard the gears clash. He had the impression that both Jacqueline and her son were already dead, that it was being driven by ghosts, or perhaps by the force of her will . . .

'Fucking hell! Aim at their heads. Only their heads,' screamed Beverley.

The two armed police officers looked at Harber, but she was transfixed. The van was now moving forward rapidly, still with plenty of speed to gain. Beverley lunged forward and made a grab for a pistol. Instinctively, the police officer whirled around and clubbed her on the side of the head with his submachine gun. She fell to the ground. The other officer was momentarily distracted and Eisenmenger implored, 'Do it!'

The man brought his submachine gun up and fired as the van was only ten metres away. The windscreen exploded in front of a sudden, billowing red mist that seemed to fill the cab; the two inside vanished within it, as if spirited away. Harber and the two armed officers jumped to the left as the van jerked to the right; Eisenmenger was trying heave Beverley's body out of harm's way but found he had put himself in it instead. He straightened up and tried to dodge but was caught on his right hip by the van's wing. He was at once whirled around, all his senses flying away from him in dizzying sickness, to be replaced by agony. He was aware of the sound of the collision of the van with the front of a tea shop only as a peripheral thing, one that came to him from beyond a heavy blanket of suffocating pain.

FIFTY-SEVEN

Eisenmenger was so uncomfortable that he felt only screaming would relieve his agitation. There was a dull, throbbing ache in his pelvis that persisted for hour after hour, through wakefulness and disturbed night, that seemed to seep into his backbone and claw its way along his legs. The pethidine injections helped, but left him nauseous and played havoc with his bowels. He felt too hot when the duvet was on, too cold and exposed when it was off; he was grateful for the privacy of being in a side ward, yet missed human contact. He was bored with daytime television, yet could not concentrate on reading anything for longer than a few minutes. It was just after lunch on his third post-operative day, and he had managed only a little of the material that passed for cuisine in that place. The points at which the internal fixation of his pelvis protruded through his skin looked angry and ready to spite him with infection. He had a urinary catheter in, which he found both uncomfortable and embarrassing.

The door opened, admitting Beverley. She looked gaunt; taped to her temple was a white dressing about five by five centimetres. 'May I come in?'

Although he wore boxer shorts, Eisenmenger hastily covered himself with a sheet. 'Of course, of course'

She came further in, standing by the end of the bed. 'I didn't bring anything; I guessed you wouldn't want flowers, and grapes just seemed a pathetic idea.'

He switched off the television that perched in the far corner of the room as if it were roosting there. 'No problem.'

He indicated the chair and she sat down awkwardly. 'When you get out, I'll cook you a meal to say "thank you".'

'What for?'

'You saved my life.'

He didn't know what to say: he hadn't thought of it like that; in fact, didn't *want* to think of it like that. 'I seem to recall I was just repaying the compliment,' he murmured.

Abruptly, she said, 'How are you?'

'Bloody awful, actually.'

'I can imagine. What, precisely, was the damage?'

'Disrupted pelvis. I was lucky, though; there's a high percentage of urethral damage and lifelong urinary problems, but I seem to have escaped that.'

'Lucky.'

The conversation petered out until he asked, 'Your head's OK, is it?'

'Nothing fractured and no concussion. Just a headache.'

After this brief spurt of life, the dialogue lapsed into some sort of indolence until Eisenmenger could stand it no longer. 'What's happening in the real world, Beverley? What's happening to you?'

She took a deep and, at its end, ragged trawl of breath. 'Still suspended. Under investigation for dereliction of duty, insubordination, attempted misuse of firearms . . . You know how it is; different day, same shit.'

'You know you did the right thing, Beverley. Remember that.'

She made a sour face. 'Thanks, but it isn't your call to make, John.'

'You saved a lot of lives and a lot more injuries; you prevented the radioactive contamination of Gloucester Cathedral, potentially saved the life of the head of the Anglican Church.'

She weighed this. 'Two people died in that crowd when the Millikans drove through it; seven more were injured to varying degrees; add to that the four people who'd already been killed during the short life of my investigation, and you've got what some people will see as a huge catalogue of serious errors.'

'I'm sure a lot of people *won't* see it like that.'

She smiled, but if there was amusement inside her, it didn't reach her lips. 'Lever's working away, making sure that every man and his dog are aware of what a crap job I did, and how, if only he'd been allowed, he could have stopped all this from happening.'

'That's a joke.'

The smile broadened but, at the same time, it became a thing so bitter that it might have been fed direct from her gall bladder. 'That's just what it isn't, John.'

'Nevertheless, if you hadn't been there at the end . . .'

'"We", John,' she interrupted. 'Not "I".'

It silenced him.

She said, 'You'll be pleased to know you were pretty well right about what had happened.'

'How do you know?'

'Jacqueline Millikan left a confession – a testament, I suppose – back in their rented house. She describes her involvement with Harawi.'

She told him briefly what the document had said. He pondered this. 'It's beautiful.'

'Is it?' She thought it typical of the man that such should be his reaction.

'From a purely abstract point of view, yes,' he replied, sensing that she did not share his appreciation. 'Everything was done at arm's length; everyone thought they knew what they were doing, and that they were in control, yet all of them were being used.' He laughed gently. 'Even Harawi, who thought he was the master-mind of it all.'

'I can't see anything beautiful in any of this.'

'Think about it. A man is persuaded to get some extra money from people-smuggling; was that, I wonder, premeditated? Did "Hammy", as Arthur Meadows knew Mohammed Harawi, recruit him specifically for that one shipment?' He shook his head and said in a voice that was almost scared, 'I rather fear he did.'

He glanced across at Beverley. 'Harawi's a dangerous man.'

'I think we know that,' was her dry response.

'The girls thought they were smuggling drugs, but they were smuggling something much more lethal. Meadows thought he was just smuggling people. Malik thought he was dealing with somebody interested in human flesh and had probably been assured by Harawi that this mysterious woman "Jacqueline" was to be trusted.'

'The girls were just disposable wrappers – "biodegradable",' remarked Beverley in a voice filled with irony.

'I wonder if Arthur Meadows would have been killed if he hadn't died?'

'We're not likely ever to find out.'

Eisenmenger thought some more. 'Harawi must have had a chess-player's ability to think so far ahead.'

'Not far enough, as it turned out.'

'Do we know where the radioactive material came from?'

'Almost certainly it was smuggled from Western Asia or perhaps Eastern Europe – there's plenty of it about, given the number of decrepit nuclear reactors the USSR left behind.'

Eisenmenger could not escape his admiration of the plan. 'Harawi talked to Meadows, he talked to Malik and he talked to Jacqueline Millikan. He manipulated them, every one, all the while staying in the background, not attracting attention to himself. In Marty, he found a supreme killing machine and, in Jacqueline, he thought he found the trigger.'

'We still don't know for certain why Harry Weston had to be killed or how the girls ended up in that barn.'

'It's probably as we thought. Weston's intervention resulted in the loss of the girls, although precisely how will never be known. Weston had to be killed – presumably because he had seen something – and then the girls had to be found. When they were, another innocent bystander had to be disposed of in the process.'

Eisenmenger took a sip of water from the plastic beaker on the table by his bed. He asked ruminatively, 'I wonder when Jacqueline Millikan decided to double-cross Harawi?'

'She doesn't say so outright, but, to judge from her words, I think she realized pretty early on that Harawi was just another in a long line of people and organizations out to use her. I think, in the end, all she wanted was to do something for herself.'

'She killed her son in the process, though. Is that mother love?'

'Her son was dead. She looked on Marty Millikan almost as a changeling, I think; an alien that had been left in her son's crib. I think she may have got some level of pleasure in using it to strike back at those she saw as oppressors.'

They fell into silence until a nurse knocked on the door and asked if she could take some observations. Beverley stood up at once. 'I've got to go. I have an appointment with my solicitor at two.'

'Of course. Good luck . . . Come and see me again.'

On the point of turning to leave, she stopped and then quickly bent down to kiss him full on the lips. His body position changed only slightly, but it was enough to spear pain through his pelvis; he didn't say or do anything. The kiss lasted a long time and he found she tasted good.